SUZANNA STIRS THE FIRE

Emily Calvin Blake

1st WORLD
LIBRARY
Literary Society

Suzanna Stirs the Fire

Emily Calvin Blake

© 1st World Library, 2006
PO Box 2211
Fairfield, IA 52556
www.1stworldlibrary.com
First Edition

LCCN: 2006936178

Softcover ISBN: 978-1-4218-3041-4
Hardcover ISBN: 978-1-4218-2941-8
eBook ISBN: 978-1-4218-3141-1

Purchase *"Suzanna Stirs the Fire"*
as a traditional bound book at:
www.1stWorldLibrary.com/purchase.asp?ISBN=978-1-4218-3041-4

1st World Library is a literary, educational organization
dedicated to:

- Creating a free internet library of downloadable ebooks

- Hosting writing competitions and offering book
  publishing scholarships.

Interested in more 1st World Library books?
contact: literacy@1stworldlibrary.com
Check us out at: www.1stworldlibrary.com

1st World Library Literary Society

Giving Back to the World

"If you want to work on the core problem, it's early school literacy."

- James Barksdale, former CEO of Netscape

"No skill is more crucial to the future of a child, or to a democratic and prosperous society, than literacy."

- Los Angeles Times

Literacy... means far more than learning how to read and write... The aim is to transmit... knowledge and promote social participation."

- UNESCO

"Literacy is not a luxury, it is a right and a responsibility. If our world is to meet the challenges of the twenty-first century we must harness the energy and creativity of all our citizens."

- President Bill Clinton

"Parents should be encouraged to read to their children, and teachers should be equipped with all available techniques for teaching literacy, so the varying needs and capacities of individual kids can be taken into account."

- Hugh Mackay

CONTENTS

BOOK III

BOOK I

CHAPTER I

THE TUCKED-IN DAY

Maizie wanted to sleep a little longer, but though the clock had but just chimed six Suzanna was up and had drawn the window curtain letting in a flood of sunshine. Maizie lay watching her sister, her gray eyes still blurred with sleep; not wide and interested as a little later they would be. Her soft little features expressing her naive personality seemed unsubtle, yet of contours so lovely in this period just after babyhood that one longed to cuddle her.

Suzanna stood a long time at the window, so long indeed that Maizie feared she was lost to all materialities. Suzanna, wonderful one, who could strike from dull stuff magic dreams; who could vivify and gloriously color the little things of life; who could into the simplest happenings read thrilling interpretations! What bliss to accompany her upon her wanderings, and what sadness to be forgotten!

Indeed Suzanna seemed oblivious. Certainly in spirit she was absent and at last Maizie could bear the silence no longer.

"Suzanna!" she cried.

Then Suzanna turned. She did not speak, however, but placed a warning finger upon her lips. Then she went swiftly to the closet and took down her best white dress. She laid it tenderly on the back of a chair till she had found in the lowest bureau drawer her white stockings and slippers, then she brushed and combed her hair, confined it lightly with a length of ribbon, washed her hands and face in the little bowl which stood in one corner near the window and leisurely donned the white dress.

Maizie sat straight up in bed watching in amazement. At last Suzanna glanced over at her little wistful sister, then in stately fashion advanced toward the bed, till close to Maizie she paused. Tall and slender she stood, with eyes amber-colored, eyes which turned to black in moments of deep emotion. Her brown hair touched with copper sprang back from her brow in waving grace; her delicate features called for small attention, excepting her mouth which was softly curved, eager of speech, grave, mutinous, the most expressive part of an expressive face.

Suzanna danced through life, sang her way to the hearts of others, left her touch wherever she went; yet, beneath the lightness, philosophies of life formed themselves intuitively, one after another, truer perhaps in their findings than those which filtered through the pure intellect of the grown-up.

At length she spoke to Maizie. "You mustn't say anything to me, Maizie, unless I ask you a question," she commanded, "because I'm a princess who lives in a crystal palace in a wonderful country with oceans and mountains."

Maizie did not reply; what could she say? Simply she stared as Suzanna moved gracefully about the room with the slow movements she considered fitting a princess.

At last she returned to the bed. She began: "Maizie, I wish you to rise, dress thyself, then go into thy parents' room and if the baby is awake, dress him as Suzanna, thy sister, did when she was here and not a princess."

Maizie rose and obediently dressed herself, ever watchful of

Emily Calvin Blake

Suzanna and thrilled by the new personality which seemed to have entered with the princess. When she was quite dressed, even to her little enshrouding gingham apron, she asked:

"Are you going to school today, Suzanna?"

Suzanna fixed her eyes in the distance.

"I'm here, Princess," corrected Maizie, "right in front of you. You can touch me with your hand. And besides, I had to ask that question. It was burning on my tongue."

Suzanna did not stir. At last: "I'm not going to school today," she half chanted. "A princess does not go to school. She wanders through the fields and over the mountains and when she returns to her palace she eats roses smothered in cream."

"Oh," cried Maizie. "Rose petals are bitter and beside we only have cream on Sundays."

Suzanna turned away. Sometimes she found it a trifle difficult to play with Maizie. She went slowly, majestically down the stairs and into the little parlor. She regretted she had no train, since she might switch it about as she walked. But she could *think* she had a train, and ever and anon glance behind to see that it had not curled up.

In the parlor she stood and looked about her. Her physical eyes saw the worn spots in the carpet, the picture of her father's mother, faded and dim, her own "crayon," the old horsehair sofa and chair, and the piano with its yellow keys and its scratched case. But with her inner eyes she beheld a lovely rose-colored room, heaped with soft rugs and satin-lined chairs; fine, soft-grained woods, and a harp studded with rare jewels.

At first she stood alone. Then by a slight wave of her hand she commanded the appearance of many ladies and gentlemen who came and bowed low before her. While she was still living in her vision, her father descended the stairs and entered the parlor. He started at sight of Suzanna all dressed in her best.

"I'm a princess, father," said Suzanna.

"A princess?" he repeated.

Her father wore his store clothes, shiny and grown tight for him. Above his winged collar his sensitive face showed pale and thin in the early morning light. His eyes, brown, soft, were like Suzanna's—they had vision. He smiled now, half whimsically and wholly lovingly at her.

"An eight-year-old princess," he said. Then the smile faded, and he half turned to the door. "Well, that's all right, your Majesty," he said. "Continue with your play. I'm going up into the attic just for ten minutes."

"You'll be late for the store, won't you, daddy?" she asked, anxiously, forgetting for the moment her role.

He turned upon her quickly. "Late for the store!" he cried, "late to weigh nails, sell wash boards, and mops. What does that matter, my dear, when by my invention the world will some day be better." Suddenly the passion died from his voice. He stood again the tall shabby figure, somewhat stooped, with long fine hands that moved restlessly. "Ah, well, Suzanna," he went on, "weighing nails brings us our livelihood."

Suzanna went and stood close to him. She put her small hand out and touched his arm. "Daddy," she said, earnestly, "this is my tucked-in day. I'm going to have two of them. Perhaps you can have a tucked-in day sometime when you can work for hours at your invention."

Again he smiled at her. "Where did you get your tucked-in day, Suzanna," he asked.

"Why, it's a great beautiful white space that comes between last week and this. It's all empty, that big space, and so I have filled it in with a day of my own. If mother will let me, I'm going to have two tucked-in days. On the first I'm a princess, and on the second, I shall be an Only Child."

"Very well, little girl," said Suzanna's father. "And now I hear others moving about upstairs. Will you stay to breakfast with us, Princess?"

"Oh, yes," said Suzanna, who began to feel the healthy pangs of hunger. "I suppose perhaps I had better set the table."

A half-hour later the house was in a bustle. The baby was crying, Peter, the five-year-old, was sliding in his usual exuberant manner down the banisters, and at the stove in the kitchen, Mrs. Procter, the mother, was filling pans and opening and closing the oven door with quick, somewhat noisy movements.

When in time all were gathered about the dining table, they were an interesting looking family. Mrs. Procter, young, despite her four children, wore a little worried frown strangely at conflict with her palpable desire to make the best of things. She darted here and there, soothing the baby with a practiced hand, pouring her husband's coffee, helping voracious Peter, her busy mind anticipating all the day's tasks. Suzanna loved and admired her mother. She loved the way the luxuriant dark hair was wound round and round the small head. She loved the rare smile, the soft blue eyes fringed in black lashes. She liked to meet those eyes when they were filled with understanding, when they seemed to speak as plainly as the tender lips made just for lullabies—and encouragements when the inventor-father stumbled, lost his belief in himself and in his Machine.

Maizie, younger than Suzanna by only a year, looked like her mother—sweet, very practical, always in a wide-eyed condition of surprise at Suzanna's wonderful imagination; a dependable little body who rarely fell from grace by reason of naughtiness.

Peter, a strange composite of his dreamy father and practical mother, sat near the baby. Peter had had a twin, a little girl, who died when she was three years old. Sometimes, even now, Peter cried himself to sleep for Helen.

The baby, now crowing in his armchair beside his mother, was a bright little chap of not quite a year. Too plump to even try his sturdy legs, he was oftentimes very much of a burden to his devoted sisters.

Mrs. Procter's eyes had taken in at once Suzanna's finery, but Mrs. Procter knew Suzanna; besides she did not always ask a direct question. Suzanna's mind worked clearly, but it worked by its own laws. So now the mother waited and toward the end of the meal she was rewarded for her patience. Suzanna put down her fork and began:

"Mother, this is my first tucked-in day to do as I please in. I know Monday's supposed to be wash day, but you said it wasn't a big wash and I did all the sorting Saturday night. I am all fixed up for a princess, and something inside me tells me I must wander about my palace and perhaps find paths leading to far-off snow countries."

It was Maizie who looked now questioningly at her mother. Could it be that Suzanna would be given her own way? In truth the entire table awaited breathlessly Mrs. Procter's answer. It came at last:

"Very well, Princess, you may have your tucked-in day."

There followed a short silence. At last:

"Mother, I must be honest with you," said Suzanna, "there are to be *two* tucked-in days. In my next space I want to be an Only Child."

Again her mother agreed. Rarely could she deny Suzanna her jaunts into the land of dreams.

So after breakfast, quite free, Suzanna left the house. The little town lay quiet, except for the rhythmic noises coming from the big Massey Steel Mills. Suzanna looked in their direction and stood a moment watching the sparks coming from the big round chimneys. Over across fields were the tumble-down cottages occupied by the employees of the Massey Steel Mills. Suzanna did not often go in their direction. The squalor made her unhappy and set in train so many questions she was quite unable to answer.

The day was early July with a spicy breeze that promised its delight for many hours. Suzanna walked out into the road, and turned to gaze at the little home in which she had been born. She loved it with its many memories. She fancied it held its head high because it sheltered her father's great Machine. At length she turned south toward the country. She breathed deeply as she went, feeling how wonderful it was to be a princess and to wander about as she pleased.

Throbbing with life and the beauty of it, the marvel of it, she began to dance. Strange thoughts flowed through her, strange understandings, that, little child as she was, she could find no words for. Only it seemed color lay within her, rich color for a thought of love; a wistful rose shade for a passing desire, a brilliant orange for the uplifting knowledge that just to be alive was great. She stopped to gather a passion flower because with its deep purple, its hidden heart that she could very gently discover and gaze into, it fitted into her mood.

Oh, to be big, grown up! All these brightly winged thoughts uplifting her, some of which puzzled her, some that frightened her, she would quite understand then! In those far-off years of absolute knowledge there would be no limitations; no commonplaces, only miracles. You could make what you wished then of all your days.

She came at last upon a little house lying far back from the road. It was like a toy house, and had stood open for years. The Procter children had often played in the rooms of the small house, and once when Peter was a baby he had fallen down the stairs, and his twin Helen, anguished because he was hurt, had cried piteously until they were home again.

Now Suzanna opened the gate, mended, she noticed, and hanging straight, and started down the garden path. Lovely old-fashioned flowers—pansies and phlox and pinks and balsam were all in their happiest bloom. Suzanna wondered who watered and tended them. As she lingered beside a pansy bed, the door of the little house opened and a rather frail little old lady came out, followed by a maid who carried a chair that was filled with pillows. She set the chair under a tree midway in the garden between the house and the road. The old lady sank into it and the maid deftly covered her with a large woolen shawl; then saying some word, and placing a small silver bell on the grass within easy reach of the lady in the chair the maid left.

Suzanna stood, unable to run. Someone then had moved into the tiny house. And who? Suzanna knew everyone in the village of Anchorville, and the old lady was a stranger. Suzanna gave up the question and started back toward the gate when the old lady suddenly turned and saw the child.

"Come here," she called, and Suzanna perforce obeyed. When she stood near the small figure in the chair she waited, while she decided that this was quite the prettiest old lady she had ever seen. The wavy silver hair lying under a white lace cap, with two little curls falling on either side made the blue eyes seems like a very little baby's at the stage when they're deciding just what color they shall be. Like Suzanna, the lady was dressed in white, flowing as to skirt, and trimmed with quantities of fine old lace. On her hand was one ring, a lovely moonstone. Suzanna at once loved that ring, not because it was a piece of jewelry, but because it did look like a stray moonbeam that the rain had fallen on.

"And who may you be?" asked the old lady at once.

Now something about her hostess called out all of Suzanna's colorful imagination. She felt an instant response to this personality.

"I am a princess, the Princess Cecilia," she answered promptly.

"Ah," the old lady straightened up and a sudden, vivid change became at once manifest in her manner. "Draw closer to me."

Suzanna obeyed, moving till she touched the old lady's hand that rested on the wings of the old-fashioned chair.

"You should be a princess," said the old lady, "for I am a queen!"

Suzanna gazed without at first speaking. "A real one?" she whispered at last.

"A real queen," returned the old lady. "It's not generally known by those who serve me, nor even suspected by my own son who lives yonder in the big house on the hill. But I'm the real queen of Spain, deposed from the hearts of her people, from the hearts of her own nearest."

Suzanna nodded. She looked over toward the hill. "That's Bartlett Villa," she said; "the people only live there part of the year. I know Mrs. Bartlett, she's the richest lady in Anchorville, but I didn't know her mother was a queen."

The old lady didn't appear to be particularly interested. She went on: "It's not generally known, I believe, that I am a queen." After another pause: "Over yonder is a camp chair. Bring it hither."

Suzanna found the chair at one end of the garden. Quickly she brought it and sank herself upon it gracefully as became a princess of the blood, but she was surprised a moment later to meet reproval in the eyes of the queen.

"It's not permissible to seat yourself in the presence of royalty," said the queen, rather sternly.

"But, I, too, am royalty and you told me to get the chair," said Suzanna. "Of course, I thought it was to sit on."

"You are merely a princess," returned the old lady. "I am your queen, and you must await my permission to recline."

Suzanna rose.

"Ask permission," said the queen, "and perhaps I shall allow you to seat yourself."

"May I sit down?" asked Suzanna.

The queen inclined her head graciously. "You may," she returned. So once more the little visitor resumed her seat. Then for a long time the old lady sat with folded hands and looking off into the distance. She was very, very still. Only the lace on her bosom moved gently to show that she breathed. Suzanna thought perhaps she had better go. But she feared to rise lest she again meet with reproof.

At last the queen remembered her guest.

"I wish to traverse my garden and in the absence of my lady-in-waiting I request your arm, Princess Cecilia," she said.

Suzanna rose quickly and bending her small arm, she offered its support to the old lady, who though now standing very straight and slender, still was scarce two heads taller than her visitor. She slipped her blue-veined hand within Suzanna's arm and they began a friendly walk up and down the path.

"Once," began the queen, "when I lived beyond the snow-capped mountains within my own palace, I was not so lonely as I now am. There was one who afterwards became my king, with whom I walked by the sea. We saw together the sapphire sparkle of the water, the golden yellow of the sands; but in reality we beheld only one another's face."

By this time they had reached the gate and both stopped and stood looking down the quiet road. But the little old lady still clung to Suzanna's arm and her eyes had a far-away look.

"And after a time," went on the queen, "we were wedded and lived together in my palace and we were happy as the birds; happy and less care free. And always we found our greatest happiness in walking by the sea or in climbing the mountains; I sometimes clinging to his ready hand or skipping before him. And once we ran away from all the pomp and ceremony that was merely surface and we found a little house right at the edge of town, and there together for some months we lived. There, too, our little prince came to us, and from there he went away.

"And one day my king, too, left, and my little prince forgot me, and I am alone. Queen as I am, I am alone!"

Suzanna was silent. Indeed, she was at a loss just how to offer comfort. When Helen, Peter's twin, went away her heart had ached, and when a little baby, soft and cuddly had gone away forever, Suzanna had wept for days and far into the nights. This queen, she found was very sad, and very longing, and very lonely, three things she thought queenhood exempt from, sadness, and longing and loneliness.

Once more they turned, and walked down the garden path till they reached the chairs under the tree. The queen sank again among her pillows and Suzanna was about to use her camp chair when the queen spoke in her old commanding manner:

"I am hungry, serf," she cried. "Go, prepare my food! All the dainties that you can find. I wish cream beaten to a froth and peaches, halved and stoned. I wish strawberries still wet with dew and reposing in their green leaves."

"But," began Suzanna, "I can't get strawberries for you."

The old lady rose to her full height. "Wilt begone, serf?" in stern accents she cried. "Wilt begone and prepare what I demand?"

Now Suzanna had a very firm idea of her own standing as a princess. Had she not earlier in the day impressed Maizie? And now, was this stranger, even though she were a queen, to demand menial service of one of royal blood? Suzanna thought not. So she said firmly, though gently:

"I am not a serf, if that means a slave! I am a visiting princess, the Princess Cecilia. I will not go into your kitchen and prepare food." And then forgetting her role, she assumed her ordinary voice. "Why, this morning I didn't even warm the baby's bottle, because mother said I needn't seeing that I was a princess and living in my own tucked-in day."

"'Tucked-in day!'" responded the queen. "What do you mean by that?"

"Why, it's my very own day, a day tucked in between last week and this week," said Suzanna.

The old lady's eyes wandered away again looking into distant countries, Suzanna had no doubt, and she hoped the strawberries were forgotten. But alas, she was wrong, for in a few moments the queen, bringing her eyes back to Suzanna's face recalled her desire:

"I will have my strawberries," she began peremptorily. And then with a complete change of voice; one with some satire in its tone she concluded: "Dost think because thou art a princess thou art exempt from all service in the world?"

"A princess does not work," said Suzanna wisely.

"I would have you know," said the queen, "that all those of the world must give service in one way or another. Dost think that when in my palace I reigned a queen I gave no service? There were those who loved me and needed me. As their queen did I not owe them something in return for their love? And could I leave their needs unrelieved?"

"But," faltered Suzanna, "you were a queen!"

The old lady's eyes lit with a sudden fire. "And 'twas because I reigned a queen," she answered, "that I must do more than those of less exalted station. In my kingdom there were little children, there were the old, and there were the feeble, and there were the poor. Could I go about unconcerned as to their welfare?" Her voice suddenly softened. She put out her hand, now trembling with her emotion, and drew Suzanna close to her. "My sweet little princess," she said, "no one in all the world stands alone. A little silver chain binds each one of us to his fellow. You may break that chain and you may feel yourself free, but you will be a greater slave than ever."

"I think I understand," said Suzanna, and indeed she had a fair meaning of the other's words. "The chain runs from wrist to wrist and is rubber plated."

With a sudden change of manner the old lady spoke again, going back to her former imperious manner: "Am I thus to starve because no slave springs forth to do my bidding?"

At this important moment the maid reappeared. She came swiftly down the garden to the old lady. She paused when she saw Suzanna. She had a very gentle face, Suzanna decided, and when she spoke to the old lady it was tenderly as one would speak to a child. Suzanna decided that she liked her.

Said Suzanna: "The queen wants her strawberries wet with dew and buried in their own green leaves."

"The queen," returned the maid, "shall have her luncheon."

"And the Princess Cecilia," said the queen, "shall eat with me, Letty."

Suzanna was very glad to hear this since for a long time past she had been hungry, and had been thinking rather longingly of the midday dinner at home.

The maid left, but in a very short time she came into the garden again and announced that lunch was ready in the dining-room.

"Walk behind me," said the old lady, and Suzanna took her place behind the queen. In that sequence they went down the path, up the four steps leading to the little house, through the open door, and paused in a short, narrow hall, through which Suzanna and her sister and brother had often walked.

"Place your coat here," said the old lady, indicating a black walnut hall-tree.

Suzanna did as she was bid and then followed her hostess into the dining-room, to the left of the small hall, where a table flower-decked, stood set for two.

Suzanna sat down at the place the queen indicated and waited interestedly. In time the maid brought on a silver tray with little cups of cream soup, and then cold chicken buried in pink jelly, a most delicious concoction. Finally there was cocoa with whipped cream and marshmallows and melting angel food cake.

The old lady ate daintily, and long before Suzanna's appetite was satisfied she announced that she was finished and demanded that the princess rise from the table with her. She did not mention the strawberries. With a little sigh Suzanna obeyed. And now, instead of returning to the garden, the old lady led the way into the parlor, which lay to the right of the hall. She went straight to the picture that hung above a marble mantel. Below the picture in the center of the mantel rested a crystal vase containing sprays of lilies of the valley.

"This was my king," murmured the old lady, and Suzanna

looked up into the pictured face. "I like him," she said immediately; "has he gone far away?"

At these words the old lady suddenly sank down into a chair and covered her face with her hands. She began to cry softly, but in a way that hurt Suzanna inexpressibly. She stood for a moment hesitant. The sobs still continued and then Suzanna, deciding on her course, went to the little shaking figure and put her hands softly on the drooping shoulders.

"Can I help you," she asked. "Just tell me what to do for you."

"Nothing," came the muffled tones, "there is no one to do for me; no one to do for me in love. I am alone, forgotten."

"Haven't you a brother or a sister?" in a moment she asked softly.

"No one," said the little lady.

"Oh, then," said Suzanna pityingly, as a dire thought came to her, "there's no one to call you by your first name!"

And then the old lady lowered her hands and looked into Suzanna's face. "No one," she said sadly, "and it's such a pretty name, Drusilla. It's many long years since I was called that."

"I'd hate to come to a time when no one would call me Suzanna," Suzanna said, and she leaned forward and touched the blue-veined hands. "May I call you Drusilla?" she asked.

"That would be sweet of you," said the little old lady. She seemed less of the queen now than before, just a fluttering, little creature to be tenderly protected and cared for.

The maid came in at this moment. She went straight to the old lady.

"I think," she said gently, "that you must take your nap now.

This is the day for Mrs. Bartlett's call."

The queen rose quite obediently. Suzanna said at once: "Well, I must be going. But I'll come again. Good-bye, Drusilla."

"Good-bye, dear," returned "Drusilla" sweetly. "I'd like to have you kiss me."

Suzanna lifted her young face and kissed Drusilla's withered cheek.

* * * * *

Once out in the road and going swiftly toward home, Suzanna pondered many things. She thought of what the old lady had said about the little silver chain binding one to another; that no one really stood alone—no one with a family, at least, Suzanna decided. It was a big thought; you could go on and on in your heart and find many places for it to fit—and then she reached her own gate and felt as always a sense of happiness. No matter how happily she had spent the day, there was always a little throb which stirred her heart when she went up the steps leading to the rather battered front door of the place she called home.

Maizie opened the door. She was as happy in beholding Suzanna returned as though weeks had parted them, for she knew Suzanna's aptitude for great adventures. Always they came to her, while another might walk forever and meet no Heralds of Romance.

"Did something happen, Suzanna?" she began eagerly.

"Yes, I found a queen and we had lunch together," Suzanna responded. "I'll tell you all about it when we're in bed."

"Are you going to play at something tomorrow?"

"Tomorrow I shall be an Only Child," said Suzanna. "Don't

you remember?"

"And not my sister?" asked Maizie.

Suzanna caught the yearning in Maizie's voice.

"Well," she said, "I'll be your closest friend, Maizie."

CHAPTER II

THE ONLY CHILD

Breakfast the next morning was nearly concluded when Suzanna made her appearance, but she met with no reproof. She had anticipated none, for surely an Only Child was entitled to many privileges; no rules should be made to bind her.

Her father was gone. It was a day of stock-taking at the hardware store, and his early presence had been requested by his employer, Job Doane. Suzanna's mother and the children still lingered at the table.

"Good morning, Suzanna," said Mrs. Procter, while the other children gazed with interest at their tardy sister.

"Good morning," Suzanna returned as she took her place; then, "Will you remind Maizie that I am an Only Child today?"

"You hear, Maizie," said Mrs. Procter smiling.

"Mustn't any of us speak to her?" asked Peter.

"No one but her mother," said Suzanna addressing the ceiling.

She went on with her breakfast, eating daintily with the small finger on her right hand cocked outward. Maizie stared,

Emily Calvin Blake

fascinated. Countless words rushed to her lips, but she had been bidden to silence, and she feared, should she speak to Suzanna, dire results would follow. Suzanna might even go away by herself in pursuit of some wonderful dream, and leave Maizie out of her scheme of things entirely.

So Maizie waited patiently.

"Since you sent Bridget away on an errand of mercy, Mother," Suzanna began later, "I'll help you with the dishes."

In Suzanna's estimation the family boasting an Only Child boasted also servants.

"I'll be glad of your help," said Mrs. Procter, "and since Bridget is away, perhaps you will be kind enough to make your own bed and dust your own room."

Suzanna's face fell. Maizie put out a small hand and touched her sister. "I'll help you," she said, "if you want me to."

"Very well," said Suzanna, and together the children went upstairs.

In the little room shared by the sisters, Suzanna went to work. Ardently she shook pillows and carefully she smoothed sheets, while Maizie, with a reflective eye ever upon Suzanna, dusted the dresser and hung up the clothes.

"Is your mother well this morning?" asked Suzanna politely.

"Why, you saw her," Maizie cried off guard. "She didn't have a headache this morning, did she?"

"I'm speaking of *your* mother," said Suzanna. "You belong to an entirely different family from me."

"Well," said Maizie after a time, "she's not suffering, thank you."

"Have you any brothers and sisters?" pursued Suzanna in an interested though rather aloof tone.

"Oh, yes," said Maizie, trying hard to fill her role satisfactorily. "We have a very large family, and once we had twins."

Suzanna looked her pity. "I'm so glad," she said, "that I'm an Only Child. This morning I was very joyous when I had whipped cream and oatmeal."

"You just had syrup, Suzanna Procter!" cried Maizie.

Suzanna cast a scathing look at her sister: "I had whipped cream!" she cried, "because I am an Only Child!" Then falling into her natural tone: "If you forget again, Maizie, I can't even be a friend of yours." She continued after a pause, reassuming her Only-Child voice, "That's why I wear this beautiful satin dress and diamond bracelets and shining buckles on my shoes."

Now Maizie saw only Suzanna's lawn dress, rather worn Sunday shoes with patent leather tips; she saw Suzanna's bare arms.

"Maybe you'd like, really, to wear a white satin dress and bracelets and buckles, but you know you haven't got them, don't you, Suzanna?" she asked.

Suzanna did not answer, plainly ignoring Maizie's conciliatory tone, and so finding the silence continuing unbroken, Maizie changed the subject.

"Will you play school with me this afternoon, Suzanna?"

Suzanna thought a moment: "I don't just know. I may go and play with some of the other girls today, and, remember, if I do that a friend can't get mad like a sister can."

Maizie began to whimper.

"All right, if you're going to act that way, I am going off to see Drusilla," with which statement Suzanna turned and went downstairs.

Maizie came running down after her. "Mother, mother," she called loudly, "I don't like Suzanna when she's the Only Child."

Mrs. Procter, busy with the baby, looked up. She was a little cross now. "I wish, Suzanna," she said, "that you would learn to be sensible and not always be acting in plays you make up."

Suzanna, who a moment before had bounded joyfully into her mother's presence, now paused, the light dying from her eyes. She looked at her mother and her mother, uncomfortable beneath the steady gaze, spoke again with an irritation partially assumed.

"I mean just that, Suzanna," she said. "Maizie can't easily follow all your imaginings; and I have enough to do without always trying to keep the peace between you."

Suzanna stood perfectly still. The color rose to her temples, while the dark eyes flashed. Waves of emotion swept through her. Emotions she could not express. At last in a tense voice she spoke: "I wish I wasn't your child, Mother."

"Go at once to your room," said Mrs. Procter, "and stay there till I tell you you may come down again."

With no word Suzanna turned, went slowly up the stairs again, drew a chair to the window and sat down. She was flaming under a bitter sense of injustice. With all the intensity of her nature for the moment she hated the entire world.

Time passed. She heard sounds downstairs, Maizie going out to play in the yard with Peter; her mother singing the baby to sleep, and still Suzanna sat near the window, and still her small heart beat resentfully.

Later, she heard her father's voice. Perhaps he cared for her. But even of this she was not sure. Then she sat up very straight. Someone was coming up the stairs.

It was Maizie. The little girl slowly opened the bedroom door, peeped cautiously in, and then on tiptoes approached Suzanna. "Mother says," she began, "that you're to come down to lunch."

"I don't want any lunch," said Suzanna. The bright color still stained her cheek. "You can just go downstairs and eat up everything in the house, and be sure and tell mother I said so."

Maizie looked her awe at this defiant sister. Downstairs she returned to deliver verbatim Suzanna's message.

Suzanna sat on. From bitter disillusion felt against everything in her world her mind chilled to analysis. Her mother loved her, she believed, and yet—she did not complete her swift thought; indeed, she looked quickly about in fear of her disloyalty. She had once thought that mothers were perfect, rare beings removed worlds from other mere mortals. Hadn't she, when a very small girl of four, been quite unable to comprehend that mother was a mere human being? "Mother is just mother," she had said in her baby way, and that sentence spelled all the devotion and admiration of a pure little heart for one enshrined within it.

And now mother had fallen short. Mother had disappointed that desperately loving, intense soul. The tears started to her eyes. It was as though on this second tucked-in day an epoch had come marking the day for all time, placing it by itself as containing an experience never to be forgotten.

After a time she realized she was hungry. So she went quietly to the top of the stairs, but no sound came up from below.

Some clock struck one, and then Suzanna heard running footsteps mounting the stairs. She sat straight and gazed out of the window. She knew the moment her mother entered the room, but she did not turn her head.

Mrs. Procter approached until she stood close to Suzanna. She looked down into the mutinous little face. She had come intending to scold, but something electric about the child kept hasty words back.

At length: "Aren't you going to speak to me, Suzanna?" she said.

Suzanna did not answer immediately. That strange, awful thought that her very own mother had been unjustly irritable held her tongue-tied. At length words, short, curt, came:

"You weren't *all right* to me this morning, Mother," she said, raising her stormy eyes. "Yesterday you were nice to me when I was a princess. Today you were cross because Maizie couldn't understand, and she never understands. You never were cross about that before." She gazed straight back into her mother's face—"I'm mad at the whole world."

What perfection the child expects of the mother! No human deviations! Mrs. Procter sighed. How could she live out her child's exalted ideal of her! She looked helplessly at Suzanna. The eyes lifted to hers lacked the wonted expression of perfect belief, of passionate admiration. That this first little daughter, so close to her heart fibers, should in any degree turn from her, pierced the mother. She put her arms about the unyielding small figure.

"Suzanna, little daughter," she whispered. "Mother is some-times tired, but always, always she loves you."

The response was immediate. With a little cry Suzanna pressed her lips to her mother's. All her reticence was gone. This mother who enfolded her stood once more the unwavering star that guided Suzanna's life.

"You see, little girl," Mrs. Procter said after a few moments, "mother sometimes has a great deal to think about—and baby was cross."

"Oh, mother, dear, I'll help you," cried Suzanna. "I'll always be good to you and when I'm grown up I'll buy you silk dresses and pretty hats and take you to hear beautiful music."

Later they went downstairs together. In the kitchen Maizie was amusing the baby as he sat in his high chair. She looked around as Suzanna entered: "Are you going to see Drusilla now," asked Maizie.

"Who's Drusilla?" asked Mrs. Procter with interest.

Now Suzanna had not told her mother of her new friend. She had wished to keep in character, and a princess, she felt, was rather secretive and aloof. But now the renewed closeness she felt to her mother opened her heart.

"Yesterday when I was a princess, living my very own first tucked-in day, I walked and walked, and at last came to a little house with a garden," she said, "and there was an old lady with no one to call her by her first name—and so I'm going to call her Drusilla."

"Is she a little old lady with white hair, and curls on each side of her face?" asked Mrs. Procter.

"Yes," said Suzanna.

"Why, she's Mr. Graham Woods Bartlett's mother, and she's a little—" Mrs. Procter hesitated believing it wiser to leave her sentence unfinished.

"A little what, mother?" asked Suzanna anxiously.

"Oh, she has fancies," evaded Mrs. Procter. "For instance, there are times when she thinks herself a queen."

Emily Calvin Blake

"What was the word you were going to use, mother?" persisted Suzanna.

"Well, then, Suzanna, such a person is called a little strange."

"Then I'm a little strange, too," said Suzanna.

"But you're a child, Suzanna," said Mrs. Procter, "and Mrs. Bartlett is a very old lady."

"Does that make the difference?" asked Suzanna. "If it does, I can't understand why. I think that an old lady, especially if she's lonely and if she grieves for her king who went far away from her, has just as much right to have fancies as a little girl has."

"Well, I don't know," said Mrs. Procter, turning a soft look upon Suzanna.

Maizie, who had been standing near listening intently, now spoke: "A girl I know had a grandfather who thought he was a cat and every once in awhile he meowed, and he liked to sit in the sun. He thought he was a nice, gentle, Maltese cat, and when he wasn't busy meowing he was awful sweet to the children, and played with them and took care of the little ones; but the big people thought they'd better send him far away, because it wasn't right that he should think himself a cat."

Suzanna's eyes flamed in anger. "I think they were cruel," she cried, "not to let him stay at home. I know the girl whose grandfather he was. Her name's Mary Holmes, and she cried because they sent her grandfather away. But she didn't tell me why."

"I'm her special friend on Wednesday recess day," said Maizie bashfully, "that's why she told me."

"I like old people," Suzanna continued. "I like Drusilla, and I like Mrs. Reynold's mother that once came to see her, and I like old Joe, the vegetable man, who made whistles for us last summer. They all seem to understand you when you talk to them, and they can see things just like you can."

"Well, I've heard it said," said Mrs. Procter musingly, "that old people are very much like the young in their fancies. Maybe that's why you enjoy them, Suzanna."

"Well, mother," Suzanna was very much in earnest now, "can't you always tell everybody who has an old lady or an old gentleman living with them that if they're not loving to old ladies and gentlemen, their silver chain will break?"

"Silver chain?" cried Maizie, puzzled. "I don't know what you mean, Suzanna."

"Why, every one of us," Suzanna explained carefully, "carries a little silver chain which binds him to everyone else, but especially, I suppose, to our very own father and mother and brothers and sisters."

"Where is the chain?" asked Maizie.

"It runs from your wrist to mine. It stretches as you move, and it's given to everybody as soon as he's born. Sometimes it's broken."

"Well, Suzanna," said Maizie solemnly, "then you've broken the silver chain that ties you to me and to Peter and the baby and to daddy and mother. You don't belong to us any more—you're an Only Child."

*   *   *   *   *

Maizie's literalness drew a new vivid picture for Suzanna. She had cut herself from those she loved. She looked through a mist into Maizie's face, the little face with the gray eyes and straight fine hair that *would* lie flat to the little head, and a big love flooded her. She went swiftly to the little sister and lifted

Emily Calvin Blake

her hand. She made a feint of clasping something at her wrist. "Maizie," she said, "I put the chain on again. You are once more my little sister."

"Not just your closest friend, but your little sister, with a silver chain holding us together?" Maizie asked.

"Always," said Suzanna. "I don't think after all that it's any fun to be an Only Child."

CHAPTER III

WITH FATHER IN THE ATTIC

A special Saturday in the Procter home, since father expected to spend the afternoon in the attic working at his invention! Once a month he had this half-day vacation from the hardware store. True, to make up he returned to work in the evening after supper, and remained sometimes till midnight, but that was the bargain he had made with Job Doane, the owner of the shop, and he stuck bravely by it.

The house was in beautiful order when father arrived at noon. He went at once to the dining-room. Suzanna and Maizie, putting the last touches to the table, greeted him cordially.

"We have carrots and turnips chopped up for lunch," announced Maizie immediately.

"And baked apples, with the tiniest drop of cream for each one," completed Suzanna.

"And the baby has a clean dress on, too," Maizie added, like an anticlimax.

Mr. Procter exclaimed in appropriate manner. He seemed younger today, charged with a high spirit. His step was light, he held his head high; his eyes, too, were full of fire. The children knew some vital flame energized him, some great hope vivified him.

Emily Calvin Blake

"Sold a scythe to old Farmer Hawkes this morning," he began, when they were all seated around the table, the smoking dishes before them. He smiled at his wife and the subtle understanding went around the board that it was ridiculous for father, the great man, to waste his time selling a scythe to close old Farmer Hawkes; also the perfect belief that Farmer Hawkes was highly favored in being able to make a purchase through such a rare agency.

Luncheon concluded, father rose. The children pushed back their chairs and stood in a little group, all regarding him with longing eyes.

"Well, children," he said at last, "if things go well with me upstairs and I can spare an hour, I'll call you. But don't let me keep you from your work, or your play. Ball for you, I suppose, Peter, since it is Saturday afternoon," he finished facetiously. Well he knew the fascination of the attic and its wonder Machine.

And Peter didn't answer. Let father have his joke; they both understood.

Father went singing joyfully up the stairs. The children listened till they heard the attic door close, then all was silent.

Suzanna found a book, and at Maizie's earnest request read a chapter from it aloud, while Peter descended into the cellar on business of his own.

"I'd rather you'd tell me a story of your own, Suzanna," said Maizie, when the chapter was concluded.

"Well, I can't make up stories today," said Suzanna. "Today is father's day, and I'm thinking every minute of The Machine."

"It's going to be a great thing, isn't it, Suzanna?" said Maizie, in an awed voice.

"Yes, and nobody in the world could have made it but our father," said Suzanna solemnly. "Father was made to do that work, and the whole world will be better because of his invention."

"The whole outside world?" asked Maizie, "or just Anchorville?"

"Oh, the whole world," said Suzanna, and then as Peter once more made his appearance: "Peter, take your tie out of your mouth. Father may call us upstairs at any moment, and you must look as nice as nice can be."

Peter obediently removed his tie from between his teeth, and just then the awaited summons came.

"Children! You may come up and bring mother."

Suzanna ran out into the kitchen. Mother had her hands in a pan of dough and was kneading vigorously. She looked up at Suzanna's message and replied: "You children run up to father; I'll come when I can. Go quietly by the bedroom door, the baby's asleep."

Upstairs then the children flew. At the top they paused and looked in. Father was standing close to The Machine; he turned as they appeared, and with a princely gesture (Suzanna's private term), invited them in.

The attic was dimly lit. Shadows seemed to lurk in its corners. It was an attic in name only, since it held no stored treasures of former days. It stood consecrated to a great endeavor. The children knew that, and instinctively paused at the threshold. They got the sense that big thoughts filled this room, big ambitions for Man.

They approached and paused before The Machine. It stood high, cabinet-shaped, of brilliantly polished wood whose surface seemed to catch and hold soft, rosy lights from out the

Emily Calvin Blake

shadows. Above The Machine rose a nickel-plated flexible arm, at the end of which hung a sort of helmet. Some distance back of the arm, and extending about a foot above the cabinet, were two tubes connected by a glass plate; and beneath the plate, a telescope arrangement into which was set a gleaming lens.

Mr. Procter opened a door at the side of the cabinet. The children, peering in, beheld interesting looking springs, coils, and batteries. He shut the door, walked around to the front of the cabinet and opened another and smaller door. Here the children, following, saw a number of small black discs. The inventor reached in, touched a lever, and immediately a rhythmic, clicking sound ensued.

Next he drew down dark shades over the low windows. The filmed glass plate above the cabinet alone showed clear in the eclipse, as though waiting.

"Now, Suzanna, come!"

Suzanna, at some new electric quality in her father's voice, sprang forward. He procured a chair, placed it directly before the cabinet, drew the flexible arm till the helmet rested perhaps four inches above the child's head but did not touch it, pulled forward the telescope and focused its lens upon her expectant face.

"Watch the plate glass," he said in a tense whisper, and Suzanna kept her eyes as directed.

A moment passed. No sound came but the rhythmic ticking. The inventor's face was white. His eyes, dark, held a gleam and a prayer. Another space, and then very slowly a shadowy line of color played upon the glass set between the two tubes; color so faint, so delicate, that Suzanna wondered if she saw clearly.

But the color strengthened, and at last all saw plainly a line of rich deep purple touched with gold. It remained there triumphant upon the glass, a royal bar.

Silent moments breathed themselves away, for the test had come and it had not failed. Suzanna, at last moving her gaze from the color registered, turned to her father. She saw, with a leap of the heart, that his eyes were wet. He seemed to have turned to an immovable image, and yet never did life seem to flow out so richly from him.

Peter broke the quiet. "What does it mean, daddy, that color?" he asked.

Suddenly galvanized, Mr. Procter ran to the stairs outside. His voice rang out like a bell.

"Jane, come, come!"

Mrs. Procter, in the kitchen, caught the exultant note in his voice. She was stirring batter for a cake, but she flung down the spoon and ran up the stairs.

"Oh, Richard, what is it," she cried, as she reached him. His eyes, half frightened, half elated, looked into hers.

"I will show you," he cried. He took her hand and led her to The Machine before which Suzanna still sat.

The wave of color still persisted on the glass. "See," he said, "registered color, for which I have worked and worked, died a thousand deaths of despair, and been resurrected to hope. This afternoon the color seemed promised, and so in fear and trembling I placed Suzanna before the machine."

"Oh, my dear, my dear, after all these years!" She lifted her face and kissed him solemnly.

And then Peter repeated his question, to which before there had been no answer.

"What does the color mean, daddy?" he asked.

"Two colors recording in that manner means great versatility; purple means the artist, probably a writer."

Peter looked his bewilderment. His mother, smiling a little, reduced the explanation to simpler form. Even then Peter was befogged.

The inventor went to a remote corner and brought forth a large book containing many pages. This he placed upon a small table, and the children and their mother crowded about him, eager to see and to hear.

Mr. Procter lit a side lamp so the light fell upon the book, then he turned the pages slowly. Blocks of color lay upon each, some in squares alone, some merging into others like a disjointed rainbow. Above each block, or merged block, were writings, interpretations of color meaning, word above word; many erasures, as though fresh thought thrust out the integrity of early ones.

Mr. Procter spoke to his wife. "Till the machine showed the possibilities of ultimate success, I have said nothing even to you of its inception. Now, however, I may speak.

"It may sound strange, but from the time I was a very young boy, I've seen others in color. That is, a vivid personality never failed to translate itself in purple to me; a pale one in blue. It was out of that spiritual sight that I built my theory of color. It took me years, but time after time have I proved to my own complete satisfaction that each individual has a keynote of color; a color explaining his purpose."

A thousand questions of details, of practicalities that his theory did not seem in the rough to touch, rushed to Mrs. Procter's lips; but she could not voice one, she could not quench his uplifted expression and, indeed, so great was her belief in him that she had faith that he would overcome all obstacles.

He went on: "After I had my system of color worked out, I

began to plan my machine, then to build it, and now—" He covered his face with his hands. Suddenly he took them down, turned to his children and with eyes alight, cried:

"For the progress of humanity have I worked, my children. To read men's meanings, the purposes for which they live, have I created this machine."

The children, deeply stirred with him, gazed back into his kindled face. His magnetism lifted them. For humanity he had worked, should always work, and with him they understood that this was the greatest service. With him they rose on the wings of creative imagination. Desire ran deep in each small heart to do something for the benefit of man. Not money, not position, but love for one's fellows, work for one's fellows! Never in all their lives were they to forget this moving hour in the attic. Its influence would be with them for always.

After a moment Maizie spoke: "How does The Machine know your color, daddy?"

The inventor smiled. "It has an eye, see?" He pointed to the lens in the telescope. Then he opened the small door. "In this place it has sensitized plates; this helmet, too, is highly sensitized." He paused and then laughed at himself as he saw the mystified expressions of his children. "Well, let us try Maizie. I know her color, but let's see what the machine says." He turned out the lamp. "Come, Maizie," he said.

So Maizie seated herself before the machine and watched to see what the glass plate should say of her. The plate remained for a moment clear, then slowly there grew a feather of color. Smoke color, a sort of dove gray, it was and so remained, despite its neutrality, quite plainly visible.

Mr. Procter lifted the helmet, hushed the machine. He went to his book, took it to the window, raised the shade a trifle and peered down. "As I knew," he said. Then closing the book and turning to his small daughter, he went on: "My little Maizie

Emily Calvin Blake

will some day nurse back to health those who are weary and worn; she will be patient, full of understanding, and she will be greatly beloved."

Maizie's face grew luminous. "And so I'll do good too, just like you," she said, with a beautiful faith.

"You will do good, too, my daughter," he answered, with exquisite egotism in his inclusion.

Peter, eager-eyed, looked up at his father.

"Do you think I have a color, too, daddy?" he asked.

"Yes, Peter. Take your place."

Peter did so.

For him there grew a tongue of sturdy bronze. In the dim light it waved across the surface of the glass plate.

And Mr. Procter said: "In time our little boy Peter will build great bridges."

"That four horses can walk across, daddy?" Peter cried in ecstasy.

"That a hundred horses can walk across, and a big engine pull safely its train of cars."

Then again into the inventor's eyes leaped a radiance. He placed his hand lovingly upon the machine as though it were alive, and indeed so it seemed to be, for into it he had put his finest ideals, his deepest hopes for the development of man.

"A few months more of work," he cried. "And then it will be ready to give to the world."

Someone came lightly up the stairs. A head appeared, then a

body, then a hearty voice: "May I come in?" it asked.

Mrs. Procter swung the door wide to Mr. Reynolds, neighbor across the way. He entered with a little hesitation. He was a large man with a heavy brick-colored face, yet with eyes that had preserved some spirit of youth. Mr. Reynolds was as great an idealist as his friend, the inventor, though his idealism gave out in totally different directions. He read all sorts of books, but reacted to them with originality. His imagination only grasped their meanings, not his intellect. He worked in another town, several miles from Anchorville, in a large chair factory, and several times a week in the evening he stood upon a soap box on a street corner, and amused a mixed audience by his picturesque setting forth of what he thought was wrong with the world; also what methods he believed would, if employed, straighten out the tangles.

Since he spoke "straight from the shoulder," as he put it, touching dramatically upon the hand of wealth as causing the tangles, he had called down upon himself the wrath of the town's richest man, old John Massey, owner of the Massey Steel Mills. Twice Mr. Massey had threatened the eloquent and fearless orator with arrest, and twice for some unknown reason he had refrained from carrying out his threat, and the authorities of the town complacently allowed Mr. Reynolds to continue his pastime.

"I knew you were at home today," said Mr. Reynolds, "and I must see the machine." He looked at the joyous face of the inventor.

"Why, have you been trying it out?" he cried.

"Yes, and with a fair degree of success. Of course, I realize it may not always work as it did today. Indeed, the colors are not so strong as I expect eventually to get them."

"A great piece of work," said Mr. Reynolds, advancing to the middle of the room and falling into the orator's attitude. "I've

Emily Calvin Blake

thought of it every day since you told me of it. When I see men in the factory working at jobs they fair hate, because they and theirs need bread—and breaking under the bondage—Oh, I say, Procter, I wish you could bring the machine to perfection soon and get others to believe in it."

Mr. Procter's eyes lost their light. "That's it, to make others believe!"

Mrs. Procter went to her husband. She put her hand on his arm and looked up into his face with a gaze of perfect faith. "A big purposeful idea like yours, that's going to make humanity happier, can't fail but some day to be brought to the world's attention. Never lose faith, my man."

The shadow of discouragement fell swiftly from him.

"And, now," she continued before he could speak, "all wait here a little while. The baby's still asleep," she flung over her shoulder as she left the room.

Shortly she returned bearing a large tray which she set down on the table. Then she lit the side lamp; it cast a soft glow over the room. "Now all draw close," Mrs. Procter invited.

So they drew chairs near the table. There was milk for the children, little seed cakes, thin bread and butter, and cups of strong tea for the inventor and the visitor.

The children, sipping their milk and eating the little sweet cakes, listening to the talk of their father and Mr. Reynolds, their expressed hopes for the success of the machine and its effect upon humanity, gazed at the invention. The sense of a community of interest filled them. They felt that they, each and all, had put something of everlasting worth into The Machine, just as it had put some enduring understanding into them.

"I feel," whispered Suzanna to Maizie, "as though we were

in church."

Mr. Reynolds caught the whisper. "And well you may, little lassie," he returned. "Your father is a fine, good man with no thought at all of himself, and some day," finished Mr. Reynolds, grandly, "his name will go rolling down the ages as a benefactor to all mankind."

A tribute and a prophecy! The children were glad that Mr. Reynolds had such clear vision.

Emily Calvin Blake

CHAPTER IV

THE NEW DRESS

An influence vaguely felt by all the Procter family lingered for days after father's Saturday afternoon at home. And then ordinary hours intruded and filled the small lives with their duties and their pleasures. Still shadowy, deeply hidden, the influence of the visionary father lay. Even small Maizie awoke to tiny dreams, her literalness for moments drowned out.

At school, Maizie and Suzanna were perhaps the least extravagantly dressed little girls. Exquisitely clean, often quaintly adorned with ribbons placed according to Suzanna's fancies, it still could be seen that they came from an humble home.

Still, in their attitude there was toward their companions an unconscious patronage, felt but hardly resented by the others, since Suzanna and Maizie gave love and warmth besides.

And this unconscious feeling of superiority sprang from "belonging" to a father who worked in his free hours that others out in the big world might some day be glad he had lived! This idealism lent luster even to his calling of weighing nails and selling washboards to the town of Anchorville.

Jenny Bryson, in Suzanna's class, bragged of her father's financial condition, and indeed she was a resplendent advertisement of his success.

Suzanna listened interestedly. She gazed with admiration at the velvet dress, the gold ring, and the pearl neck beads. She loved them all—the smoothness of the velvet, the sparkle of the gold, the soft luster of the pearls. But she felt no envy. She loved the adornments with her imagination, not with desire. And though she could not say so to Jenny, she rather pitied her for not having a father to whom a future generation would bow in great gratitude.

Then too, as mother said, if you merely bought clothes, you lost the joy of creating. Witness the ingenious way, following Suzanna's suggestion, that mother had draped a lace curtain over a worn blue dress, and behold, a result wonderful.

It was fun then to "make the best of your material," as mother again said. Mother, who, when not too tired from many tasks, could paint rare word pictures, build for eager little listeners castles of hope; build, especially for Suzanna, colorful palaces with flaming jewels, crystal lamps, scented draperies.

Joys sometimes come close together. Father's day, then Sunday with an hour spent in the Massey pew with gentle Miss Massey, old John Massey's only child, setting forth the lesson from the Bible, and then the thrilling announcement by the Superintendent that a festival was to be given by the primary teachers some time in August, the exact date to be told later.

Miss Massey, taking up the subject when the Superintendent had finished, thought it might add to the brilliance of the affair if Suzanna were to recite. So she gave Suzanna a sheet of paper printed in blue ink, with a title in red. "The Little Martyr of Smyrna," Suzanna spelled out.

"You are to learn the poem by heart, of course, Suzanna," said Miss Massey, "and if you need any help as to emphasis or gesture, you may come to me on any afternoon."

Suzanna flushed exalted. "I don't believe I'll need any help, thank you, Miss Massey," she said. She could scarcely wait then till she reached home to tell her mother the great news.

"You'll have to study hard," said Mrs. Procter after she had read over the verses, "but Suzanna, you have nothing suitable to wear."

"The lace curtain dress, mother?" asked Suzanna, hopefully.

"Beyond repair," returned Mrs. Procter.

Father, sitting near, looked around at his small daughter. "I have two dollars that I couldn't possibly use. Take them for a dress, Suzanna."

"But, dear—" began mother, and went on haltingly about a pair of new shoes she believed father had been saving for.

But father did not hear, and so behold Suzanna and her mother the next day at four o'clock in the afternoon in Bryson's drygoods store deciding upon a pink lawn and a soft valenciennes lace. And later, green cambric for a petticoat. And then on Wednesday the cutting out of the dress with suggestions and help from Mrs. Reynolds, the very kind neighbor across the way. On Thursday, baking day, mother put in every waking moment between the oven in the kitchen and the sewing machine in the dining-room.

"Mother dear, don't work so hard," Suzanna begged once. She held the fretful baby in her arms and tried to soothe him. He was always fretful, it seemed, when mother was very busy.

"The dress must be finished this week," said Mrs. Procter, basting away furiously.

"But there's two weeks yet to the festival, mother," said Suzanna, as she hushed the baby against her shoulder.

"Next week, Suzanna, the bedrooms must be thoroughly cleaned, the carpets taken up. O, please take the baby out into the yard and keep him amused."

Two red spots burned on Mrs. Procter's cheeks. Suzanna saw them. Ardently she wished mother would stop and rest. Such driving haste, such tenacity, meant later a nervous headache with mother put aside in a darkened room. Suzanna sighed as she took the baby out into the yard.

She put him into his carriage and wheeled him about till he fell asleep. Then she called Maizie to watch him, while she tiptoed back into the dining-room. Her mother still sat, dress in hand. Now she was drawing out the bastings. The red spots still burned.

"The baby's asleep, mother," whispered Suzanna. She longed ardently for the return of the loved one who could laugh and say something funny about sleep claiming the baby when he had made up his small mind to remain exasperatingly wide awake.

But instead—"Take out the stockings, Suzanna, and darn them. I'll call you when I need your help for supper. Keep your eye on Peter."

That was all. Suzanna lingered, but no further word came.

Suzanna dragged a low rocking chair into the yard, emptied the bag of freshly washed stockings on the ground beside her, selected a pair of Peter's, slipped the egg down, threaded her needle and began the task of filling in the huge holes. Then she called Maizie from beside the still sleeping baby.

"Maizie," she began, "listen to me say two verses of 'The Little Martyr of Smyrna.'"

Maizie sank down at her sister's feet. She listened in awe as Suzanna dramatically repeated the first part of the poem. Her gestures were remarkable, her voice charged with feeling.

"It's beautiful, Suzanna," said Maizie. "Everybody will listen and look at you in your new dress."

"O, it isn't a dress, Maizie," cried Suzanna, the while her small fingers dexterously wove the needle in and out. "It's a rose blossom. And when I recite in it on the last day of school my heart will be a butterfly sipping honey from the flower."

"I thought it was only a pale pink lawn at ten cents a yard," said Maizie. She spoke somewhat timidly now, fearful of Suzanna's scorn.

"You think everything is just what it is," answered Suzanna reproachfully. "Go see if the baby is still asleep, and look down the road for Peter."

Maizie went off obediently, but she returned in a moment with the news that the baby still slept and Peter was playing near Mr. Reynolds' gate. She seated herself as before. She wanted to hear more of Suzanna's fancies, but Suzanna remained silent, having been chilled a little by Maizie's practicality. So Maizie put out her hand and touched her sister. "Will the petticoat be a petticoat?" she asked, and wondered excitedly into what beauty Suzanna's imagination would transmute this ordinary piece of cambric.

Suzanna's spirits rose again. "It'll be a green satin cup for the rose," she answered, gazing dreamily before her. She let Peter's stocking fall to the ground while she clasped her hands ecstatically. "O, Maizie, it's almost too much joy! To wear a flower dress and to recite something that makes you so happy and yet you want to cry too."

Maizie nestled a little closer. "Do you think, Suzanna, when the green petticoat's nearly worn, that it'll come down to me?"

Suzanna pondered this for a moment. "Yes, it'll go down to you, Maizie, but not for years and years," she answered, finally. "Things do last so in this family."

Maizie, by a sad little shake of the head, agreed with this statement, and the sisters were silent. In different manner, however, for Maizie simply accepted an unpleasant fact, while Suzanna worked mentally to a solution of any situation. She found the solution at last.

"I'll tell you what I'll do, Maizie," she said. "Once a month, when we love each other madly, I'll let you wear my petticoat."

"I hope it'll come on Sunday when we love each other that way," said Maizie, wistfully; "I'm sure mother wouldn't let you lend the petticoat to me for an every-day."

"We can fix that, too," said ready Suzanna. "Some Friday you can begin to fuss about washing Peter. I'll have to wash him myself if you're *too* mean. And Saturday morning you can peel the potatoes so thick that mother'll say: 'Maizie, do you think we're made of money! Here, let Suzanna show you how to peel those potatoes thin.' And then I'll be so mad I'll give you a push, and I won't speak to you for the rest of the day."

"Yes, go on," said Maizie, her eyes shining.

"And then on Sunday morning, just before breakfast, you'll come to me and put your arms around my neck and say: 'Dear, sweet, *lovely* Suzanna, I'm so sorry I've been so hateful. I'll go down on my knees for your forgiveness. *And I'll sew on all the buttons this week!*'"

Maizie drew away a little then. Suzanna went on, however. "And I'll say: 'Yes, dear sinner, I forgive you freely. You may wear my green petticoat today.'"

There fell an hour of a never-to-be-forgotten day when the pink dress lay on the dining-room table, full length, finished, marvelous to little eyes with its yards and yards of valenciennes lace that graduated in width from very narrow to one broad band around the bottom of the skirt.

Emily Calvin Blake

Suzanna, Maizie, Peter, and even the baby bowed before the miracle of beauty.

"How many yards of lace are on it, mother?" asked Suzanna, for the sixth time, and for the sixth time Mrs. Procter looked up from her sewing machine at which she was busy with the green petticoat and answered: "A whole bolt, Suzanna."

The children at this information stared rounder-eyed and then turned to gaze with uncovered awe at Suzanna, the owner.

"Do you think, mother," asked Maizie, "that when I'm older I can have a pink dress with no trimming of yours on it?"

"We'll see," said Mrs. Procter, who knew how strictly to the letter she was held to her promises.

Now Suzanna reluctantly left the dress and went to her mother. "Mother," she cried, softly, "when I recite 'The Little Martyr of Smyrna' up on the big platform, I'm afraid I won't be humble in spirit. It's too much to be humble, isn't it, when you've got a whole bolt of lace on your dress?"

Mrs. Procter, quite used to Suzanna's intensities, answered, running the machine deftly as she spoke: "Oh, you'll be all right, Suzanna. The minister means something else when he preaches of being humble. What bothers me now is how to manage a pair of shoes for you. Yours are so shabby."

"Can't I wear my patent leather slippers?"

"You've outgrown them, Suzanna. They're too short even for Maizie, you remember."

"I could stand them for that one time, mother."

"No," said Mrs. Procter decidedly; "I should be distressed seeing you in shoes too small for you."

"Mother, you could open the end of my patent leather slipper so my toes can push through and then put a puff of black, ribbon over the hole!" The idea was an inspiration, and Suzanna's eyes shone.

Mrs. Procter saw immediately possibilities in the idea. Years of working and scheming and praying to raise her ever increasing family on the inadequate and varying income of her inventor husband had ultimated in keen sensibilities for opportunities. "Why, I think I can do that," she said. "I'll make a sort of shirred bag into which your toes will fit and so lengthen the slipper and cover the stitching with a bow. I hope I can find a needle strong enough to go through the leather." Her face was bright, her voice clear. She was all at once quite different from the weary, dragged mother of the past few days, determined against all odds to finish the dress so the cleaning might be started the following week.

Suzanna gazed delightedly. With the fine intuition of an imaginative child she understood the reason for the metamorphosis. It was the quickening of the senses that rallied themselves to meet and solve a problem that brought a high glow; stimulated, and uplifted. She herself was no stranger to that glow.

She put her arms about her mother's shoulder.

"Isn't it nice, mother, to have to think out things?"

A little puzzled, Mrs. Procter looked at Suzanna. Then her face cleared.

"O, I understand. It is—can you understand the word, Suzanna—'exhilarating' sometimes."

"I feel what the word means, mother—like catching in your breath when you touch cold water."

"Exactly. Now please get the slippers."

Suzanna ran upstairs. Returning, slippers in hand, she found the other children had left.

"Has Maizie got the baby?" Suzanna asked anxiously.

Her mother smiled. "Yes, I carried him out to the yard. He's kicking about, happy on his blanket."

Suzanna, relieved, handed the slippers to her mother.

"And I brought my old black hair ribbon. That will do for the shirring, won't it, mother?"

"Nicely."

Together they evolved, worked, tried on, completed.

"It's more fun doing this than going to Bryson's and buying a new pair, isn't it, mother?"

"Well, I believe it is, daughter."

"I feel so warm here—" Suzanna touched her heart—"because we're doing something harder than just going out to the store and buying what we'd like."

Mrs. Procter gazed at her handiwork reflectively. "Well, it does make you feel that you've accomplished a great deal when you've created something out of nothing."

Mrs. Procter rose then, touched the new dress lovingly, and said: "So, we can put it away now, Suzanna; it's quite finished. The petticoat needs just a button and buttonhole."

Suzanna stood quite still. At last she looked up into her mother's face and put her question: "When will you begin to cut the goods out from under the lace, mother?"

Mrs. Procter, her thoughts now supperward, spoke

abstractedly: "Oh, we'll not do that."

There was a silence, while the room suddenly whirled for Suzanna. Recovering from the dizziness, with eyes large and black and her face very pale, Suzanna gazed unbelievingly at her mother. For a moment she was quite unable to speak. Then in a tiny voice which she endeavored to keep steady, she asked: "Not even from under the wide row round the bottom, mother?"

"No, Suzanna," Mrs. Procter answered, quite unconscious of the storm in the child's breast. She moved towards the door.

"But, mother, listen, please." Suzanna's hands were locked till they showed white at the knuckles. "If you don't cut the goods away the green petticoat won't gleam through the lace! You see, it's a rose dress and a rose has shining green leaves, just showing."

The plea was ardent, but Mrs. Procter was firm. Indeed she did not glance at Suzanna. The reaction from her days of hard and continuous work was setting in. She merely said: "Suzanna, we must make that dress last a long time. I made it so that it can be lengthened five inches. We can't weaken it by cutting the goods away from under the lace. Now, dear, go and see that the children aren't in mischief. I must start supper."

CHAPTER V

SUZANNA COMES TO A DECISION

The children were playing contentedly in the road, Suzanna assured herself. And finding them so, she wandered disconsolately back to the front porch, where seated in a little rocking chair she stared straight before her. She felt as one thrown suddenly from a great height. One moment she had been thrillingly happy, the next, the bitter fruit of disappointment touched her lips. So events occur lightningly quick in this world. The day itself was as beautiful as it had been an hour before, yet its sun had ceased to shine for little Suzanna, since the crowning touch of The Dress, the poetic completeness of it, was denied her.

Years ago it seemed she had wakened in the morning after dreaming of a rose gown with its glimpses of cool green flickering through rows of open lace; but no more could she dream, since that lace was now condemned to blindness, unable even to hint at concealed beauties, and this because Economy, the stern god of the Procter home, so ordained.

Two tears at last found their slow way down her cheek. Not the least of her woe was caused by the realization that now the dress was ingloriously what Maizie had termed it, a pale pink lawn at ten cents a yard, bearing no appeal to her imagination, fulfilling no place in Suzanna's great Scheme of Things.

Suzanna's distress, as the days passed, did not abate. She never spoke of the dress, nor did she go to look at it as it hung shrouded in cheese cloth in the hall closet upstairs. No longer did she look forward with delight to the day when feelingly she should recite the troubles and the heroism of "The Little Martyr of Smyrna."

Instead she went quietly about performing her customary duties, finding for the time no real zest in life.

Mrs. Procter, innocent of the cause of Suzanna's listlessness, spoke no word. She wondered why the child had lost interest in the festival, indeed in all things pertaining to the occasion. It was difficult, she finally decided, to know how to cope with a child so complex, so changeable. She determined to treat the new mood with indifference, as being the most potent method. So she asked of Suzanna the performance of daily duties just as usual. When she discovered Suzanna gazing at her, Maizie close beside her with the same degree of reflection in her gray eyes, Mrs. Procter grew uncomfortable, then a trifle irritable. Both children seemed to regard her as an alien, one, for the time, quite outside their pale.

Suzanna, then, had taken Maizie into her confidence.

"One needs be clairvoyant," Mrs. Procter told her husband one evening, "to know what passes through small minds."

"Clairvoyant and full of patience," he answered, looking up from his color book. "I can remember even now my own sensations when at times my mother failed to go with me into my land of dreams."

Mrs. Procter cast her memory back over the events of several days.

"I can't think what has so changed Suzanna," she said at last; "I've disappointed her, I fear, about something or other. Dear me, what insight versatile children do demand in a mother. And Suzanna takes everything so very seriously. And Maizie stares at me too, with a little bewildered expression. It's strange that Maizie, with all her literalness, can understand at times Suzanna's disappointments when her fancies are not given due value. For, of course, it is some fancy of Suzanna's that I've either not noticed, or perhaps laughed at." She paused to smile at her husband.

"Such children come of giving them an inventor father, an 'impractical genius,' as I've heard myself in satire called."

She flushed up angrily at this.

"You've done wonderfully well," she said, and believed the assertion; just as though at forty to weigh nails correctly and to sell so many yards of garden hose a week was a fine measure of success. "And your name will go ringing down the ages." She would never let him lose confidence in his own powers. Circumstances alone had thrown him into a mediocre position in a small town, but they should never hold him down.

He grew beneath her look; beneath her belief in him. And so the conversation ended on the personal note; ended with hands clasped and fond eyes seeing each the other's charm after many years.

Suzanna, arranging the pantry the next morning, sought her mother upstairs with a domestic announcement.

"The vinegar bottle is empty," she said.

"And the gherkins all ready," cried Mrs. Procter. "Will you run over to Mrs. Reynolds and ask her for some vinegar, Suzanna?"

Listlessly, Suzanna returned downstairs, and from the pantry procured a cup. Slowly she left the house, walked down the front path and across the road to Mrs. Reynolds' home. Arrived there, she went round to the back door and knocked with slack knuckles.

Mrs. Reynolds, a white cloth tied about her forehead, opened the door. She gave out redolently the pungent odor of the commodity Suzanna sought to borrow.

Mrs. Reynolds was stout and comfortable looking ordinarily. A quaint and interesting personality, sprung from Welsh parentage, she fitted into the life of Anchorville only because of a certain natural adaptability. She seemed to belong to a wilder, more passionate people than those plain lives which surrounded her.

Suzanna knew her tenderness, her tragic depressions. She loved her deep voice, her resonant tones, all her quick changes of mood, and her occasional strange ways of expression, revealing her understanding of men and women's vagaries.

Mrs. Reynolds adored Suzanna. She had said often there was one thing she coveted from her neighbor, and that was her neighbor's child.

Mrs. Reynolds had no children and in that deplorable fact lay her keenest unhappiness.

She greeted Suzanna cordially.

"Come in, Suzanna, come in," she said. "I've been using vinegar and red pepper all morning," she continued, as she went her way to the pantry with Suzanna's cup. "I've one of my old headaches."

"Oh, I'm so sorry," said Suzanna, with immediate sympathy. "Have you been worrying?"

"Not more than usual, Suzanna," said Mrs. Reynolds with a sigh. "Here's your vinegar. Hold it steady. Vinegar's a bad thing to spill."

"Thank you," said Suzanna, politely, as she received the cup. And then: "I don't see why you should worry. You have no

Emily Calvin Blake

children. It's mother's many children that sometimes give her worry."

"Your mother'd have worries even without you all," returned Mrs. Reynolds. "Won't you sit down a spell, Suzanna?"

"No, I can't, mother's waiting." Suzanna walked toward the door, pausing on her way to glance about her. "My, but you're very clean here," she said, appreciatively. "Your cleanness is different from ours. Ours doesn't show so."

"There's no little hands to clutter things up," said Mrs. Reynolds, but her voice wasn't glad.

Suzanna, intuitively sensing the real trouble, said: "Reynolds slammed the door this morning, Mrs. Reynolds. We heard the slam in our dining-room and my mother jumped." Suzanna quite innocently borrowed Mrs. Reynolds' way of referring to her husband.

Mrs. Reynolds' face darkened. "Yes, I know he did. That man is getting more like a bear every day."

"He liked our twin that went away, Mrs. Reynolds. He wasn't like a bear when he played with her."

At this statement Mrs. Reynolds suddenly threw her apron over her head and sobbed: "That's just it, Suzanna, that's just it; there aren't any little cluttering fingers about."

Suzanna set the vinegar cup carefully down on the table, the while her keenly sensitive mind worked rapidly. Those gifts which by dint of their frequency in her own home seemed rather overdone were actually missed here! A strong, deep sympathy for Mrs. Reynolds' disappointment grew within her, but did not entirely crowd out the thought that through this very disappointment her own burning desire might be brought to pass. She now went swiftly and touched the weeping woman.

"Mrs. Reynolds," she began, "will you tell me how you feel about cutting pink goods away from under lace. Can you afford to do that?"

Mrs. Reynolds' apron came down with a jerk, and for a second she stared her perplexity at the upturned, earnest little face. Then with quick understanding which revealed her real mother-spirit, she answered: "Why land, Honey-Girl, Reynolds makes pretty good money at times. I guess we can do about as we please in most simple ways."

"Well, then, keep your apron down," advised Suzanna; "and just think this thought over and over: 'Reynolds is not going to be cross any more!' Thank you again for the vinegar, I must be going now."

It was not without misgiving that Suzanna started immediately to put her secret plan into execution. And her judicious side urged the completion of all details before she said anything to those most nearly concerned in her new move. Only to Maizie, whose constant attendance she skillfully managed to elude while she made her simple preparations, did she at last give any confidence, and it was in this manner she spoke:

"There's going to be a great change, Maizie; and tonight you must manage to stay awake to do something for me."

Maizie, at once interested, grew wildly expectant. Though she could send up no airships of her own, she loved to contemplate Suzanna's daring flights.

"I'll do anything, Suzanna," she promised.

So Suzanna gave Maizie her news. Hearing it, Maizie's lips quivered, but she kept back the tears by the exercise of great control. They were upstairs in their own room. It was late afternoon. Peter was out playing. Mrs. Procter, the baby with her, was downtown ordering groceries.

"Now, you mustn't cry, Maizie," said Suzanna; "it all had to be, and what is to be is for the best." Suzanna quoted from Mrs. Reynolds. "Go downstairs and get father's dictionary."

Maizie obeyed, returning quickly with the desired book.

"And now stand at the window so as to tell me when you see mother coming."

So Maizie took her stand while Suzanna labored hard with the pen. An hour passed. Once Suzanna flew downstairs to the kitchen, then returned to her work. At last, Maizie in excited tones announced that her mother and the baby had turned the corner. Suzanna laid down her pen.

"Well, it's all finished," she said.

Maizie looked at her sister. Now the tears came, blurring the big gray eyes.

"You mustn't cry, Maizie," said Suzanna, trying to subdue her own emotions.

"Couldn't you just wear the dress as it is?" asked Maizie in a small voice, touching the crux of the whole matter, the cause of the great change.

"I just couldn't," Suzanna returned. "It wouldn't be a rose blossom, you see, Maizie, *when it could just as well be one.*"

Maizie nodded. Perhaps she understood Suzanna's sense of waste. Undoubtedly her grief at Suzanna's contemplated step had sharpened her sensibilities. Vague stirrings told her that the artist in Suzanna had been desperately hurt; and for the once her imagination thrilled as did her sister's to the dress as a Rose Blossom. She knew with passion that it could not remain simply pink lawn cut and slashed into a mere garment.

So she went softly to Suzanna and touched her gently.

"I'll help you all I can, sister," she said.

So it was that just as the clock was striking nine, little Maizie stole from her room—shared as long as she remembered with Suzanna—crept down the stairs and into the parlor where her father sat studying, as always, a formidable book, the while her mother sat sewing, her chair drawn close to his. Maizie went straight to the quiet figure.

"Mother," she said, "Suzanna told me to stay awake till the clock struck nine and then to give you this."

"This" was a note folded into the shape of a cocked hat, which Suzanna thought very elegant. Mrs. Procter, accustomed to Suzanna's ways, unfolded the note, smiled at the large printed letters, sighed a little at the thought of the great effort put into their forming, read once, twice, then sat up very straight. The note thus told its own story:

My Loving Mother:

I have given myself to the Reynolds for there own. Mrs. Reynolds is not happy with Reynolds' slams of doors and crossness be cause they have no child. They will be pretty sprised to see me to night and glad with my big shiny bag witch I have borrowed from my once very loved father. I have my pink dress witch will soon be a rose in it and my other things. I wore my hat and coat even if it is warm. You will not miss me much because the last baby went away and a baby always makes more work. And anyway one little girl out of a big family wont make any difrunce. But if you want any fine errands ran, you can borrow Mrs. Reynolds new child. Tell father I am loving my naybor as myself. It hurt me till something stopped inside to see Mrs. Reynolds put her apron over her head at Reynolds slams. Perhaps the mother angel that stops at our house all the time will pause at Mrs. Reynolds' next time and leave a bundle, thinking when I'm there a family don't have to be started which is always hard, I

Emily Calvin Blake

suppose. Mother, please don't forget about borrowing. It is not polite to come 2 often even to borrow me for some thing big. It took me an hour and twenty minutes to write this while you were at the butshers and grosers and Maizie at the window. I had to stop too, to watch the beans on the stove. I have labored over some of the big spelling with fathers dicsionary on my knee, remembering to make all my i's big I's.

Farewell forever,
Suzanna *Reynolds*.

P. S. Mrs. Reynolds can afford to cut away the goods from under all lace, which makes my heart jump! Perhaps tho even tho I'm sorry for her, if she hadn't promised to cut away the goods from under the lace in my pink dress, I wouldn't have adopted myself out to her. So I shall see you when I recite "The Little Martyr of Smyrna" with the green showing through the windows of my many yards of lace. O, Mother, I couldn't bare to ware that dress which is just a *dress* when it could be a *rose*.

"What's the matter?" asked Mr. Procter, attracted by the strange, almost solemn silence. "What's the trouble, Jane?"

She handed the note to him, waited while he read it through not once, but many times, as she had.

He passed it back to her. "Shall we go for her?" he asked.

But she shook her head. "Sometimes I don't know just how to act where Suzanna's concerned," she said. She folded the note. "No, sometimes I feel just helpless."

CHAPTER VI

SUZANNA MAKES HER ENTRY

Mr. and Mrs. Reynolds were in the kitchen, she belatedly washing the supper dishes, he smoking his pipe near the window. She lent, through her vivid personality, color to him. Big, hearty, he was not picturesque. He seemed to take note of realities more than she did. Perhaps springing from emotional folk, she stood with a quality of rich background denied to him by a line of unimaginative ancestors.

He read his big books, she found truths in her own heart. She found a quick, tender language springing from her understanding. He used his words like bludgeons.

Still they loved one another, and her deepest hurt was that he wanted that which she could not give him. So she placed his longing before hers and grieved most for his lack.

The front door-bell rang. They looked at one another wonderingly, then Mr. Reynolds slowly withdrew his feet from the window sill and went as slowly down the hall. He opened the door to Suzanna, who stood waiting, conventionally attired in hat and cloak, pale, and with eyes wide and dark.

"Good evening, Reynolds," said Suzanna.

"O! good evening, come in, come in," urged Mr. Reynolds hospitably, but totally at a loss as he looked at the little figure.

"Come right out to the kitchen."

Suzanna followed him. When once in the kitchen, she stood for a moment blinking in the light streaming from the hanging lamp under which Mrs. Reynolds stood; then she said:

"I've come to you, Mrs. Reynolds, to stay. I've adopted myself out to you."

"Well, I never, dear love!" was all Mrs. Reynolds could say as she wiped her hands on a convenient roller towel.

Mr. Reynolds laughed. "Oh, you think you'd like a change of homes, Suzanna?"

Suzanna turned to him then. She spoke quietly, but decisively so he might perfectly understand. "No, that's not it, Reynolds. I love my little home; but first I don't want Mrs. Reynolds to throw her apron over her head at your slams. And second it's for myself I come, because you can afford to do something for me my own mother thinks she can't on account of little money."

But Mr. Reynolds caught only the first reason. "What do you mean, young lady, about slammin'; that's what I want to know." His tone was belligerent. Mrs. Reynolds threw him a withering look. "Here, Suzanna," she said; "give me the bag, and you sit down. Take your hat off, my brave little lass. 'Twas but you and you alone could think of this sweet thought."

"I'd rather have things settled before I take my hat off," said Suzanna. She relinquished the bag, however, and seated herself in the chair Mrs. Reynolds pulled forward. Then she went on: "You know, Reynolds, you do slam doors and make Mrs. Reynolds cry. And you know, anyway, you oughtn't to blame Mrs. Reynolds because you get no visits. It may be just as much your fault because the mother angel don't like your ways."

She paused a moment before continuing. "And, anyway, my father never blames mother for anything, only when she's tired and cries he remembers to love her even if he's on the way upstairs to the attic to his wonderful Machine, and he puts his arm about her waist, though mother says it's much larger now than it was years ago. That's what my father that used to be, does."

"Why bless my soul!" blustered Mr. Reynolds, his face a fine glowing color; "bless my soul!" he repeated, removing his shoes and slamming them down, as he always did under stress. "Women, my dear, will make up all sorts of stories. If I did give the door a bit of a slam, it was because the bacon didn't set right, perhaps. And a woman's always fancying things."

"But you don't put your arm about her, you know that, Reynolds. I was born in this town and I've never seen you put your arm about her."

Mrs. Reynolds' apron was over her head again, but she made no sound. Her husband knocked the ashes from his pipe, and ran his fingers through his thick hair. Then he stared helplessly at Suzanna. She rose valiantly to the occasion.

"If you say, 'There, there, don't cry, you should have married a better man,' she'll say: 'There couldn't be a better' and take her apron down." Thus innocently Suzanna exposed a tender home method of salving hurts, and her listener, as near as his nature could, appropriated the method. He rose from his chair and went softly to his wife. At her side he hesitated in sheer embarrassment, but as she began to sob, he hurriedly repeated Suzanna's formula: "There, there, dear, don't cry. I'm a bad 'un, I am—"

Mrs. Reynolds lowered her shield. "You know better than that, Reynolds," she denied, almost indignantly. "You're a good provider, with a bit of a temper."

"Well, out with it then. What *is* the trouble? I'm willing to do what I can, even occasionally to doing what the little lass suggests." And with the words, his big arm went clumsily about his wife, the while he looked at Suzanna for approval. She nodded vigorously, her eyes shining.

"It's just this, then, Reynolds," the words were now a whisper, and the big red-faced man had to stoop to hear. "It's that I'm achin' all the time to hold one in my arms; and always to you I've let on that I didn't care. An'—an'—I know the hunger in your own fine heart, my lad."

Mr. Reynolds' face grew wonderfully soft; indeed, tender in a new understanding. "I didn't know, Margie, that you grieved. Come, look up. You and me are together anyway."

"And you have me, now, too," broke in Suzanna, eager to help. "I'm going to stay with you forever'n forever, only except when my mother that used to be wants to borrow me back. Now, I'll go to bed, if you please."

And then one swift, cuddling memory of little Maizie alone in bed across the street brought the hot tears to Suzanna's eyes, but she winked them resolutely back as she lifted the black, shiny bag.

"Tomorrow," she said to Mrs. Reynolds, "you can cut the goods away from under the lace on my pink dress, can't you?" She went on, not waiting for an answer. "Shall I go right along upstairs?"

Mrs. Reynolds spoke gently: "Yes, Suzanna. Did you tell your mother you were coming to me to be my own lass?"

"I wrote her a letter."

Suzanna on her way upstairs waited a moment while Mrs. Reynolds whispered directions to her husband: "You run across to the little home while I put her to bed." Then looking wistfully up into his face: "Do you think she'll let me undress her?"

"That young'un will do anything to make you happy, Margie."

From the top of the stairs the words floated down: "Are you coming—*mother*—"

Suzanna's voice choked on the word, but Mrs. Reynolds heard only the exquisite title. She lifted her face, glowing like a heaven of stars.

"I'm coming, Suzanna," she called. And she went swiftly up the stairs to the little girl. "This night you sleep under the silk coverlet—and more I couldn't do for royalty!"

CHAPTER VII

REGRETS

Suzanna woke the next morning to a realization that she was in a strange place. She occupied a large bed, too large, it seemed to her, for one small girl. And even the silken coverlet failed to assuage the sudden wave of homesickness which threatened to engulf her.

She lay thinking. A clock on the dresser showed her the hour to be seven. Maizie would be up and downstairs. She would have buttoned Peter and would be carrying the blue dishes from the pantry to the dining-room. Father would be in the attic for a glance at his beloved Machine before obeying mother's cheerful call to breakfast.

Suzanna choked back a lump insistent upon rising to her throat. Across the way was home and she had adopted herself out of it! Here all was quiet, and comfortable, very comfortable. The mattress was thick, her small body quite sank into its depths; the bed she shared with Maizie, she had realized on occasions, had lumps, and no silken coverlet spreading itself brilliantly. Still there were rare and beautiful compensations for the lack of thick mattresses and silken coverlets—and greatest grief to her of all was that she stood no longer a daughter to a great man!

The tears came perilously near. Suzanna choked them back as she heard "Reynolds" close the front gate with what to him was a gentle click. She felt that in a moment Mrs. Reynolds would summon her downstairs to a breakfast hot and delicious.

Why had she left home if she loved it so!

The sentence formed itself in her mind.

Well, she hadn't realized that home and those in it were so dear till she left. And her reason was a good one. It had seemed she could scarcely live possessed of a dress whose sweet possibilities were denied by a mother's spirit of economy. Never had she so intensely wished for anything as for the goods to be cut away from under the rows of lace.

Still now, lying there alone in her strange surroundings, that desire was losing its poignancy. It didn't seem quite to fill her entire universe.

Mrs. Reynolds put her head inside the door. She wore a crisp blue and white dress, her black hair was drawn smoothly back from her brow. Her eyes dwelt lovingly on the little girl.

"Quite awake, Suzanna?" she asked.

Suzanna nodded. She couldn't trust herself to speak.

"Well, then," said Mrs. Reynolds, "I'm going to give thee a treat." She went away quite unconscious that she had fallen into her original quaint method of speech.

Presently she returned, carrying a tray covered with a white and red napkin.

Suzanna sat up, received the tray in her lap and waited unexcitedly while Mrs. Reynolds removed the enshrouding napkin.

There lay an orange cut up and sugared; a poached egg on a

slice of perfectly browned toast, and a glass of rich milk.

"For my little girl," said Mrs. Reynolds in her contralto voice. "Now eat thee, my dearie, and take your time. I'll leave now."

Alone once more, Suzanna surveyed the tray. She lifted a spoon with the tiniest piece of orange on its tip, and found strangely that when she attempted to swallow the fruit her throat quite closed up.

Suddenly there came a memory of Drusilla. Drusilla had told of the little silver chain, binding all to one another. Surely the chain binding Suzanna to her mother was doubly thick, yet she had broken it! She put the tray to one side and sprang from the bed. Her desire, recently so keen, so all absorbing, seemed little indeed beside the yearning now to be back across the way once again her Mother's Child.

Mrs. Reynolds, returning, found her little guest at the window, bare feet on the cold floor; the white gown held tightly at the neck by a small, trembling hand. A glance at the tray on the bed revealed a breakfast practically untasted.

"Why, my lamb," began Mrs. Reynolds, "not a bite gone down!"

Suzanna turned, a desperate little face she showed, eyes wide and appealing.

"I just couldn't eat, Mrs. Reynolds." No thought now of bestowing the beloved title.

"And the food brought fine to bed to you."

"Not even then."

"Well, come then, dear heart; you must be dressed. I put your clothes away neat and tidy."

Mrs. Reynolds opened a closet door and brought forth an armful of garments. Suzanna surveyed them as though they had no relation to her.

Mrs. Reynolds went suddenly and picked up the little figure, carried her to a rocking chair and with no word held her close.

"What is it, my little girl?" asked Mrs. Reynolds after a time, softly.

Her little girl! Suzanna winced. But she *was* Mrs. Reynolds' little girl now. Hadn't she broken all ties with the loved ones across the way?

She tried to find comfort in Mrs. Reynolds' joy. "I am your little girl, aren't I?" she asked softly, calling valiantly on her sense of justice.

Mrs. Reynolds looked searchingly into Suzanna's face. With no child of her own, she was still a mother-at-heart. She was full of understanding.

"As much, my own lassie," she answered, "as any other woman's child can be. You see," she went on after a pause, "there's a bond 'tween mother and child that can't ever be broke."

"But I adopted myself out to you," said Suzanna, though her heart was beating with hope.

"Yes, you did," admitted Mrs. Reynolds; "but you didn't at that break the tie that binds you to your own mother. You could never do that, Suzanna, lassie."

As Suzanna looked up into the kind face, new thoughts came surging to her. She couldn't separate them, couldn't arrange them. They all jumbled together, like vivid picture impressions, full of color and feeling. One thought at length cleared itself, stood out.

Love and the chain binding you to those you loved was the biggest thing in the world.

So she told Mrs. Reynolds about Drusilla's chain. And Mrs. Reynolds, greatly impressed, said: "Yes, it's a blessed thread that holds us together. Reynolds calls it the 'sense of brotherhood.'" Her voice lowered itself: "He's a Socialist, Reynolds is, Suzanna." There was pride and fear mixed with a little condemnation in her voice.

"A Socialist—it's a nice word, isn't it?" said Suzanna, settling more comfortably into the hollow of Mrs. Reynolds' arm.

"And I'm going to see Drusilla, as you call her," said Mrs. Reynolds, "and take her some of my crab jelly. I've seen her many's the time sitting out in the yard with naught but a trained maid by her. Poor, poor old soul, with a rich daughter-in-law."

"And a King that's gone to the Far Country," said Suzanna; "and she longs for him. Oh, she's a lonely old lady."

"She must be that and all," said Mrs. Reynolds, wholly sympathetic.

They sat rocking then in silence. Suzanna was the first to speak.

"Mrs. Reynolds," she began in a low voice. "I think I'll dress now, and after I've helped with the breakfast dishes I'll go and see my mother."

The heartbreak in the small voice touched Mrs. Reynolds deeply. "Why, small lass," she cried: "You mustn't think I'll hold you to your giving yourself away to me. No, not even for a bit of time. Sweet, you gave me joy last night. I pretended that you were my own. I undressed you and put you to bed, and heard your prayers. You did something for me, and I be vastly grateful to you."

Suzanna's eyes brightened. "Oh, thank you for saying all that, Mrs. Reynolds."

"Yes, you came to me in the night with your shiny bag, and you told in your little way some truths to Reynolds. You made him see clear and farther than he has for many a day, the fine man though he is, and I'll always hold you in my heart as my dream child."

"Your dream child—and I'll dream for you—that you should have your heart's desire like the fairies say," finished Suzanna.

"Ah, lack-a-me," cried Mrs. Reynolds. "Who e'er gets his deepest heart desire in this drear world?"

Suzanna sprang to her feet.

"Oh, but heart's desires change."

"Change!"

"Yes. You can have new ones every day. Why, for many days my deepest heart's desire has been to have the goods cut away from under the lace. Now, I don't care so much for that—not so much—Now I want most in the world to see—my—mother—"

Fearful that she had hurt Mrs. Reynolds by her confession, she put out her hand and stroked the capable hand lying near.

But Mrs. Reynolds wasn't hurt. She was smiling. "Well, it's a hard thing at times to learn to put one wish in place of another. But I guess life teaches you that; it hurries you forward so you have to put wish on wish." She stood up. "And now, the morning's well started, Suzanna. Dress quickly and come down to a warm breakfast."

She raised the tray and Suzanna knew that now she was hungry.

"Come down when you're ready, my wee bit girl," said Mrs. Reynolds, as she left, carrying the tray with her.

So Suzanna in a short time descended. How restful the house was; no insistent voices of children, no clattering of dishes.

"It's so quiet and nice here, Mrs. Reynolds," said Suzanna, as she entered the kitchen. "At home there's lots of talking and sometimes the baby cries."

"Do you like quiet, Suzanna?"

"Ye-es," Suzanna stammered. A recurrent attack of homesickness was upon her; that dreadful pulling of the heartstrings; that sinking feeling that she had cut herself loose from all to whom she belonged rightfully.

She stood still watching Mrs. Reynolds who was busy at the stove. She admired the deftness with which an egg was broken and dropped into boiling water, and in a few seconds brought to the top intact, to be placed upon the awaiting toast.

"You're awful quick, Mrs. Reynolds," she started to say when a knock sounded upon the door.

The door slowly opened and, alone, Suzanna's mother entered.

She stood just looking in. She was pale, her eyes wide, languid, shadows beneath them as though she had not slept. But those same tired eyes lightened as they fell upon Suzanna.

"Mother-eyes," the phrase grew in Suzanna's heart. She should never in all her life forget that look of longing, of love.

And somehow another impression, new, almost unbelievable, came to Suzanna. Her mother was *young*, for wasn't that yearning note in her voice; that tentative little gesture; her whole questioning attitude, all her seekings, but expressions of her youngness? She wasn't after all far removed from her little daughter, not for this minute, anyway. A delicious sense of comradeship with this mother flooded the child.

And the mother stood and looked at her child, almost as for the first time, at least with a sense of newness, as though Suzanna had been born anew to her.

In the night a far reaching understanding had come to her. It came out of her conclusion to strike a blow at the child's oversensitiveness by a full dose of ridicule; by accusing her of affectation, a clever playing to the gallery; this when the night was early, and the mother still aching with weariness from the day's many tasks. And then as the hours wore on, and the quiet soothed her weary nerves, the knowledge came, flashing out of the ether, as often it does for serious mothers, that the gift of keen sensibility, of intense desire was too valuable to be quenched.

What if Suzanna began to question her own motives; what if she should lose belief in her own spiritual integrity; learn in time to look in on herself with a spirit of morbid analysis instead of living out her natural qualities beautifully and spontaneously!

All these truths stirred her again as she looked at her child.

While Suzanna didn't move from her place, she wanted to stay at some distance that she might look her soul's full at her mother—*her mother!*

At length she spoke: "Mother—I want to be your little girl again. Will you take me back?"

Would she take her back? Mrs. Procter's arms opened wide. Into them Suzanna flew.

Mrs. Reynolds regarded the cold poached egg, the second one spoiled that morning. Furtively she wiped the tears from her eyes. At last she cleared her voice and spoke:

"I'll go upstairs and pack your bag, Suzanna," she said.

CHAPTER VIII

SUZANNA MEETS A CHARACTER

That summer was a happy one, filled to the brim, as Suzanna often said, with joyful times. In her pink lawn dress with the petticoat after all showing through the lace, she recited "The Little Martyr of Smyrna" and brought much applause to herself.

And then following close upon that happy occasion, Miss Massey invited her pupils to a "lawn party." Once again the pink dress was to see the day.

"I'll be very careful with the dress, mother," Suzanna promised on the day of the lawn party. "Perhaps it'll wear just as long if I take extra care of it as though the goods weren't cut away."

"Enjoy your dress," said Mrs. Procter. She had learned another truth which had sprung from the episode of the pink lawn. Economy might, indeed must dwell in a little home like hers, but sometimes, recklessly, the stern goddess must be usurped from her place. For the child love of beauty, the child's capacity for fine imaginings, could not be killed at the nod of economy.

The children were both ready and waiting anxiously at the front window long before the hour. Maizie was the first to make her announcement.

"Miss Massey's coming down the path," she cried.

They all crowded to the window. Miss Massey, looking up, waved her hand gaily, and the children delightedly waved back.

"Oh, Miss Massey, we're all ready for you," Maizie exclaimed at once as Miss Massey entered.

"Lovely," Miss Massey returned. Glancing casually at her, she appeared young, yet looking closely it might be seen that her first youth was over. She was perhaps in her middle thirties. Her hair beneath the simple blue chip hat, had gray strands. There was a hesitating quality about her, as though she had never done so daring a thing as reach a decision; a wavering, indefinite figure, with a wistfulness, a soft appeal, quite charming. That she had never come in contact with realities showed in the wide innocence of the childlike eyes; the sometime trembling of the lips as when a thought as now engendered by the Procter home and its humbleness, its lack of many real comforts, forced its way into the untouched depths of her mind.

She was the only child of old John Massey. He was a large figure in the small town, and one not cordially admired. He was masterful, choleric, some claimed, unjust. Owner of the steel mill which stood just outside of the town limits, the employer of hundreds of men, he had failed to gain the esteem of one human being. Fear, for many depended upon him for their livelihood, was the emotion he most inspired.

Fairfax Massey, his daughter, inspired a deep sympathy, perhaps because her leading characteristic was a pitiable holding to her ideals. She painted her father as a good and loving man hiding his real tenderness beneath gruff mannerisms. When he denied her friendship with the man she secretly loved, she put upon that denial a high value. He could not bear to run the chance of losing her, his one close possession. To that chivalrous thought of her father, she sacrificed her friend and went her way, undramatically, uncomplainingly.

She spoke in a low sweet voice. "The children will have a happy time, I'm sure, Mrs. Procter," she said, as she left, Suzanna and Maizie clinging to her.

Other little girls were waiting in the phaeton. They greeted Suzanna and Maizie and moved to make room for them. Miss Massey took her place near the driver, from which vantage spot she could watch her little guests, and with a great flourish off they started.

"Are you quite comfortable, Suzanna?" Miss Massey asked once.

Suzanna looked up quickly, a puzzled line between her eyes. After brief hesitation she answered, merely in good manners, "Yes, thank you."

The phaeton stopped several times till eight little girls filled the vehicle to overflowing. Then with no more pauses, they were off to the big house on the hill.

The day was wonderful. A soft little breeze caressed the children and the sky overhead was like an angel's breast, thought Suzanna. But she did not say this, even to excited Maizie; she was gathering impressions and burnishing them with her vivid imagination. Once her gaze fell on Miss Massey's long, slender, tired-looking hands. Her mother's hands, Suzanna recalled, were tired-looking, too, but in a different way. Her mother's, she decided after a time, were just plain tired-looking, while Miss Massey's were a sorry tired, as though they missed something. They were never quiet, always doing futile little things. And yet, Miss Massey lived in a wonderful house and wore pretty dresses and hats with gorgeous, real-looking flowers. Suzanna pondered unanswerable questions.

The driver, with the air of a brave knight, swept round the last corner. He commanded his horses to stand still, when even the smallest girl knew he would have to urge and coax for a full minute before the fat, complacent animals would start again. But Suzanna liked his play. It was in keeping with this wondrous event. She even forgave the driver his wrinkled red neck, from which as she sat behind him, she had earlier deliberately turned away her eyes.

The children sprang to the ground and stood looking up at the big pile of stone, this great show house of the town. Miss Massey swung back an iron gate and led the way first through an arbor, sun-shaded and fragrant; then out again into a garden glowing with crimson flowers. "The garden I love best," she said. This from simple, dear Miss Massey into whose whole life no great color had fallen, or if there was once a promise that life should blossom for her into a full, joyous thing, the promise had fallen very short of fulfillment.

And just then the disaster befell Suzanna. There in the wonderful red garden, a dire sound fell upon her ears and her eyes following the direction of the sound were just in time to see one white toe burst through the confines of the black ribbon lengthening her slipper.

She stood a moment, gazing down. Then in an agony lest the others should discover her plight, she tried to draw the toe back within the slipper, but with no success. As Miss Massey and the little girls walked on, Suzanna stopped and pulled the ribbon over the protruding toe, tucking in the ravelled edges. Mercifully, the ribbon stayed in place since Suzanna cramped her toe back that it might not force its way through again. Hastily hopping along, she entered the massive front doors held wide by a solemn man with brass buttons. He pointed down the wide hall. "To the right," he said.

Would the ribbon hold! was Suzanna's only thought as she later found herself in a room called the library, with books and soft-toned pictures; with a great fireplace banked now with greens, from above which looked down the lovely face of a lady, Miss Massey's mother whom the daughter scarce remembered.

If only she had worn black stockings instead of her one beloved pair of white, went on in thought, unhappy, humiliated Suzanna. If only—but in conjecture Suzanna was lost. The cramped toe exerting its right, thrust itself through again. One fleeting, horrified glance told the child that two toes now peeped out on a world that would be scandalized should it peep back.

No time now for any furtive maneuver an active little mind might suggest to remedy the situation, for Miss Massey at the end of the room turned her head and looked toward Suzanna's place. In a second her eyes might fall on the white toes! Quickly Suzanna sank into a large velvet armchair and drew her foot beneath her. Just in time, for Miss Massey said: "Shall we play the game of 'Answers?' You know the game, Suzanna, don't you?"

Suzanna moistened her lips: "I know it, Miss Massey, but I don't care to play games, thank you." How could she move, since doing so would necessitate putting confidence in Miss Massey? Telling her that once discarded slippers too small even for Maizie had been made to do duty by cutting the toes and lengthening with black ribbon, ribbon which in a miserable moment failed in its work? But how eventually to extricate herself from the miserable predicament? She could not sit forever on her foot!

Other games were suggested and played by the children, but Suzanna still sat in the big armchair, one long thin leg dangling, the other bent under her. She grew fertile in excuses when asked to join the others. She like to "watch," then she felt a little tired, until Miss Massey at last sensing that something was wrong did no more urging.

Once little Maizie sought her sister. Why wouldn't Suzanna

play? Was she mad at something?

Suzanna gulped hard, then with manifest effort she whispered: "You know where mother put the ribbon bag so my slippers would be long enough? Well, my toe's stuck through the ribbon, and I mustn't move."

"Oh!" Maizie was sorry. "Can't you tell Miss Massey and let her fix it?"

Suzanna shrank back. "No, no," she cried. "You mustn't say anything, do you hear, Maizie? Promise me."

Maizie solemnly promised. "Will the other one hold?" she asked then.

Thus the little Job's Comforter gave Suzanna food for unpleasant questionings. Would, indeed, the other slipper hold?

Then said Miss Massey: "We are going into the garden, Suzanna. Would you rather stay here till we return?" Her question was very gentle, her understanding would have been very sure had Suzanna told her trouble. But Suzanna only answered eagerly:

"Yes, I'd like to stay here." She was almost happy in the moment's relief.

"If you wish to come later you can find us. Just ring this bell and Mrs. Russell, the housekeeper, will take you to the South Garden," said Miss Massey. She leaned down and touched Suzanna's face with her soft lips. And then Suzanna was left alone.

Now what to do! Suzanna set her fertile little mind to work on the problem. She settled into the chair and lowered the foot on which she was sitting. She was intently regarding the torn slipper, when she heard distinctly an unpleasant sound. A sound which gathered volume, till Suzanna realized that something or someone was approaching the library. She resumed her former position, and waited!

The brocade curtains were drawn aside; a little man in a sort of uniform stood with head bowed, while a large man limped into the room.

"Fix my chair, you simpering idiot," he shouted at the little man, "and then take yourself off!"

The small man glided to a great easy chair near the fireplace. He heaped pillows in it, stood aside while the loud-voiced one lowered himself, groaningly, into the downy nest. Then the valet disappeared. Suzanna involuntarily glanced at his feet. Did he move on velvet casters?

A moment, then the big man gave a twist of pain. A rheumatic dart had seized him, had Suzanna known, but she could not know, and a little exclamation was drawn from her. At the sound, the other occupant of the room started and glanced around till finally his eyes came to rest upon the small girl in a large chair thrust well away in a shadowy corner of the room.

"Well!" at length he ejaculated. And then: "Are you one of the Sunday School class?"

"Yes, I'm Suzanna Procter. The other little girls have gone out into the garden."

He grunted and continued to glare fiercely at her. But Suzanna knew no fear. She felt strangely a sudden high sense of exhilaration, just as once when she had been caught in a brilliant electric storm. Some element in her rose and responded to the big flashes; just as she had responded to Drusilla's play of imagination. Now a force was roused in her that claimed kinship with the big, thunderous man opposite. She sat up very straight, and stared right back at him. Then she said very calmly:

"You look like an eagle!"

"Then you're afraid of me!" He flung the words at her with a certain triumph.

"I'm not! I don't like the way you shout, but *I'm* not afraid of you."

He sank back among his pillows, but did not take his eyes from her face. At last he asked: "What are you sitting bent up that way for? Are you hiding anything?"

Suzanna flushed. "You're not supposed to ask a visitor if she's hiding anything; especially when her leg's asleep and she's suffering."

A spasm crossed his face. Perhaps he was trying to smile. He said only: "Well, put your leg down, then. Seems to me you're old enough and ought to have sense enough not to sit on it when it's asleep. Put it down, I say!"

She did not move. "Will you please turn your head away a whole minute?" she finally asked.

He did so, somewhat to his own surprise. He was unaccustomed to obeying others. When he turned again, she uttered a cry: "Why didn't you keep your head turned the other way till I told you to look," she exclaimed, indignantly. "You don't play fair."

"See here, little girl," he commenced, when his eyes fell to her foot, which for the moment she had forgotten, a small black-shod foot with two protruding toes. "Eh, what's that!"

"My toes!" she answered. Her face flamed, then with sudden anger against him, against circumstances, against everything that had conspired to spoil this beautiful and long-dreamed-of day: "They're sticking through my slipper. That's why I had to sit on my foot. That's why my leg went to sleep. That's why I couldn't go out in the garden with the others."

He began to laugh, silently, mirthlessly, but it was laughter nevertheless. Suzanna regarded him, her quick temper getting beyond her control. At last she burst forth: "You're a rude man! And it isn't funny to miss beautiful things, the flowers and the baby squirrels, and perhaps lemonade."

He didn't answer for a moment. Then he said:

"Agreed! But it's certainly funny to see your toes sticking through your shoe. No wonder you sat on your foot." Still, despite his discourteous words, his tone changed; it was almost apologetic.

Suzanna's face lost its clouds. "Of course, I had to sit on my foot," she agreed. "I couldn't let Miss Massey see how mother put a black ribbon bag on my slippers to make them longer, could I? She wouldn't understand like you do, would she?"

"Do I understand? I wonder. Well, why did your mother put on the black ribbon?"

"The shoes were too short!"

"She should have bought you a new pair."

Suzanna sprang from her chair and went to the big man.

"Do you know what rent week means?" she asked, lifting her earnest face to his and standing so close that her hand touched his knee.

"I think I do," he answered.

"Well, this is rent week and Peter's coat was out at the elbows and two of us needed shoes and the insurance was due on all of us and mother can't let that go. It came in very handy when Helen, Peter's twin, went away."

Emily Calvin Blake

"What do you mean by 'went away?' Don't lean on that knee, that's where the rheumatism is—do you mean died?"

Suzanna flinched. "We say 'went away,'" she answered gently; "you think then that someone you loved has just gone away for a little while, and is waiting somewhere for you."

The man's gaze wandered up to the lovely, smiling face above the mantel and stayed there a space before his eyes came back to Suzanna.

"And so," she finished, "because everything came together, rent and insurance and shoes, and a coat, I had to wear these slippers." Suzanna was quite cheerful again, only very eager that he should understand the situation.

At this moment the timid little valet appeared in the doorway. "Anything you wish, sir?" he began. "Are you quite comfortable?"

"You infernal idiot!" bawled the man in the chair. "Can anyone be comfortable with rheumatism in his knee?"

The little man precipitately retired. "You're awful cross," Suzanna commented. "What does the man mean asking if you're 'comfortable?' That's what Miss Massey asked me in the park carriage. I was sitting down, and nothing hurt me."

"In other words," he answered, strangely catching her meaning at once, "one chair is like another to you."

"Well, is there any difference?" she queried. She was very much interested in this question, for the subtleties of refined comfort held no place in her life. Knowledge of luxuries was quite outside the ken of the younger members of the Procter family.

The big man said: "Yes, there is a difference; a decided difference." He was thinking of his household with its retinue of trained servants, each helping to make the days revolve smoothly.

"Why aren't you at work?" asked Suzanna then. "My father works every day in the hardware store and sometimes way into the night on his invention in the attic. *He* doesn't have a chair filled with pillows to lean against. Does God like you better than He does us?"

"Eh, what's that? What do you mean?"

"Because you don't have to work! And you think one chair is better than another to sit in, and you can shout at the little man and make him afraid."

"Well, we'll not talk of that," said the big man testily. "And now I'll ask you a few questions. What does your mother do when rent week comes round? Cry, and throw up to your father the fact that she can't make ends meet? That's what women generally do, I've heard and read."

"Oh, no, my mother doesn't do that," said Suzanna, shaking her head. "She just looks sad at first and sits and thinks and thinks and then after awhile she says: 'Well, if everybody was thoughtful we'd all have enough. But when some people waste, then others must pay the piper'—'pay the piper'—I like the singing way that sounds, don't you?"

"And who does she mean by other people?"

Suzanna smiled confidently: "Oh, she just says that; so no one really is blamed, I guess. There really isn't anyone of that kind living; 'cause nobody in the world could waste if they knew some children needed shoes and some little boys' elbows stuck through their coats; would anyone?"

The man looked at her suspiciously. "Have you been listening to Reynolds haranging on his soap box?" But seeing her innocence, he went on: "Well, we don't know about those things. There's some reason why." He went on more vigorously: "Of course, some people are privileged because they're stronger; they've better judgment."

But Suzanna didn't understand that. She put the matter aside to think over later, and, if she could remember the words, to repeat them to her father for his explanation at a time when he wasn't hazy and far away from realities.

"What does your father do?" Suzanna's companion resumed after a moment.

"He weighs nails in Job Doane's hardware store," said Suzanna, "and he sells washboards to ladies. My father's a great man. He's an inventor! He has a wonderful machine in the attic and sometimes when he's thinking of his invention, he doesn't see us at all, and mother tells us not to talk then to disturb him."

"What's your father's name?"

"Richard Procter," said Suzanna. And then:

"You are like an eagle; that's why I like you. You'd fight, wouldn't you, if you had to! But I shouldn't mind your shouting. And I'd rather you'd see my toes sticking through my shoe than any person in the world outside my family. Now, get me a needle and thread before they all come back," she finished.

The man stared into her upraised flower-face. His own turned red for the visible second of hesitation. Then he raised his voice and called. The timid one appeared. His master said: "Get me some black thread and a needle; also a thimble. Don't stand there gaping! I'm waiting."

With some difficulty, the amazed valet gained volition over his power of locomotion. He returned shortly bearing the desired articles reposing on a silver tray, and retired once more, his eyes still dazed.

"Now hurry up," said the big man to Suzanna, "if you want to get into the garden at all."

Suzanna threaded the needle, then removed her slipper. "I'll overcast the ribbon, like mother does seams," she said. "Will you hold the slipper? There, that's easier. You see I need both hands."

Silence, till the work was finished. "Now," said Suzanna, stopping to bite the thread, no scissors being at hand, "I guess no toe in the world could push through that, I've stitched so tight. You think it will hold, don't you?"

Very carefully he looked at the mended place. "I should say, if my judgment's worth anything, that it's a very decent job. But see here, you've taken up such a large seam; the shoe will be too small again."

Suzanna smiled at him. "Oh, that doesn't matter, just so the toes can't burst through again," she answered. "You don't mind hobbling a little bit when you have to."

He cleared his throat. "Well, I'll call the housekeeper and she'll take you to the other children."

"Good-bye," said Suzanna friendlily. And then very politely, "Thank you for helping me."

"Well, I suppose I might say you're welcome."

But he watched the small figure, that did after all "hobble" a little all the way down the room as the summoned housekeeper led the way. And, left alone, he sat quite still for a few moments. Once or twice he smiled grimly, but several times he frowned.

* * * * *

Suzanna was full of her experience with the Eagle Man, and in spite of her mishap she had greatly enjoyed her day. Hadn't the fierce one, the one of the loud voice and cross face, been kind to her and helped her to mend her slipper? And hadn't he told the housekeeper to give her a great bunch of the purple grapes especially procured from the city for him, she was told?

She thought of all this when she and Maizie left the low phaeton in which they had been driven home. For some indefinable reason she was elated, and excited—an emotion far above the usual happy fatigue felt after a day of pleasure. She meant to tell her father and mother all about her talk with the Eagle Man when the supper dishes were washed and put away. She would show her father just how her toes had thrust themselves through her slipper and how she had sat upon her foot till it went to sleep. Not, however, till the setting was right would she tell her story. Suzanna's unconscious dramatic sense rarely failed her.

At the supper table that night the baby fell asleep in his high chair. Peter, after a hard day of play, was nodding in his place. Maizie, replete after her third dish of rice pudding, was quiet; a little sleepy too, if truth must be told.

It was then Suzanna told of her visit with the Eagle Man. She left out no detail, from the time her stocking burst its confines to her interesting intimacy with the Eagle Man.

"You told old John Massey, you say, Suzanna," said her father at length, his eyes bright, "about my machine?"

Suzanna nodded. Then a little fear stole upon her. She slipped from her place and went to her father.

"Did I talk too much, daddy?" she asked, mindful of former such indictments.

His arm went about her waist. Then he drew her close and kissed her.

"No, Suzanna, little girl," he said; "I guess talk from the heart rarely hurts." He paused. "Perhaps it was meant you should talk to him."

CHAPTER IX

A LEAF MISSING FROM THE BIBLE

Suzanna thought a great deal about the Eagle Man. She was extremely puzzled as to the exact place he filled in the world. While she admired him, indeed was strongly drawn to him, still she considered him in some ways quite inferior to her father. And so she wondered why he could live in a big house, could have servants who sprang at a word to do his bidding, and could eat all the fruit he wanted as evidenced by the great bunch of purple grapes, one of many bunches, while her father lived in a very small house, had no servants, and had little fruit to eat. She knew instinctively that the Eagle Man had no need to worry about rent day, and the many other similar things she felt harassed her father, and over and over again she pondered on this seemingly unjust state of affairs. It would have been so much better, she thought, if the Eagle Man occupied with his one daughter just a little cottage while the large Procter family had the bigger house. Though she dearly loved the little home, there had been times when it seemed very small for the growing Procter family.

But she concluded at last that for the present there were many perplexities which must remain perplexities till that wonderful time when she would be a woman, and everything made clear to her. Experiences, too, had shown her that a troublesome question of Monday often had resolved itself by Wednesday. So she went contentedly on her way.

On a morning following Suzanna's talk with the Eagle Man, Mrs. Procter and all the children except the baby who was taking his early morning nap upstairs, were in the kitchen busy at their tasks, Suzanna polishing the stove, and Maizie peeling the potatoes for supper, a task Mrs. Procter insisted upon being performed early in the day. Peter, exempted, because of his sex, from household duties—and very unfair this exemption Suzanna thought privately—was trying his awkward best to mend a baseball. Maizie broke a rather long silence.

"Mother!" she cried, and then waited.

Mrs. Procter looked up from her kneading.

"What is it, Maizie?" she asked.

"Didn't Jesus ever laugh?" asked Maizie.

No one spoke. Maizie, engaged in peeling a large potato, went on quite unconscious of the variant expressions pictured in the faces of her audience: "He's always so sad in our Sunday School lessons, mother. Even when He said, 'Suffer little children to come unto me,' He didn't smile—or they never say so when they read the chapter," she finished.

Mrs. Procter looked helplessly at Suzanna. And Suzanna rose to the occasion. "Maizie," she said, "you know Jesus was born in a manger so His mother didn't have much money and it was hard to make both ends meet. And, besides, there wasn't anything to smile about in those days when the world was so fresh."

"I guess that's right," Mrs. Procter agreed. "What with going round and trying to persuade people to be good and understand what He was trying to tell them, there couldn't have been much excuse for smiling."

Maizie, however, was tenacious. "Mother, you know at times

even when things have all gone wrong you've laughed at something the baby did," she said looking up from her work.

"Yes, I know," put in Suzanna, as though Maizie had spoken to her. "But mother doesn't have to go round turning water into wine and doing lots of other wonderful things."

"Well, I wish He had smiled," Maizie persisted.

Suzanna looked searchingly at her sister. "Why do you wish that, Maizie?" she asked.

"Oh, I'd think then He was more like a big brother," said Maizie. "Now, sometimes I kind of feel afraid of Him."

"If you didn't feel afraid of Him, Maizie," Suzanna asked, turning back to the cold stove and vigorously polishing away, "do you think you'd be a better girl?"

Maizie flushed resentfully. "I'm good enough now," she answered.

"But you get mad for nothing, Maizie," said Suzanna; "you always get mad when you don't see things."

"Anybody would get mad," Maizie exclaimed. "Why just yesterday when we were playing in the yard you said, 'Behold, the lion marcheth down the yard. Maizie, quick, quick, out of the way,' and when I said, 'I don't see any lion, Suzanna,' you said, 'Well, he's there, right beside you. Don't you hear him roaring?' and there wasn't any lion there at all."

"Well, Maizie, you can't see anything unless it's there," deplored Suzanna.

"You mean, Suzanna," put in Mrs. Procter as she covered the dough with a snowy cloth, "that you have more imagination than Maizie."

"Well, anyway, Maizie," said Suzanna after a time, "I'm going to try and make you a better girl."

"Make her stop saying that, mother," said Maizie, "I'm good enough as it is."

Suzanna said nothing more then. She finished her stove, and then, when Maizie had peeled all the potatoes, Suzanna went into the parlor and dusted all the furniture very carefully. Maizie followed and stood watching her sister.

"How could you make me better, Suzanna?" she asked, after a time, curiosity elbowing pride aside.

"I meant to tell you a story," said Suzanna; "about something you've never heard before." She went on dusting.

"Would the story make me a better girl?"

"Yes, and happier, too."

"Is it a nice story, Suzanna?"

"Awfully sweet."

"When could you tell me, Suzanna?"

"We'll go out into the yard after I've finished dusting and then I'll tell you the story, Maizie."

"All right."

So when the dusting was accomplished, the children sought the back yard. Suzanna procured a soap box, placed it beneath the one tree, while Maizie drew another very close to her sister that she might lose no word, and settled with keen anticipation to listen to Suzanna's story.

The day was hot, with scarcely a breeze stirring. Still, with the quiet there was a freshness in the air that made the children draw in deep breaths.

Suzanna began very softly: "Maizie, do you see that big rose nodding near the fence over there at Mrs. Reynolds'?"

Yes, Maizie saw the rose.

"Well, yesterday when you were wheeling the baby and I was sitting on this very box putting buttons on Peter's waist, that rose all at once walked across the road to me! It stood by my side for a long time, and then it said softly, 'Suzanna,' and it looked at me and it was all pink and very sweet, and it said to me, 'Suzanna, how old are you?' and I said, 'I'm nearly eight, Lady Rose, and Maizie is nearly seven. Mother had hardly got over my coming to her when Maizie came along.'

"And the rose said, 'Maizie? Is that the little girl that is going to ask tomorrow whether Jesus ever smiled?' And I said, 'Yes, Maizie will be peeling a big potato, and I'll be polishing the stove, and mother will be kneading bread when Maizie will ask that question.'

"'Well,' said the rose, 'you must tell her that once upon a time Jesus *did* smile, but they didn't put it in the Bible because it didn't seem 'portant to grown folks, and they didn't think that all the little children in the world would sometimes wish He had smiled.' And then the rose went on to tell me the story of the dear smile."

Maizie gazed wide-eyed at her sister. "Did you really see the rose with your eyes, Suzanna?"

"Yes," Suzanna answered; "truly with my eyes." She suddenly sat up very straight and pointed a small finger, "and there it's coming again. It's nodding its head at me. Look, Maizie!"

Maizie jumped.

"There, see, Maizie, it's walking right through Mrs. Reynolds' gate. Isn't it graceful?"

"How can it walk on one stem?" asked Maizie, the literalist.

"Well, it does, doesn't it? You can see it. Now, it's coming into our yard." Suzanna waited, then: "Good morning, Lady Rose," she greeted in a high treble voice. "Come and stand near Maizie." Maizie moved quickly to make room. "You see it now, don't you, Maizie?" Maizie hesitated. She stared hard at the spot near her, then up with wistful eyes into Suzanna's face.

"I can't see it, Suzanna," she said at length. "Do you think mother'd better take me to the doctor and have my eyes examined like Mrs. Reynolds had hers?"

Suzanna felt flowing over her a sudden wave of pity. "No, Maizie, dear," she said, putting her arms about Maizie and drawing her close. "Maybe I see the rose with something inside of me. But never mind, lamb girl—isn't that pretty, Mrs. Reynolds calls me that—the rose has gone home again. Listen close and I'll tell you the story that was left out of the Bible, just as the rose told it to me."

Maizie settled herself again, expectantly.

"This will be told, Maizie, in the way the Bible is written. Funny words that we don't know the meaning of, but can guess; terrible threats."

"Oh, don't," cried Maizie, "don't, I don't want 'terrible threats.' It sounds awful."

"Well, then," conceded Suzanna, "I'll leave out the terrible threats, Maizie. Now I'm beginning:

"There came to the city of Jerusalem one day a Little Boy with a halo on His head. It was on a Monday that he came. The

Emily Calvin Blake

mothers were all washing and those that were not washing, behold, they were hanging clothes out in the yard, and as He walked He carried a message, and His message was this: 'Beware of green tea, handsome to the eye, but destructive to the human system.'"

Maizie's memory was pricked wide awake. "Why, that's written on mother's tea canister, and you read it aloud a thousand times one day," she cried.

"That saying has come down the ages," responded Suzanna quickly. "And any more breaking-in and I'll not tell the story."

Maizie subsided, and Suzanna continued.

"Now when all the mothers heard this wonderful saying, there came sorrow and fear into their hearts. 'Yea,' said one, 'have I not used green tea?' And the Little Boy with the halo said, 'Thou art never to do so again,' and all the mothers bowed their heads.

"And the Little Boy grew and grew till He came to be a man. A man that looked very much like our father. He played the harp, the one he afterwards took to Heaven with Him. And He wore a long, white, flowing gown, that His mother washed out every morning and ironed carefully after it was dry. 'Behold,' she said, 'Yea, nay, no other hands but mine must touch this gown.' There were no laundries in those days.

"The Man with the halo walked by the sea at day, and walked under the stars at night. Then He came on back to His mother. She said to Him: 'Is it that Thou art tired that Thou dost not smile?' And He said, drawing Himself up to a big height, 'There is nothing to smile at.' And His mother said, 'Behold I have made for Thee something nice to eat, with an orange in front of Thy plate!' But even then He did not smile. And next day, He went off into the fields and took care of His lambs. And the day after that, yea, He went into His father's shop and He said to His father, 'I must away,' and then the earth trembled and rocked beneath their feet.

"Then the Man with the halo left, and for a long time His mother didn't see Him any more. And out in the world, in Galilee, I think it was, He didn't even there find a chance to smile. Everything was too sad and people too bad, and then one day, behold, the Man with the halo was busy making ten fish out of one little tiny minney for Peter who was hungry, and had a 'normous appetite like our Peter's, when a woman came running down the road. Everybody looked at her, but she went on. And when she came near the Man with the halo, she fell on her knees and He stopped his work. He had just half a fish in His hand when this woman spoke. She said: 'Pardon me, Master, but I have heard of lots of wonderful things Thou hast done, and now I must ask a favor of Thee.'

"The Man with the halo put down the fish that wasn't finished and turned His big eyes upon her, and He said, 'Speak, woman.' And she said: 'Wilt Thou come with me?' He waited a little, but felt pity in His heart for her and so He went with her, His halo shining like the sun and making a wide light path for everyone to walk in, and lots of people walked behind Him, but no one in front.

"And they came to a little house, like ours set back from the road, where lots of children lived. And there in the middle of the room, lying in a white box, fast asleep was the littlest baby that had ever gone to Heaven. And though the woman had lots of other babies, and maybe lots more would come to her like they come to us all the time, she wanted that one tiny little baby to open its eyes and look at her.

"And so she fell on her knees, and she said to the Man with the halo: 'Will you wake that lovely baby of mine for me? Oh, please, Master, waken it—even though it should cry all night. Perhaps it's happy in Heaven, but I am lonely. Dost Thou think I can have it back?'

"And just then Peter came into the room. He had followed the

Emily Calvin Blake

Man with the halo. 'But it's only a little thing,' Peter said. 'And it made so much noise when it was awake. Its big sister had to warm milk for it, and take it out in the buggy and to wash its clothes, sometimes when its mother was busy or had been up the night before. Is it not better for all that it is in Heaven?'

"And then she said, 'I'm not speaking to you, Peter,' and she looked again at the Man with the halo. And at last He spoke and His voice was like music, thrilly and gentle. And He said, 'All mothers want their babies and we've got plenty in Heaven, and I'll give this one back to you.'

"And He went to the white box and He looked at the baby, and pretty soon the baby got pink like my coral beads, and then its eyes opened and it looked up into His face and it raised its arms up to Him.

"*Then He smiled!*—and He lifted the baby up and held it close, so He warmed it all through. And then He put it into its mother's arms and said, 'Well, I must be going.'

"And this is what I'm going to tell you, Maizie, *that you were that little baby*, and Jesus smiled at *you* to wake you up."

Maizie did not speak. Her eyes were shining, her lips trembling. Her small soul was touched to its depths. After a long time in a whisper she spoke: "Oh, was I really the baby that made Jesus smile? I'm happy, Suzanna, but—it hurts me, too—"

Suzanna put her arms about her sister. The emotions she had aroused in that little sister warmed her, thrilled her through and through. They sat on in silence. Soon a question began to puzzle Maizie. She gave it voice. "I didn't know I'd been a baby more than once, Suzanna."

"You're a baby every hundred years," said Suzanna promptly.

"Oh, I see." Then: "I do love Him now, Suzanna. I'll always love Him 'cause once He woke me up. Suzanna, do you think the rose will come to you and tell you another story?"

Suzanna believed the rose might.

CHAPTER X

A PICNIC IN THE WOODS

For days Maizie lived in the sanctity of the thought that the Master of all had smiled at her. But even so marvelous an occurrence, so sweet a marking out of her above all the children in the world, failed completely on one occasion to help her overcome a mood of sullenness.

She awoke late one morning, and found that Suzanna had arisen and gone down stairs. She heard sounds indicating breakfast, but there was a little dull feeling at her heart. Her customary joyous anticipation of living a whole day, ripe with possibilities, was quite absent. She decided to remain in bed, but at her mother's voice calling her name she was prompted to put out one small foot, then the other, and soon, as another call came up peremptorily, she went lazily ahead dressing herself.

Ready then for the day, she went to the window and looked out. The sky was hazy, with little dull clouds floating on its breast. From far away came grumbles of thunder. Over to the east the sky seemed to open in a long thin path of vivid light and then close again, leaving the heavens gray, bleak. Maizie wanted to cry; it was with an effort she controlled her tears.

At last, languidly she moved from the window, went down the stairs, through the tiny hall and into the dining-room, her little face downcast still, with no smile lightening it to greet the other children. Suzanna and Peter sat at the table awaiting the laggard.

"Father had to leave early this morning, Maizie," said Suzanna at once. "He ate his breakfast all alone."

Maizie did not answer; silently she sank into her chair as her mother appeared with the baby and took her usual place, after placing him in his high chair. Maizie gazed for a moment at the oatmeal in her own blue plate, then with a little petulant gesture, she pushed the plate away.

"I don't like oatmeal with a pool of syrup in the middle," she said slowly, not addressing anyone directly, but keeping her eyes on her plate.

"You've always liked it before this morning," her mother answered. "I think you're just cross, Maizie."

"I don't like syrup in the middle of my oatmeal," repeated Maizie; "I want milk on it like father has."

"Oh, Maizie," said Suzanna, "father *must* have milk on his oatmeal."

"Why?" asked Maizie.

"Because he is our father and he must have the nice things."

"Well, we're his children," pursued Maizie, apparently unconvinced. "And I don't see why we shouldn't have some nice things to eat, too."

"But there's so many of us," said Suzanna.

"Why did father leave orders for so many of us then?" said Maizie looking up. Belligerence was now in her tone, in her very attitude.

"Now," said Mrs. Procter, firmly. "We must not talk this way. Father doesn't like syrup. It doesn't agree with him. You're a very naughty little girl this morning, Maizie."

Maizie was again on the point of tears. Lest they overflow she rose quickly from the table and left the room.

"Maizie's in a bad humor today," said Mrs. Procter to Suzanna.

"Maybe she feels bad today, mother, because it's Wednesday."

"Well, what in the world has the day to do with it!" Mrs. Procter exclaimed.

"Well, Wednesday you know is the shape of a big black bear. It's not like Thursday, that's the shape of a great snowy white ship on a sparkling sea. I don't like Wednesday myself, mother."

"Well, I'm sorry," returned Mrs. Procter. "But it's not in my power to shape days to please you children," she spoke crisply.

"Are you tired, mother?" asked Suzanna, after a pause.

"I think I'm always tired these days," Mrs. Procter admitted, "but I'm particularly tired this morning. The baby was very restless last night."

"If you were like Mrs. Martin on the other side of the town," said Suzanna as she rose from the table and began to gather up the dishes, while Peter escaped into the yard, "who has only one little girl, you wouldn't be kept awake." Suzanna's eyes were widely questioning. Did her mother regret owning so many children?

Mrs. Procter stood up. She lifted the baby out of his high chair. "You're every one dear and wonderful to me," she said. "But we're all human, dear, and apt to grow tired."

Suzanna walked into the kitchen and put the dishes down on the table. On her way back to the dining-room she glanced out of the window. The early September day had changed. Miraculously every dull gray cloud had scurried away, leaving a sky soft, yet brilliant. Birds flew about, carolling madly, as though some elixir in the air sent their spirits bounding. Suzanna's every fiber responded. The desire whipped her to plunge into the beauty of outdoors, to run madly about, to shout, to sing. But alas, she knew there was no chance to obey her ardent impulse, since Wednesday was cleaning day, a day rigid, inflexible, when all the Procter family were pressed into service; that is, all but Peter, belonging to a sex blessedly free from work during its young, upgrowing years.

Mrs. Procter spoke: "Bring the high chair into the kitchen, Suzanna, near the window for the baby; then we'll start cleaning."

Suzanna obeyed reluctantly. She turned from the window. "Mother," she said, "when I'm grown up I'll have no steady days for anything."

"What do you mean?" asked Mrs. Procter.

"Well, I won't wash on Monday, and iron on Tuesday, and clean on Wednesday, and bake on Thursday. I'll let every day be a surprise."

"Yes," said Mrs. Procter, "and a nice mix-up there'd be. You must have set times for every task if you expect to accomplish anything."

"But isn't it 'complishing anything if you're happy?" asked Suzanna, really puzzled.

Mrs. Procter hesitated. "But you can be happy working, too."

"But I know, mother, that I'd be happier today out in the sun."

"But the truth remains, Suzanna, that if we don't wash on Monday we'd have to wash on Tuesday, and that ties up everything at the end of the week," said her mother.

Suzanna sighed. She couldn't by mere words combat her mother's arguments. They seemed indeed unassailable if you applied plain reason to them. But something deeper, finer than reason, made Suzanna believe that to be out in the sun, to be under the trees, to be dreaming in the perfume of flowers, was more important than cleaning and dusting; anyway in a glorious, straight-from-Heaven day like this Wednesday. So she returned unconvinced to the dishes, while her mother after tying the baby in his high chair cast an appraising eye around, wondering just where she should begin her upheaval.

Suddenly a loud, heart-rending outcry was heard, and Peter, who a moment before had been playing peacefully in the yard, came rushing into the house. Out of the medley of his piteous cries, Suzanna at last made sense. Not so her mother who asked anxiously:

"What in the world is he crying so for, Suzanna? Is he hurt? Will he let you look him over?"

"No, he's not hurt," returned Suzanna. "He is crying because *never in all his life will he be able to see his ears.*"

Mrs. Procter stared dumbfounded. But she soon recovered. She was accustomed to originalities of this sort in her family.

"So! Well, what am I to do about it?" she asked the small boy.

Peter looked at her stolidly. "I want to see my ears," he repeated. "And I can't only in the mirror."

"Have you lived for five years," asked Mrs. Procter, "without discovering that your ears are attached to your head, and that I can't take them off in order that you may see them?"

"And you can't see the back of your neck either, Peter," cried Suzanna at this juncture. At which disastrous piece of information Peter cried louder.

"Now, Suzanna," exclaimed Mrs. Procter in some exasperation. "What did you tell him that for? Isn't it enough for him to learn in one day that he'll never see his ears without telling him about the back of his neck? Stop your crying, Peter. It's bad enough to have you cry for things that can be mended."

Maizie, attracted by the noise, unable to control her curiosity, appeared at the door. Her face was still sullen, but it also bore a rare expression of stubbornness. Satisfying her curiosity as to the reason for the commotion, she then made her announcement.

"Mother," she began, "I'm not going to wash the window sills upstairs this cleaning morning."

"Now, Maizie," said Suzanna, conciliatingly, "don't you remember Who smiled at you once?"

"M-hm, I remember," said Maizie, without change of expression, "but I'm not going to wash the window sills."

A little silence ensued. Then Suzanna offered a suggestion.

"Mother," she said, "none of us feels right, do we? Can't we have a picnic?"

"A picnic?" exclaimed Mrs. Procter. "A picnic!" She was about vigorously to refuse the request when she paused. She looked at the three earnest little faces before her. Suzanna resenting steady days for doing steady tasks; Maizie hating her porridge, and Peter grieved because he couldn't see his ears; the baby too, not his usual sunny self. But set against the strange and varied emotions of her young family, loomed the house with its stern demands upon her. Should she postpone her tasks then vengeance in the double form of cleaning and baking day would descend upon her tomorrow!

Then suddenly the truth pressed in on her—the children had rights upon her time, her thoughts, her understandings, her sweetnesses! What if for this week the window sills upstairs did remain unwashed, the rugs downstairs stay unshaken? She stole a glance out of the window at the one tree in the yard, green and gently swaying in the soft breeze, and she spoke with the impulse of youth. "Well," she said, "where could we go?"

"We could have it in the yard if you say so, mother," cried Suzanna, mentally forecasting consent in her mother's question. "But I know some lovely woods not very far away. We could push the baby in his cart."

The baby from his high chair gurgled joyously.

"And take lunch," said Maizie, brightening.

"And my baseball," completed Peter.

"Well," said Mrs. Procter, the brief spark that had lifted her dying, "if I'm going to have grumbling all the time, something the matter with each one of you, I might as well let the work go for once, I suppose."

But though the consent fell leaden in its delivery, it *was* consent and in a miraculously short time they were all ready to start away; even the lunch basket was packed and the baby put into his carriage and wheeled out to the front gate to wait till the entire family was assembled.

Mrs. Procter locked the doors, ran across the street to ask Mrs. Reynolds to buy certain vegetables from a daily huckster and then away they all went down the wide white road to the woods.

Soon the joy and beauty of the day stole into Mrs. Procter's heart. She breathed in the invigorating air deeply. Cares seemed to fall from her. Materialities were banished into the background. She looked at her children as they went singing down the road. She had meant to bind them to sordid tasks within four walls when a jewel of a day beckoned to all! She visualized her house clean and in perfect order, but the children cross, she herself irritable and tired out, and wondering a little bit about the meaning of things. Was it worth while to let inflexible rules remain victors at such a cost. She knew a sudden thrill of gratitude for Suzanna, who had suggested the outing, and putting out her hand she drew the little girl to her.

Suzanna looked up. She caught the deep and tender look in her mother's face, so she voiced a plea which had been in her heart, but kept from utterance in fear that she might ask too much.

"Mother, if we're going on a real picnic we ought to take the lame and the halt with us. And I know a little girl who has cross eyes, and she's a weeny bit pigeon-toed. She's the lame and the halt, isn't she? Because when she looks at me I never think she is looking at me. I tried to teach her one day how to look straight but it wouldn't do. Could I invite her, do you think?"

"Where does she live?"

"Oh, just the other side of the fork road," Suzanna replied, pointing out the direction. "If you'll go on I'll run and get Mabel and then catch up with you. She's that new little girl. Her folks haven't lived here long."

"Very well."

In a short-time Suzanna returned, holding tight to little Mabel's hand. "I told her mother we had enough to eat with us and that we'd take good care of her. So here she is," said Suzanna.

Emily Calvin Blake

Little Mabel looked up obliquely at Mrs. Procter.

"Her hair doesn't grow thick around her face," said Suzanna a little apologetically; "and I told her mother to rub Gray's ointment into it, like you did for the dog that came off in spots. The one Peter found, you remember."

"It didn't do any good—" began Maizie.

Mrs. Procter plunged in to prevent further discussion about the unfortunate dog. "Do you think you can walk quite a distance, Mabel?" she asked.

Mabel put her finger in her mouth.

"Don't talk to her right away, mother," begged Suzanna. "She's a little bit shy."

So they went on, little Mabel contributing no word to the talk. They passed fields full of yellow daisies and they walked by one group of gentle, cud-chewing cows. "But I hope there'll be no cows in your woods, Suzanna," said Mrs. Procter.

And her wish was granted. Indeed all, sky, flowers, breeze, absence of dust and curious animals, helped to make this a day of days. When they reached Suzanna's little patch of woods with many spreading oak trees that invited rest beneath their sheltering branches Mrs. Procter exclaimed in delight.

"Isn't it lovely, mother?" cried Suzanna. "See, there's a tiny brook, too. I've been here often when I wanted to think of poetry."

"And I've never had time," her mother murmured.

"Now you just sit right down here with your back against this tree," Suzanna went on with a delicious air of protection, "and I'll take care of the baby. Close your eyes, dear mother-love, and forget that God sent you a big family and that you've got to do your best by us all like you told Mrs. Reynolds last week."

Mrs. Procter's eyes were suddenly overflowing. Children! How rare and fine a gift they were. How many truths they could teach! She sank down upon the grass and Suzanna put the baby down beside her, first spreading out a thick shawl.

Mrs. Procter caught the small loving hand within her own: "I don't know, Suzanna; sometimes I wonder if I'll be able to do all I'd like to do for you all," she said in a low voice.

"Why, mother, *you love us*!" Suzanna exclaimed. "Don't you remember last Sunday when I put on my leghorn hat with the bunch of daisies over my left eye—"

"I remember," said Mrs. Procter, somewhat at a loss as to the connection between thought and thought.

"Well, when I said, 'good-bye, mother, I'm going to Sunday School,' you looked at me and *smiled* from your soul! And I forgot that there was Maizie and Peter and the baby, and I didn't even remember father, and I said to myself: '*That's my very own mother!* Just as though we just belonged to one another with nobody else in the whole world."

"Kiss me, Suzanna darling," said Mrs. Procter, after a long moment.

Suzanna stooped and kissed her mother very tenderly.

"Now run away and play," said Mrs. Procter, leaning against the supporting tree and closing her eyes, blissfully conscious that she could rest undisturbed for at least twenty minutes.

An hour later she opened her eyes and sat up straight. She had fallen asleep, though her position was not a particularly comfortable one, and slept sweetly, soundly. The baby still lay peacefully quiet, his little blanket covering him. And small bees

Emily Calvin Blake

had been working about her. Spread before her, reposing on a red table cloth lay a tempting meal. In the middle of the table cloth, to give an air of festivity, was a bunch of daisies. But most appealing of all to the mother was the sight of the four children, her own three and little Mabel, seated quietly near the table; they had evidently been there some time, waiting patiently till she should open her eyes.

"Oh," cried Maizie, great relief filling her at sight of her mother stirring, "Suzanna made us stay so quiet till you woke up, mother, and we're all awful hungry."

"Yes, I want that fat sandwich," said Peter.

And then they fell to eating with much laughter and gaiety.

"Out in the woods you don't have to pretend you hate to eat, do you, mother?" said Suzanna.

"Nor anywhere else that I know of," said Mrs. Procter, smiling.

"But I don't like to see anyone eat as though he liked to eat," said Suzanna. "May I have two or three grapes, mother?"

She received her grapes. And quiet fell, while each did his best to clear the table. At length when the meal was concluded, and the basket repacked, and the pewter knives and forks carefully wrapped in a napkin, the children begged Suzanna for stories.

So she began, and seemed never to fall short of material. Her mother listened, dreamily contented, till another hour passed and the baby awoke. He was a smiling, happy baby and crowed with delight when his mother allowed him a cracker and a cup of milk.

"Shall we play games?" asked Suzanna next, when just at the moment the sound of wheels was heard and shortly there came into sight a low carriage drawn by the two prosperous, fat brown horses, and seated in the carriage was Suzanna's Eagle Man.

Suzanna darted out into the road. As the carriage did not stop she called out: "Mr. Eagle Man! Oh, Mr. Eagle Man!"

The coachman involuntarily pulled in his horses. He didn't know what peremptory signal would be given him to move on, or what inquiry as to his sanity would scorchingly be made, but Suzanna's eager voice impelled him to stop. Mr. Massey leaned over the side of the carriage.

"I never dreamed you'd ride by our picnic," said Suzanna, all excited. "We've got my mother here and our baby."

"Well, well," said the Eagle Man. "And how are you, little girl?"

"I'm awfully well," returned Suzanna. "But today was cleaning day at home and we all started out wrong; the baby kept mother awake last night and Maizie hated her oatmeal with the syrup in the middle and Peter cried hard because he couldn't see his ears, and never in all his life can see his ears."

She paused tragically. "Never in all his life—and neither can you, or anybody."

"What a terrible loss, for sure," said the Eagle Man, after a look darted at his coachman's imperturbable back. "And what did *you* cry about?"

She stared at him in horror. "I never cry," she said. "I mean I never let the tears fall down my face. I cry in my heart sometimes, but never out loud, on top. But I felt funny this morning because I wished we didn't have to wash on Monday, and iron on Tuesday, and clean on Wednesday, and bake on Thursday, and mend on Friday, and clean again on Saturday."

"Well, ask your mother to wash on *Saturday*," the Eagle Man suggested easily.

"Oh, I don't think mother would," Suzanna cried, in a little horror herself at that idea. "She's awful set about washing on Monday. Still I'll ask her if you say so, Eagle Man, because Saturday is kind of a wet day anyhow. You see Saturday is just the shape of a big, immense, round ocean. Shall I bring my mother over here to look at you?" suddenly recalling the conventions.

"I don't think I'm fit to look at this morning," the Eagle Man muttered.

"Oh, I think you are," said Suzanna, earnestly. "I like your shiny shoes and your very high collar. I know mother would like you, too."

The Eagle Man looked down at his shiny shoes, hesitated and was lost. He opened the carriage door, seized his cane and struggled to the ground. "Now, let's see your wonderful family," he said to Suzanna, as he hobbled forward toward the little group under the trees.

Suzanna looked up at him. "Oh, you're the lame and the halt, too! We took Mabel along on our picnic because her eyes don't match, you know. They don't seem to work together. We *are* obeying the Bible today, aren't we?"

Old John Massey did not answer, since he was intent upon covering the ground with as little wear and tear on his nerves as possible, and so in silence they walked till they reached Mrs. Procter, still leaning against the tree, but now holding the baby in her arms.

Maizie, Mabel, and Peter all looked with vivid interest at the newcomer.

"Mother," began Suzanna, "this is the gentleman I told you about. He's John Massey; you've seen him on Main Street. *He loves to be comfortable.* And he doesn't work during the day, either, but he sits in a chair and shouts at a little man, and the little man hops mighty quick, I can tell you."

Mrs. Procter's face went crimson. "How do you do?" she said. She did not meet his keen eyes.

"How do you do, madam," the Eagle Man responded. "Out for an airing with your family?"

"Yes," said Mrs. Procter. "The children were all in a bad humor this morning and so we thought we'd have a picnic."

"Oh, no, mother," said Maizie earnestly, "we weren't in a bad humor. We just didn't like things at home."

"Well, we'll put it that way," smiled her mother, "and so Suzanna suggested a picnic." Mrs. Procter attempted to rise.

"Stay where you are, madam," said the Eagle Man. Mrs. Procter sank back against the tree.

"You sit down, too, Eagle Man," said Suzanna cordially. "We've got another shawl. Here it is." She spread it down on the ground and the Eagle Man quite gladly accepted the invitation, though his face whitened in the downward process of reaching the shawl.

"Well, madam," he began again, "most people can't afford big families these days."

Mrs. Procter smiled, but did not answer. Suzanna, sensing a criticism, spoke quickly.

"Mother can't afford them either, but she's not asked anything about it. The doctor who has charge of giving out babies stops at our gate often and looks into mother's eyes. Then he knows she'd be awful sweet to a little baby and so next time he gets around he brings one to us. Maybe one that no one else will have."

"I see," said the Eagle Man. He turned to Mrs. Procter. "Your daughter is very apt with explanations."

Mrs. Procter smiled.

"Her explanations," he continued, "are a trifle more honest than the ones I often hear."

Another little silence. The Eagle Man appeared to be thinking deeply. First he cast a glance out into the road to where his capacious vehicle stood, then he looked over at Mrs. Procter.

"I wonder, madam," he said, "if you and your family would do me the honor to drive with me."

Suzanna's eyes grew like stars, Maizie wrung her hands in a very eloquence of prayer as she awaited her mother's answer; Peter just stared, speech stricken from him; Mabel turned in her toes in her agony. The baby only was unconcerned. Finally Mrs. Procter answered:

"We'll be very glad to, I'm sure, Mr. Massey." And in less time than it takes to tell, Mrs. Procter, the baby on her knees, sat beside Mr. Massey in the carriage, while the three little girls sat on a seat facing Mrs. Procter, a seat that could at will be let down or pushed back. Peter, to his everlasting delight, sat beside the coachman.

"Out into the country, Robert," said Mr. Massey to his coachman, and so away they started at a leisurely pace, since the complacent horses refused any other. Sometimes vagrant chickens wandered into the road, exhibiting a daring that enthralled Peter. His opinion of chickens rose when, the fat horses almost upon their tail feathers, they disdainfully moved off.

"We couldn't run one down, I suppose," he asked Robert,

hopefully. "Just take a feather off, you know, to learn 'em a lesson."

"I scared a pair of 'em good and proper, once," returned Robert, who had been, known to coddle an ailing worm, but at the moment he was just a little boy with Peter, in very proper high spirits. And while braggingly he went on talking to his delighted listener, the rest of the party were silently, but with keen enjoyment, watching the passing country side. It was a ride to be long remembered; the smooth roads wound alluringly away, Suzanna wondered, to what beautiful hidden country. The breezes fanned their cheeks with delicate, fragrant breath; the birds sang overhead, or flew gaily about, adding harmony and color to the atmosphere. And yet, to Suzanna's horror the baby, apparently quite insensible to all the beauty and totally oblivious of the gratitude due the Eagle Man, soon fell fast asleep, engagingly sucking his fat thumb.

"He's not very old," whispered Suzanna to her host; "and he doesn't know he must be truly thankful to you."

"Well, let him rest comfortably," said the Eagle Man, and he moved in such a way that the baby's head rested against his knee.

"There, that's better," he said to Mrs. Procter. "I didn't suppose you wanted its neck to be broken," he ended gruffly.

"You can't talk that way to mother," said Suzanna, very gently. "She's not used to it, you see, and she might think you meant it, though I know you better. Father, when he isn't thinking of his invention, speaks very kindly and sometimes he says, 'Are you tired, Little Woman?'"

Mrs. Procter attempted to speak, but again the Eagle Man stopped her—very gently, for him.

"It's all right," he said. "It's rather interesting to find someone, if only a child, who's not afraid to be absolutely sincere."

They came to a small hill where Robert stopped his horses. The breezes had gone whispering away and stillness was upon all. Soon the birds ceased their calls; over in the west the clouds were soft delicate folds of bronze; and even as one looked they broke into bars of distinct color, orange, purple, coral. An opal sunset.

"Oh, how beautiful!" cried Mrs. Procter.

"A daily incident," returned the Eagle Man, but he, too, gazed at the glowing sky.

"And now, I suppose we must return," he said at length, and so Robert turned his horses upon the homeward journey.

It was nearly dusk when, after leaving Mabel with her mother, the little cottage came into sight, and then Mrs. Procter said to the Eagle Man: "This has been one of the happiest days of my life. I thank you for helping to make it so."

"That's very kind of you to say so," the Eagle Man answered in his usual gruff voice.

They reached the gate and leaning upon it was Mr. Procter. He stared his amazement at sight of his family returning in such state.

"Father, we had a picnic," called Maizie, springing from the carriage.

"And once I drove," cried Peter, almost falling from his seat, "and scared a chicken."

"We've had the grandest day, father," finished Suzanna, running to him. "We went on a picnic and we took the lame and halt along, Mabel and the Eagle Man, and they had a good time, too."

"And twice today, father," said Maizie, taking her father's

hand, "I remembered Who smiled at me."

"Who smiled at you?" asked the Eagle Man, who heard everything, it seemed.

"The Man with the halo, Jesus, you know," Maizie answered reverently. "When first I was a baby on this earth He came to smile at me and to wake me up. Suzanna told me so."

Silence. Then the Eagle Man turned to Mr. Procter. "Glad to have met your family, sir."

"Glad you've had the opportunity," said Mr. Procter.

"You sold a quantity of nails to me a few weeks ago, good nails, too; not underweight either, I noticed," said the Eagle Man at last. "Your little girl tells me you are an inventor."

"Yes, I'm working on a machine," Mr. Procter flushed. "It is nearly finished. That is, sometimes I think so; other times completion seems far away."

The Eagle Man paused. "I'd be interested in seeing your invention," he said, and stopped. Yet there was promise, too, in his voice, in his eyes.

Again the color rushed to Mr. Procter's face. He stared unbelievingly at the other, and then said: "I'll be glad any time to show my machine; to tell you all about it—" He hesitated. "There'd be a great chance for you, should you become interested in it."

"Well, if that's the case, expect me any time. Good-bye."

Suzanna spoke cordially: "You must come and see us very often," she said warmly, "only not on Tuesday nights, if you're coming to supper, because we have stew then made from the last of Sunday's roast."

"I'll remember," said the Eagle Man gravely, as he gave the signal to Robert to drive away.

The little family went down through the yard and on to the house.

"I must hurry with your supper," said Mrs. Procter. "I'm sorry you were kept waiting." She felt rested enough not to dread preparing the meal.

"Don't hurry, I found some crackers," said Mr. Procter, and added, "Why, I've not seen you look so happy in many a long day."

"Well, I really must thank Suzanna," said Mrs. Procter. "She insisted upon a picnic because the day started wrong. The house is all upset though," she finished, as they went into the kitchen.

"The house?" he returned, gazing vaguely about. "It looks all right to me. Suppose, Jane, he should really be won over to believe in the machine. Oh, I never hoped I could interest him!"

"It may be the beginning of a great day," she answered. He put his arm about her.

"What should I do without you to encourage, to help," he said.

"That's my privilege," she said softly.

Bending, he kissed her.

BOOK II

CHAPTER XI

THE INDIAN DRILL

Mid September and school days.

"I like my new teacher, that's why I'm happy," Suzanna told her mother at the end of the first school day.

"I saw her," said Maizie, who was a pupil at public school for the second year. "She holds her arm funny."

Suzanna flushed darkly. "She's beautiful," she averred; "she's my teacher."

"But didn't you see her arm?"

"No," said Suzanna, "I did not."

Maizie cried out triumphantly: "Well, that's the first time you didn't see something I saw."

Suzanna did not answer. She could not voice her emotions.

"Well, I don't want you or anyone in the whole world even to notice Miss Smithson's arm," she flung out, and so Maizie was silenced.

Emily Calvin Blake

Suzanna glanced through the window.

"Why there's father," cried Suzanna; "I wonder why he's coming home so early?"

Mr. Procter came hurriedly down the path, pushed open the front door, and with no word sprang up the stairs. To the attic, the children knew.

"He must have thought of something to do to The Machine," said Maizie.

"Yes," Suzanna answered; "whenever he has that still look on his face he has a new idea."

"Someone must be taking his place at the store," said Mrs. Procter. "I'm glad the baby's asleep. Be very quiet, children. Father may have a splendid thought—why there, he's coming downstairs again."

He entered the kitchen at once, his face aglow.

"Just the turn of a screw!" he exclaimed. He spoke directly to his wife. "Oh, my dear, it's coming on. Nearly ready to show to John Massey."

"Oh, I am happy for you," she cried.

He spoke to Suzanna and Maizie: "Would you chicks like to take a walk down town with me?" He fumbled in his pocket. "Here's a ticket good for ten dishes of ice cream." He held up a small card.

"Oh, daddy, where did you get it?" cried Maizie.

"From Raymond Cunningham, leading druggist," he announced slowly. "His soda fountain was out of order and I fixed it for him. I didn't want money for a small act of kindness, so he issued this ticket to me."

The children were delighted. Mrs. Procter smiled too. In generosity of spirit, she forbore to point out to her husband the fact that Raymond Cunningham was known from one end of the town to the other as one who would "skin a gnat for its teeth."

Without doubt the man now beaming upon his little daughters had saved the druggist a bill of ten dollars for which he had issued a ticket worth sixty cents!

But she simply smiled, and going to her husband she brushed an imaginary dust speck from his coat. He caught her hand.

"Wait, Dear One, till the invention is ready," he said; "all shall give homage to my wife."

She did not answer him in words, but he seemed satisfied with the silence. Such moments of love, of high hope, were beautiful to both.

The little group started away for their trip to town.

Just as they reached the drug store, Suzanna pulled her father's sleeve. She was all excitement.

"See, daddy," she cried, "that tall lady dressed in black standing near the lamp post is Miss Smithson, my new teacher."

"Well, let's go and say a word to her," suggested Mr. Procter, easily.

"Oh, father, I don't think she talks outside of school," said Suzanna, her voice falling. She fell into prim step as they neared Miss Smithson.

Miss Smithson, seeing Suzanna, smiled.

"This is my father," said Suzanna proudly.

Emily Calvin Blake

"I should know that at once by the close resemblance," returned Miss Smithson.

"Yes, Suzanna and I do look alike," said Mr. Procter, "and I think I've sold tacks to you." He rarely failed to speak of his work. He was so exalted a being, Suzanna thought glowingly, that he lifted his daily labor to the dignity of a fine art. People must think so too, because they always looked closer at him when he spoke of weighing nails, or wrapping wringers and washboards.

"We were going on to the drug store for some ice cream. Will you join us?" asked Mr. Procter of Miss Smithson.

Suzanna's face went white as she waited Miss Smithson's answer. Teachers, being purely ethereal she felt, never descended to the discussion of materialities. She wondered at her father's overlooking this truth.

But, "Thank you," said the teacher, very calmly.

So together they all entered the corner drug store, Suzanna still very quiet. Mr. Procter found a table large enough to accommodate them all. Suzanna sat next to Maizie.

"I'm going to have a chocolate ice cream soda," whispered Maizie.

"No, you can't, Maizie," Suzanna returned in an agony; "take lemon ice cream soda."

"But I don't like it."

"Well, that doesn't matter, Maizie. Chocolate is too dark; and besides you smear it all over your lips and it looks dreadful; pale lemon ice cream soda is sweet looking. We must do something to honor Miss Smithson, who's here just because she wouldn't hurt father's feelings."

But Maizie looked belligerent.

Suzanna's temper threatened to flame forth. With a mighty effort she controlled it. She turned to her father. "Father, don't you think Maizie had better have lemon ice cream soda?" she asked.

"Anything she wants; anything she wants," Mr. Procter answered and not lowering his voice, even in Miss Smithson's presence: "What do you think you'll have, Suzanna?"

"I'll have a lemon ice cream soda," said Suzanna primly. And she had difficulty in restraining her tears when Maizie deliberately gave her command for chocolate ice cream soda. When the orders came Suzanna scarcely touched her glass. Covertly she watched Miss Smithson; she saw, how daintily that lady ate her plain vanilla ice cream; perhaps, after all, even teachers found it necessary to find some subsistence and Miss Smithson had hit upon ice cream as the most aesthetic. At least Suzanna was forced to believe this in her endeavor to keep intact her ideal of Miss Smithson.

Then Miss Smithson said in a pleasant, every-day voice:

"I'm glad to have this opportunity, Mr. Procter, of asking you if Suzanna may take part in an Indian Drill I expect to give at school next month."

"Why, I can see no reason against her taking part," said Mr. Procter. "You would enjoy such an occasion, would you not, Suzanna?"

"She will need an outfit," Miss Smithson went on, treading delicately, since in part she guessed the state of the Procter finances and she wished to be very sure before implicating Suzanna in any embarrassing situation, "including dancing slippers, though I may be able to rent the Indian costumes from a masquerader in the city, and then the cost will be lessened."

"That will be all right," said Mr. Procter immediately. "Just tell us the clothes she will need and her mother will get them."

"That's very nice," said Miss Smithson, though she felt still a little uneasy.

"When will the affair take place?" Mr. Procter asked.

"On the fifteenth of October. We have ample time for rehearsals."

A little later Miss Smithson shook hands with Suzanna's father, murmuring something conventional about his being fortunate in the possession of such an interesting family. Then she was gone.

The children, bidding father good-bye, hastened on home. They burst into the house, anxious to tell mother all about the meeting with Miss Smithson.

Mrs. Procter listened interestedly. "And father said I might take part in the Indian Drill," said Suzanna. "I shall have to have an outfit perhaps and dancing shoes."

"What did father say about that?" asked Mrs. Procter, an anxious little frown growing between her eyes.

"He said you would get them for me," Suzanna returned. She, too, looked a little anxiously at her mother. "But Miss Smithson said perhaps she could hire the Indian costumes."

Mrs. Procter's expression lightened.

"Well, perhaps she can," she said.

"And if she can't, mother?" Suzanna breathlessly awaited the answer.

"Well, we'll manage some way."

And Suzanna was satisfied.

A week later Mr. Procter returned home, carrying a mysterious looking parcel.

"For you, Suzanna," he said, his eyes sparkling. "But let's not open it until after supper."

Suzanna reluctantly put the package to one side. That supper would never end that evening she had a firm conviction.

And yet the end was reached, and she was opening the package, attended by the entire family. At last her eager eyes swept the contents, and her little beating heart for the moment palpitated strangely in her throat, for there lay a pair of shoes.

"Shoes," said Mr. Procter, "for you to wear in the Indian Drill. I saw them thrown out in a little booth when I went into Lane's shoe shop for a piece of leather to be made into washers. They really were marked at so ridiculously low a figure that I thought at once we could surely afford them for Suzanna. They are, I should judge, the very thing for the Indian Drill."

To all of which Suzanna listened gravely. Her heart had gone back to its normal rhythm, but her eyes could not leave the atrocities lying before her. Truly, they were of fine leather, but with their high French heels, and flat gilt buttons, they might have been in style when Suzanna's mother was a very little girl, and, to be really candid, they would have lain under the anathema of being out of date even then. But over and beyond the painful vintage of the shoes was the fact that Miss Smithson had announced that all the girls taking part in the Indian Drill should wear the same kind of shoes. She had gone farther and told the children that the right kind of shoes could be obtained at Bryson's for a dollar and forty-eight cents a pair, a really reduced price because fourteen pairs were to be purchased. She had finished by giving the children the number to be called for, "A-14116." Suzanna knew the number well; she had repeated it mentally over and over again.

Finally Suzanna found her voice. "They're very nice, daddy," she said.

"Yes, they are very nice," he said. "See, you can turn them up. They're as soft as a kid glove."

"Well, since you've bought the shoes," said Mrs. Procter, "and probably at a very reasonable figure—" she paused, and Mr. Procter finished:

"Yes, they were only forty-eight cents, a remarkable bargain, I think."

"Remarkable," said Mrs. Procter, picking them up. "Why, I believe they're a handmade shoe! Well," she went on, "since the shoes are accounted for, I think if I have to I can quite easily manage the rest of the outfit."

Suzanna's heart sank lower. She only wondered miserably if her mother, seeing a piece of inexpensive goods of almost any shade, and finding a pattern easy to manage, would make up what she thought would do quite well for the Indian Drill costume. Then her thoughts returned to the shoes. Perhaps after all they wouldn't fit! She was enabled by that emancipating thought to turn a happier face to her father and again to thank him.

But alas, the shoes fitted perfectly.

"I think," said Suzanna desperately, "that perhaps they're a little bit too small—narrow, I mean."

"Do they hurt you?" asked her mother.

Suzanna had to confess that they didn't hurt.

"They certainly make your foot look very nice and slender," said her father.

Well, Suzanna thought miserably, she should have to wear them, and in that belief all interest in the Indian Drill left her. She simply couldn't, she felt, take her lead on the eventful day wearing those shoes. Every eye in the audience, she knew, would be fixed upon them, so different from those of the other girls, so terribly old-fashioned, as instinctively she sensed them to be.

Mrs. Procter carefully wrapped the bargains in the original tissue paper. She was happy in the thought that her little daughter was provided with a pretty and appropriate pair of dancing shoes.

But it was very perfunctorily that Suzanna went through the ensuing rehearsals at school. Her spirits were not lifted even when Miss Smithson announced that the costumes were to be obtained through a masquerader at the small cost of twenty-five cents for each pupil. But at length, the child's natural persevering force had its way, and she set her mind to studying the question of how to avoid wearing the unsuitable shoes and still preserve her father's confidence in his own good judgment. Usually she asked no help, working alone on the problems which assailed her, but suddenly the thought of her friend Drusilla came to her. She would ask Drusilla what she thought about the matter.

CHAPTER XII

DRUSILLA'S REMINISCENCES

One afternoon immediately after school, Suzanna, taking Maizie with her, went to call on Drusilla. Twice since her first visit in July she had gone to the little home, but on both occasions Drusilla had been ill, unable to see anyone. But today the pleasant faced maid admitted the children.

"Go right up to the attic," she said. "Mrs. Bartlett is there looking over some old trunks."

In the attic, a tiny place with slanting roof and unfinished walls, the children found Mrs. Bartlett, sitting on the floor beside a huge, overflowing trunk. Old-fashioned dresses, high-heeled satin slippers, dancing programs, painted fans, were all heaped together.

"We've come to see you, Drusilla," said Suzanna at once. "I've been twice before, but you didn't know it. This is my sister, Maizie. I've got a very important question to ask you."

Drusilla rose from the floor. "I'm glad to see you both. I've often thought of you, Suzanna. Close the lid of that trunk and sit on it and your little sister Maizie can sit in that old easy chair in the corner. That is, if you want to stay up here in the attic."

Suzanna looked about her. The attic was rather sad-looking,

she thought, not full of its own importance as the one at home, but still, very interesting. Old portraits hung on the slanting walls. In corners were piles of old furniture looking strangely lifelike in the shadows.

"We'd rather stay up here, Drusilla," she said. "And we'll stay a long time with you, if you like."

"Very good," said Drusilla. She drew forth a low rocker and seated herself.

Suzanna suddenly remembered her manners. "Perhaps we shouldn't have come today anyway," she said. "You were busy with your trunk when we came up."

"I was just looking over some old dresses and relics I've kept for many years," said Drusilla. "There's a dress in there," she said, "that I wore when as a young girl I lived with my parents way back across the ocean."

"A big city?" asked Maizie. "Not like Anchorville?"

"A big city," returned Drusilla. "You see that glass case in the corner? Go and look at it."

Suzanna and Maizie sprang up and went to the dusky corner. On a table stood the glass case, and under it was an apple, a pear, a bunch of grapes, and a banana, all made of wax.

"That came from the city across the water," said Drusilla. "It was given to my grandmother by our old herb woman."

The children left the wax fruit and went and stood quite close to Drusilla. "What's an old herb woman?" asked Maizie, interestedly.

"Why, she was our doctor in those days. She had an old shop buried away in a part of the town that we reached by crossing a canal. Many is the time my grandmother took me to that old shop with its rows of dried herbs hanging from the ceiling; with its old worn corners, and its barrel of white cocoanut oil standing near the door. Oh, I loved that place. I loved the smell of the herbs and I loved the little old woman who could brew teas from her herbs that would cure any ailment in the world, I thought. And then right next to the old herb shop was a pawn shop with three tarnished golden balls above the door."

"A pawn shop?" The children wanted to know the meaning of that kind of shop.

"A shop," said Drusilla, warming to her keen audience, "to which you could bring anything, from a worn out dress to a piece of jewelry, and get money for it and a ticket. And if you wanted the dress or the jewelry back again, then you brought the ticket and the money and a little interest.

"The old pawn shop was a landmark. It had stood next to the herb shop, my grandmother told me, for a hundred years; during all these years owned by the same family. When I was a little girl a woman kept the shop. She was very tall, very thin, with quantities of black hair braided and wound round and round her head. She wore always a Paisley shawl of faded colors, and her hair coiled as it was made me think always of a crown.

"The shop was long and narrow and full of wonderful rare, old curios—old violins, cameos, and uncut stones. I was allowed to go all over the shop; to open quaint cases, to go upstairs and out upon an old gallery and to lift from their drawers silken crapes, and to find, buried away, whispering sea-shells and crystal bottles, and irregular pieces of blue-veined marble and alabaster. Oh, the happy, thrilling hours I spent in that place! My grandmother told me that scholars came from every part of the country to see this tucked-away, historic old pawn shop."

Drusilla paused, but in a moment to the children's relief she went on: "Then on a quite busy street, back this side of the canal, the side we lived on, was a large place called an ovenry.

And there we sent our bread to be baked."

The children's eyes widened.

"Yes," went on Drusilla, "we put our dough to rise at home, made it into little loaves, pricked our initial—or some other distinguishing mark—on top when it lay in its pans, and then a big red-faced man with a wagon drawn by a donkey called for our bread. Once my grandmother let me ride with him, and I stayed all afternoon in his ovenry, though the fire from the big ovens made it uncomfortably hot. I watched him and his helpers put the pans of bread on big shovels and heave them into yawning caves of flames. When they were finished, another red-faced man delivered them baked brown, and smoking, to the customers. We paid a penny a loaf for having our bread baked."

"Oh, and that saved you buying so much coal, didn't it?" asked Maizie. "I wish we had an ovenry in Anchorville."

"Yes," said Drusilla, "I think, myself, some of these old-fashioned ideas were economical."

"There isn't a pawn shop anywhere near, is there?" asked Suzanna. She was thinking about the shoes and what a blessing it would be to dispose of them.

"I don't believe so," Drusilla answered. "Anyway, there couldn't be another like that wonderful shop of my youth."

There ensued a silence. Suddenly leaning forward, Suzanna began very earnestly:

"Drusilla, I have a very important question to ask you. Which would you rather do, be honest or suffer?"

"Be honest or suffer?" repeated Drusilla. "I don't quite understand."

"Well, you see, it's this way," said Suzanna. "Now, Maizie, I see you're listening with your eyes wide open, and I want to tell you now that you mustn't say anything to father of what I'm going to tell Drusilla." Having delivered this ultimatum, she went on and told of the Indian Drill and of the costumes, and then of her father's recent purchase of the shoes. "I can't tell daddy that the shoes would be different from everybody's else," she said, "because it will hurt his feelings. But, oh, Drusilla! My heart jumps into my throat when I think of wearing those shoes so different from everyone else's."

"The shoes cost forty-eight cents," elaborated Maizie, "and so you can see Suzanna has to wear them whether she likes them or not."

"Yes," said Suzanna, "forty-eight cents is very near to half a dollar and we can't afford to lose that. I thought, Drusilla, that you could give me some advice. That's all I want, just that you tell me which is best, to be honest or to suffer. You told me once about the little silver chain and that has helped me a lot."

Drusilla looked puzzled. "The silver chain?" she asked.

"Yes, don't you remember that day you were queen and told me about the chain?" asked Suzanna.

In a second a remarkable change came over the old lady. She rose to her feet. Then she turned to Suzanna, her shoulders straight and her head held high.

"My crown," she demanded. "Is that to be lifted from me in these the full years of my queenhood?"

"I've never seen you with a crown on," said Suzanna.

"Enough, serf!" cried the queen haughtily. "Procure me my crown." Suzanna looked about her. An old dried-up Christmas wreath hanging on a rafter attracted her attention. Quickly she procured it and held it out to Drusilla. "Here is your crown,

Queen," she said. And then, her voice changing, she said: "You'd better let me put it on, Drusilla, it's liable to crumble if you're not careful. Lower your head, please."

The old lady did so and Suzanna placed the crown upon the silver hair.

"Now," said the old lady, "if you have sought me to gain advice, repeat your question, that I may answer in a manner worthy my exalted station."

"Well," said Suzanna for the third time, "I want to know whether it's best to be honest or to suffer?"

"What shall be your course if you are honest?" asked the queen.

Suzanna pondered. "I think I'll tell daddy, perhaps tonight," she said at last, "that to wear the shoes will hurt my feelings dreadfully; that I tremble when I think of being the only girl in the drill without low shoes with two straps. Something like moccasins. If I tell daddy this, then I'll be honest."

"And if you decide to suffer?"

"Then I'll wear the shoes at the drill and from the time I put them on till the drill is over, I'll be full of pain. I'll know that everybody will be just looking at my feet, and I'll not enjoy the dance one bit."

The queen knit her brows. Then her answer came: "Be not honest in the way you describe, neither suffer."

"But, Drusilla," Suzanna objected, "I don't understand."

"*And can you not be brave?*" asked the queen with a note of scorn in her voice. "Is it left to one who feels the time approaching when she will be deposed from her throne and all she holds dear, alone to have courage?" She looked straight

Emily Calvin Blake

into Suzanna's dark eyes. "Your father knows joy in thinking he has given you your heart's desire. Why, then, hurt him by telling him that the shoes are not your desire? Why not, with head held high, lead the dance you speak of, and forget shoes, and remember only the movement of the dance, the lilt of the music?"

"Is that bravery?" asked Suzanna.

"The greatest bravery," returned the queen, "will be to say to yourself, 'Am I so poor a maid that I cannot by the very beauty of my dancing keep the eyes of the watchers lifted clear above my shoes? For shoes, what are shoes? Leather and wood. Inanimate, unthinking *stuff*! They are not worth one heart pang, one moment of misery to me or mine. But *I, I am alive*. I can see and think and understand. I can go so joyously through the mazes of the dance that the watchers may forget their sordid cares.'"

Suzanna, listening, was carried away. She cried with eager response: "Why the night of the Indian Drill I can believe I am a fairy, dancing over snow-topped mountains, and singing, flying clear up into the clouds!"

"You might fall, Suzanna," said Maizie, "you know you haven't wings."

But on this occasion Suzanna was not to be recalled to earth, and besides in her queen's interested, understanding face, she felt a quick fellowship to the spirit that dwelt within her.

And then breaking harshly into the wonder of this moment came the tinkle, tinkle of the electric bell.

"Oh," cried Maizie, "someone is coming."

"I shall brook no intruders," cried the queen.

"No matter who it is?" asked Suzanna.

"No matter who it is. I desire to be alone with my court. However, you can peep over the banisters and see who dares come thus upon us."

Suzanna went to the top of the stairs. The maid was ushering in a lady and a boy.

"Go right upstairs," Suzanna heard the maid say. "Mrs. Bartlett's in the attic with two of the Procter children."

The visitors appeared at the top of the stairs and paused to glance in.

The lady was beautifully dressed, quite exquisitely, from the dainty little toque upon her haughty head to her small gray cloth shoes. Her eyes, flashing from pansy shades to lightest blue, were cold. Her white skin seemed to hold no possibility of color. Yet, even as she stood, the milk of it turned to rose when Drusilla gazed at her with no warmth of recognition in her glance.

The boy, about twelve, Suzanna surmised correctly, stood forward. There was some of his mother's haughtiness in his bearing, a great deal of her beauty. But added to both, a rare, high look as though always he were seeking what lay beyond his grasp, and perhaps his comprehension. He seemed altogether like a child whose emotional values did not stand clear. He gazed half prayerfully at his grandmother, as though asking and bestowing at the same time.

Breaking into the embarrassing silence, Suzanna spoke:

"Drusilla has her crown on," she said. "You see, she's a queen now, and she's been answering some questions of mine."

The lady in the doorway looked at Suzanna meditatively. Then she spoke directly to Drusilla.

"May I come in, mother?" she asked. "You see I've

brought Graham."

Drusilla began: "Court was in session. However, I shall be glad to have you remain." The boy, who had remained quiet, now spoke.

"Oh, bully, mother; grandmother's playing again. I want to stay."

But his mother put out a detaining hand as he attempted to enter the attic.

"No—we can't stay now—" She spoke directly again to Drusilla. "We'll come again—when you are more—yourself."

In a moment she was gone down the stairs, leaving after her a soft fragrance. The boy obediently followed her. In the hall below she encountered the maid. She whispered a few hurried words before taking her departure.

The maid went up immediately into the attic.

Drusilla was again talking eloquently while Suzanna and Maizie stood listening spellbound.

"I think," said the maid, breaking in quietly but firmly, "that you little girls had better go home now. Mrs. Bartlett is tired and I want her to lie down."

She approached the queen. "Come, Mrs. Bartlett," she said, "you must rest now." She raised her hand as though to remove the crown of faded leaves.

"What means this sacrilege?" cried the queen, stepping backward.

"She likes to wear her crown when she's a queen," said Suzanna, much distressed.

"But she can't lie down in her crown, you know, little girl, it will hurt her."

"Well, that's true, Drusilla," Suzanna conceded. "Will you put your head down and I'll take the crown off very carefully and we'll put it away for another day."

The queen obediently lowered her silver head to Suzanna. Suzanna very carefully removed the wreath and hung it on its old nail.

"I *am* tired," said the old lady, now in a voice that trembled a little. "But you'll come again soon, won't you?" she asked, appealing to Suzanna.

"Yes, just as soon as I can," said Suzanna. "Come, Maizie. Good-bye, Drusilla, and thank you very much for helping me."

Drusilla brightened. "That's nice, to know that I can still help someone," she said.

CHAPTER XIII

MRS. GRAHAM WOODS BARTLETT

The great house stood on a hilltop quite two miles from the station, and cut into the immense iron door standing guard to the grounds was the name "Bartlett Villa."

Here for a small part of the year the Graham Woods Bartletts lived. The family consisted of mother, father, and son, named for his father. In the city another house as large and more palatial received the family when they tired of the country home.

Mr. Graham Woods Bartlett held large interests in the Massey Steel Mills. That he might be on the ground part of the time he had built Bartlett Villa. In his heart he loved the small town. It was like a retreat to him to come back to its quiet after feverish hours spent in the crowded city. Here he seemed to recall in part a few of his vanished dreams—those dreams so bright, so well-nigh impossible of fulfillment, which as a young man fresh from college he had cherished. While young, he met and loved the girl he married. That she had visions he perfectly believed. That her visions were unworthy no power then could have made him believe. She came from an impecunious family whose lineage was older and greater than his. How she could have thought the high-browed, sensitive-faced young man the one who could fulfill her grasping desires is not to be fathomed. She had believed so, and he did bring to pass all her aspirations. That in doing so he killed his finest ideals mattered not.

Young Graham, too, was always glad when the time came for a stay at Bartlett Villa in Anchorville. He loved the big upstanding elms; loved the many gardens, and the flaunting flowers. He loved the two people who belonged properly in the environs of Bartlett Villa—old Nancy, who had been his mother's nurse and his own, and David, the gardener, with his little daughter Daphne.

Nancy, old, with hard rosy cheeks, was still so real. She worked and sang, loved and sometimes resented on behalf of those whom she served. Often, when quite a little boy, Graham would seek her in the old nursery of the city home and climb into her lap, rest his curly head against her loving breast, and sometimes contentedly fall asleep.

He never so cuddled with his mother, no matter how fervent the longings that filled his heart. She was always finely dressed; and her eyes were never for him alone. They were fixed on some distant and glittering goal, quite beyond the boy's understanding.

Then there was David, big of stature, big of mind. David, given over to many long, silent periods, because David had lost a loved and cherished one.

There were times when David would take Graham with him on long rambles, and then he would talk. He knew everything about the birds, their habits, their peculiarities, their fears, and their courage. He put into Graham a great love for the little creatures. Often together near a nest they would stand, and, scarce breathing, watch the first lesson given by a mother bird to a frightened young one.

"She's greater, that mother, than some humans," David said once, when they were on their way home.

"Why?" asked Graham, interestedly.

Emily Calvin Blake

"Well," said David, slowly, "we most of us hold on too long when it's time for those we love to try their wings."

"You wouldn't hold on, would you, David?" asked Graham, his boyish eyes upturned in perfect faith to his friend.

"I might, Graham; human nature is weak and wants always its own."

Upon reaching home Graham would ask: "Will you have time to go riding this afternoon, David?"

And David would answer: "Perhaps, my lad, if there's not too much work in the gardens."

Once Graham asked: "Why do you do such work, David? You could be in the city making lots of money." Thus Graham, who through heritage had been innoculated with that thought, that money meant everything.

And David had turned with a swift gesture: "Why should I mistreat my spirit, kill my brightest self trying for money, young Graham? Here among my flowers, working in the soil, I find time to think."

Graham looked strangely at David. Time to think! On what? Well he knew that David would tell him some day, and then he would weigh in his own mind the question of whether it were wise to work hard at something that took all your time in order to make lots of money; or to work at something that while you worked gave you time to think and grow.

David had an uncanny way of knowing another's thoughts. "It's not altogether what you work at, lad," he said, "it's what your ideals of life are." And turning, he left Graham to ponder.

On the day that he and his mother had paid the visit to his grandmother in the attic, the boy's mind was deeply concerned with the scene he had witnessed in his grandmother's attic. He envied the Procter children, since there grew in his imagination the treasure a grandmother could be. She probably knew "bully" stories of long-ago days. Certainly as she stood, crowned, she seemed the best sort of a playfellow, since she could pretend as well as any child.

His mother drove him home and then went to pay a call in a near town. He had gone directly to his own room. A telegrapher's outfit, in which he was then greatly interested, needed his attention. He was anxious to resume work on it; still his undermind, even as he drew forth the machine and began to work, was busy.

Suddenly he remembered the time last year when his mother had made elaborate preparations for an extended sojourn in the South. They were then in their city home. He had ardently wished that she would decide to take him with her, but the thought evidently did not occur to her. He had said good-bye to her with a strange, empty feeling at his heart.

And then quite unexpectedly she had returned, her contemplated stay cut enchantingly short. She had talked with him, taken long walks with him, even accompanied him to several ball games.

For a month she had been a friend, a good friend interested in boyish sports, in active games, and once in an open moment she had asked him if he had ever been lonely.

He answered, not wishing to hurt her: "Sometimes, when you stayed for months in Italy. But I was only a very small boy then. Father had to be away most of the time too, and the tutor you got for me wouldn't allow me to talk with other children until he knew all about where their fathers and mothers came from and how much money they had."

She was touched. She meant then to see that her boy should have more of the normal boy life of fun and roughness.

Emily Calvin Blake

But gradually her old desire for social leadership pressed in on her. And it took all her time and energy to dress, to entertain, to outdo her social rivals. And Graham went his own way again, only wishing that it was not necessary for both father and mother to be so occupied with outside interests that they had little time for their one child.

After a time he left his machine to look out of the window, and as he stood, he saw his mother. She had left her small runabout, and David was leading the horse to the stables.

He saw her enter the house. In a moment he heard her talking in her sweet voice to one of the servants before she mounted the stairs to her own room. She would then, Graham knew, be in the hands of her maid for a long time, since she was giving a formal dinner party that evening.

When the shadows were lengthening Graham left his room and wandered aimlessly around the house. Finally he reached the kitchen, where he sat for a time, watching the imported French chef's noble efforts for the coming dinner, efforts that must result in the wide proclamation of Mrs. Graham Woods Bartlett as an original hostess. But in the kitchen it was made manifest that Graham's presence was not welcome. At last, feeling this truth, he left.

The maid, coming from his mother's room and meeting him in the hall, told him that his dinner was to be served at six in his own room. "Your mother thought you'd like that," she finished.

Graham nodded without speaking and went on once more to his own room. He felt lonely, dispirited. Old Nancy, to whom he might have turned, had gone to her old home to visit some grandchildren. David, he knew, would be very busy.

At six the boy's dinner was brought, and with the hearty appetite of boyhood he ate. Afterwards he read a little, and then, feeling tired, he concluded to retire. But he did not go to sleep at once. Occasionally he heard interesting sounds from below, music from a string orchestra, laughter of women, and the bass voices of men.

At nine o'clock he was still lying awake when he heard a little running step outside his door. Out of an impulse he called softly, "Mother."

Mrs. Graham Woods Bartlett, on her way to her private safe for a piece of jade she wished to show one of her guests, paused at the call. Then she pushed open Graham's door, which was slightly ajar, and went in. Graham sat up. By the glow of a small electric light near his bed he could plainly see his mother. She was a beautiful vision in her soft white gown, quite untouched by any color, her hair piled high upon her small, finely shaped head.

"Did you call me, Graham?" she asked.

"Yes," he said, "I wanted to see you all dressed."

She went quickly and sat on the edge of the bed. "Did they serve you a nice dinner, Graham?" she asked.

He nodded. "Very nice," he answered.

"I thought you'd be asleep long ago," she said. "Otherwise I should have looked in on you."

"I couldn't sleep," he answered. Then impulsively: "Mother, I know you have to go downstairs again soon, but I've been thinking so much of grandmother. Wouldn't it be possible to have her come to live here with us? We've got such a big house, and she must be very lonely."

She drew herself a little away from him. "Perhaps I haven't explained to you, Graham," she said, "that your grandmother is given to periods of hallucinations. That is, she has peculiar fancies, one of them being that she thinks herself a queen."

Emily Calvin Blake

"Well, does it hurt if she does think she's a queen?" asked the boy.

"In this way it does. It's not pleasant to have in close proximity one who isn't what is called just normal. I think she is much better cared for as she is and in her own home. You'll admit it would be very unpleasant if she lived here, and appeared before guests in one of her unnatural moods."

"But she is lonely," persisted the boy, sticking to the one line of thought that had remained with him all afternoon, and had aroused his mind to dwell insistently upon his grandmother. "You don't mind, mother, do you, then since she can't come here, if I go to see her often?" He hesitated before continuing: "Father told me he wished I would, as he hasn't the time to do so."

"Of course, you may go to see her, Graham, if you like. I didn't know you cared so much."

She rose from the bed and walked away to the window, looking through its leaded panes to where she knew lay the broad road leading out into the country with farm houses and plowed fields. After a moment she turned to gaze at the little lad who still sat up in his bed; who still regarded her with wide eyes very much like her own, but holding a depth and a promise that hers did not seem to hold.

"Perhaps it's not the proper time to tell you now, Graham," she said, "but I think I might as well do so. I'm making arrangements to leave for Italy some time soon."

"To be gone long, mother?" asked the boy.

"Well, for three months anyway. I met some interesting people there on my last trip and they have invited me to pay them a prolonged visit," she said.

Graham did not answer at first. Then: "I suppose you'd better go downstairs now, mother," he said.

His mother left the window. Passing the bed she once more paused and looked down at him.

"Well, little son," she said at last, "good night. I've been up here an outrageous time." She put her arms around his small shoulders and drew him to her.

But for the first time in his short life she felt no response in her child. Indeed, she recognized his withdrawal from her, more poignant in its effect upon her because it was unconscious on his part. In that one moment the instinct of motherhood leapt full within her, a sudden bewildering emotion, totally new to her in its aliveness, its vividness. And then cold truth swept in on her that by some act she had wiped from his young heart in one moment his ideal of her.

She sank on her knees beside his bed, realizing dimly how great a crown his love had been. After an appreciable length of time, his hand crept out and rested a second lightly on her arm, and at the touch she raised her head. "I've disappointed you, Graham," she said. He did not answer. She waited, and then as he was still silent she rose. She shook her unwonted mood from her and her face hardened into its habitual brilliance.

"Good night, Graham," she said and went away.

Emily Calvin Blake

CHAPTER XIV

THE STRAY DOG

Miss Smithson had had years of experience with children. She knew their sensitiveness, their capacity for suffering through those incidents which adults term trifles.

She had questioned Suzanna with much adroit delicacy concerning the shoes, and had elicited the story of the father's purchase. Though she read correctly the child's real shrinking from the thought of being the cynosure of many amused eyes, she felt herself helpless.

That one odd pair of shoes in the company of participating children! In imagination Miss Smithson visualized the unsuccessful efforts of their owner to hide them, to find her place in the background. The kind-hearted teacher really suffered in her anticipation of Suzanna's pain.

So when the great night arrived and the music sounded the approach of the Indian maidens, Miss Smithson, sitting in the front row beside Suzanna's parents, kept her eyes steadfastly lowered. At length, not hearing the expected titters from children in the audience, she found her courage and looked up. Her eyes were immediately drawn to Suzanna's face and rested there.

For pictured there in place of depression, self-pity, troubling self-consciousness, she found sparkle and joy. Miss Smithson gasped in astonishment and relief. With perfect abandon Suzanna moved through the dance; she seemed as one quite set apart from her companions; and so she was.

All that Drusilla had told her lived with her, inspiring her, lifting her beyond mere mortals. She might have been frolicing upon a cloud in her little bare feet, so far away from her consciousness was the thought of the shoes.

The dance ended, and with flushed cheeks and heart beating happily, Suzanna took her seat. The applause lasted a long time.

Then came a recitation and a piano solo given by a greatly embarrassed boy, though certainly a greatly talented one. Suzanna recognizing his anguish felt very sorry for him. She wished he had had a Drusilla to advise him, to make him see that he was for the time greater than his audience. That he had music in his soul. She understood now that the greatest gift was to forget yourself and love your art so much that it reigned supreme.

Then looking out at the people seated before her, she recognized that they were *kind*. That they had come not to criticize, but to enjoy and to acclaim. She felt growing within her heart a great love for all humanity.

Her eyes sought out her father's. Just in front he sat, looking up at her, his eyes filled with pride. She had made him happy. Her heart was very full.

Her eyes after a time went again over the audience. And behind her father sat a boy, the one she had seen at Drusilla's. His eyes seemed to be searching her face. She smiled at him and he smiled in return.

The evening was over. Suzanna was down in the audience. "Did you like the dance, daddy?" she asked.

"It was beautiful," he answered with gratifying response. "I was very proud of my little girl—and the shoes—I was so glad you could have them—they were the prettiest in the drill."

"I think they were, too," Suzanna answered, with real truth.

Out in the street she saw the boy. He was standing near the gate of the school yard, by his side a tall, dark young man.

"How do you do?" said Suzanna.

He snatched his hat from his head. "Oh, I liked your dance," he said. "This is my tutor," he finished.

"How do you do," said Suzanna politely to the young man. She wondered what a tutor was. Then to the boy: "Drusilla's your grandmother, isn't she?"

"Yes; do you live in this town?"

"Yes, right down that road. Your big house was closed for three years, wasn't it—since I was a little girl of five. That's why we haven't seen one another, I suppose." Then: "How did you think of coming to the Indian Drill?"

"Why, one of the school trustees had to see my father on business and he spoke about the entertainment. I thought I'd like to see it."

"Well, I'm glad you came. Good-bye."

A carriage drew up. The boy and his companion stepped into it and were driven off.

"That's young Graham Woods Bartlett," said Mrs. Procter as they started home. "They live in the big house on the top of the hill. This is the first time it's been open for some years."

"And Drusilla's his grandmother," said Suzanna. "He's an

awful nice boy."

"His father and old John Massey are business associates," put in Mr. Procter.

"Such a fine big house to be occupied only a few months of the year, and then not every year," put in Mrs. Procter. "And they rarely stay so late in the season as they're staying this year—way into October."

"I'll take Maizie and Peter and go and see him tomorrow," said Suzanna.

"Oh, Suzanna, I don't believe—" began Mrs. Procter. Then sensing immediately that her small daughter would be totally unable to understand social distinctions, she did not finish her sentence.

So it was that the next afternoon right after school, Suzanna, who never lost time in carrying out a resolve, prepared for her visit.

"I wonder where Peter is?" Mrs. Procter asked.

As if in answer to his mother's question, Peter opened the kitchen door. He wore primarily a guilty expression. His hat was on one side of his head, the suit which two seasons before he had outgrown, was short in the legs, tight as to chest, and there was a very symphony of entreaty in his eyes. By a frayed string he held a stray dog, the fourth one since spring.

Mrs. Procter looked at him sternly. As mothers do, she took in with one glance Peter's prayerful attitude and the appealing one of the shrinking animal.

"You take that dog right away and lose it!" she commanded.

"Oh, mother," began the small boy entering the kitchen, the dog perforce entering also. "He followed me all the way home and we're awful good friends already. Can't he stay?"

"Not one minute," returned Mrs. Procter. She regarded the animal scornfully. "He's not anybody's dog," she said. "He's simply a stray, and I'm tired of feeding every stray dog that comes into the neighborhood."

Peter turned reluctantly away. "He'll be awful lonely out there," he said, "and he's hungry, too. No lady ever thinks a dog eats. Can't I give him a bone or something before I turn him loose?"

"Take him out on the back porch and give him that soup bone left from supper last night. And then I don't want to see him again. Now, Peter, this time I mean it."

Peter made one last effort. "He's a fine breed, his roof is black," he said. "He'd make an awful good watch dog."

"Well, we really don't need a watch dog," his mother answered, and half smiled.

Maizie, advancing from the dining-room, stared at the intruder on his way out.

"Oh, but this dog has hair, mother," she cried. "You remember one of the others hadn't."

"Hair, or no hair," Mrs. Procter returned determinedly, "that dog is not going to stay in this house. I've had enough of stray animals to last me for quite awhile."

Peter stood holding the rope and still looking at his mother. But his hopeful expression, brought on by Maizie's words, was fast ebbing.

"Hurry up," said Mrs. Procter. "Take him away."

"Can't he stay for one night, mother?"

Suzanna, silent during the colloquy, now spoke.

"Maybe we can find another home for him, Peter. We were just going over to Graham Bartlett's, and perhaps he'd keep the dog. We'll ask his mother," she said.

Peter brightened a trifle at that. He really wanted more than anything in the world to keep that friendly dog. But if he was not to be allowed to do so, finding a good home for it was the next best thing.

So away the children started. It was a long walk, but the October day was cool and exhilarating. The children kicked the fallen leaves before them, and once Peter gave chase to his dog. Maizie sang little tunes, and Suzanna felt new wonderments rising within her at the beauty of the world.

They came at last to the Bartlett home, but no one was about, only several carriages stood in the road. Suzanna swung the big gate wide and with the children following her, and the dog held in Peter's firm grasp, she came to the house, mounted the steps and seeing the carved front door wide open, they all walked in. In the empty hall with the high ceilings they stood a moment embarrassed.

From a side room came sounds of laughter and soft voices. Suzanna turned. Heavy Persian rugs hung at the entrance to this room and Suzanna hesitated one moment. She wished someone were about to direct her. But alas, at this critical moment the hallman had escaped kitchenward. It was Mrs. Graham Woods Bartlett's at-home day, and the function in full blast, and as his services might not be required for perhaps half an hour he had flown, believing discovery could not fall upon him.

So Suzanna, Maizie, Peter and the dog stepped within the gorgeous room.

Soft music came enchantingly from a hidden orchestra, ladies beautifully gowned and bejeweled stood about in graceful postures. Mrs. Graham Woods Bartlett attired in a flame-colored velvet gown with a wonderful satin-lined train hanging straight from her shoulders, stood near a table at which two very pretty girls were serving little cups of tea and dainty cakes.

Suzanna, Maizie, and Peter holding tight the frayed rope with the hungry-looking dog on one end, gazed awe stricken at the fairylike scene. At length Mrs. Graham Woods Bartlett turned and beheld her late guests.

The children stood irresolute; some expression in Mrs. Bartlett's face halted their advance. That look made Suzanna strangely self-conscious. Maizie was undeniably shy, and Peter with dread at his heart for fear Jerry (a quickly bestowed name that the dog had learned immediately to answer to) might not act in a gentlemanly fashion when he should pass the tea table. With all these different emotions in their hearts, the children finally started across the beautiful room. The ladies fell back from the dog lest in his passage he might touch their gowns, and all gazed in wonder at the small cavalcade. When at last the children stood before Mrs. Graham Woods Bartlett, Suzanna spoke, broke into the dead silence of the room, for even the orchestra had stopped its music.

"We thought you might like a dog," began Suzanna. "He's a very nice dog and very loving, although if I'm to be honest, I can't say he's a good-looking dog." She felt her courage ebbing at the icy stillness which greeted her statement.

For a long time Mrs. Graham Woods Bartlett remained speechless, and as the dog once had looked at Mrs. Procter, so he looked imploringly at her who might eventually be his new mistress. Little Maizie, moved to a show of bravery for Peter's sake, spoke up:

"We've only got a little house, and you've got a big one, so we thought you wouldn't mind."

"And," concluded Peter, "he really is a fine dog. You can buy a nice collar for him and maybe cut his tail—" Mrs. Graham Woods Bartlett made a little wry face—"and you'd be surprised to see how elegant he'll look."

A laugh rang out from one end of the room. It came from a fine-looking old lady who stood near the window surrounded, it would seem by admiring satellites, and at the little musical sound Mrs. Graham Woods Bartlett's face cleared magically, for the stately old lady was a very important personage to all present, envied usually too, and if this little incident seemed to amuse her then the matter was beautifully altered. So Mrs. Graham Woods Bartlett found her voice. "Go out into the grounds and see the gardener. If he can find a place for the animal, let him keep it."

The children felt themselves dismissed. On the way out Suzanna kept her gaze quite away from the table with its alluring load of dainties. But Maizie paused an infinitesimal fraction of a second and let her eyes stray over the fascinating cakes, the glasses of pink ices, and the Maraschino cherries and nuts and white candies. But it was Peter who neither looked aside nor paused, but as he went by the table he addressed the ceiling.

"My dog's very fond of cakes," he said. "But mother says dogs can do without cakes, especially stray dogs."

One of the pretty girls laughed merrily, and sweeping from a silver plate a handful of cakes she thrust them into Peter's hands. "Thank you," he said simply. And then the children left with the dog gamboling in expectancy behind his small master. He knew well the cakes were for him.

Out in the grounds they met Graham. He had been to the stables to look at his pony, a new gift from his father. He paused astonished at sight of the children.

"Oh, Graham," Suzanna cried at sight of him, "your mother

said we should see the gardener about this dog. She thought he'd like to have him."

Graham, though startled, asked no questions.

"I guess it's David mother means," he said. "Wait here and I'll see if he's in the back garden."

After Graham had gone Peter began to conjecture. "If David won't take Jerry," he said, "what'll we do?"

"You'll have to take him out and lose him then," said Maizie calmly.

Peter turned a considering eye upon her. He couldn't understand her. Quite as a matter of course she suggested his taking the dog out on some prairie and turning it loose, to know hunger, and perhaps abuse. And yet, he had seen this same tender-hearted little Maizie crying because a spider had been swept down from the porch. No, in his boyish soul he decided that should he live a thousand years, he never would understand women with their inconsistencies and their peculiar viewpoints. Their tendernesses in one direction and their complacent cruelties in others.

"Let's go and sit on the steps of that cottage," said Suzanna, pointing to a small house at the foot of the side garden. Maizie consented, but Peter preferred not to move. He wished to stay with his dog as long as possible. In the cottage might be a lady who would look with the same horror-stricken eyes upon his friend as had Mrs. Graham Woods Bartlett.

So Suzanna and Maizie left him with his dog. They had just ensconced themselves comfortably on the steps of the cottage when a distressing accent struck upon their ears, and simultaneously they turned in the direction of the sound. There on a tiny verandah, almost hidden behind a large fern growth, a little girl sat on a low chair crying softly and pathetically as though her small heart were broken. The children stood for a moment not knowing just what to do. Then Maizie, the same one, thought Peter satirically (he could see all that went on from his place beyond) who had suggested his losing his dog on a prairie, went to the pathetic figure and sitting beside it said in a tremulous low voice, full of sympathy and pity:

"What's the matter, little girl?"

The one thus addressed took her hands down from her face and looked around at her questioner. Her eyes were dark, with black lashes, and she had wonderful, curly hair. When she had finished looking at Maizie, which was a long moment, she put her hand behind her and produced a doll, sadly deficient as to features. Indeed, noseless, entirely, and with one eye gone. But in a very fever of love, she held it to her.

"Are you crying because your doll is broken?" asked Suzanna, now coming a little closer and standing straight and slim before the child.

"No, she's not broken," said the little girl, "but she's got the whooping cough and she keeps my father awake nights coughing."

Suzanna instantly responded. "Oh, that's too bad," she said. "Can't your mother fix her some flaxseed tea?"

Now down once more went the little girl's head upon her knee, and once more she was shaking with sobs. And at this moment young Graham returned and in his wake, David.

"David says," began Graham cheerfully to Suzanna and Maizie, "that he can find room for an extra dog, so you may leave yours. Where's your brother?"

"He is right over there," pointed Maizie.

Then the gardener's glance fell upon the little girl, with her head bent as she still wept.

"She's crying awfully hard," said Suzanna to the gardener. "Do you know whose little girl she is?"

"She's mine," said the man with a big world of tenderness in his voice. "She's my little Daphne."

"We thought she was crying because her doll was broken," said Suzanna. "Then she said it had the whooping cough and kept you awake all night and I asked her why her mother didn't make some flaxseed tea for it."

A swift shadow darkened David's fine face and he shaded his eyes with his hand. Then he went to the little girl and raised her as though she were one of his carefully cherished flowers. Her sobs ceased as she found herself in her father's arms.

"You see," said her father, "she has no mother!"

Now the children knew by his tone and by the extreme sadness in his eyes that the little Daphne's mother had gone away never to return. And they knew it must be the saddest thing in the world to be without a mother; one who was always ready to understand even if you had to wait till the baby was hushed, or the bread looked at in the oven. The understanding did come, sure and tender; a mother who sometimes smiled at you in that complete, deep way, as Suzanna's mother had smiled at her the day she wore her leghorn hat with the daisies.

"Can Daphne play with us?" asked Suzanna after awhile. "And can we take her home to see our mother?"

The man's face brightened at this. "Why, that will be fine," he said. "Perhaps you'd like to play here in the grounds for awhile. Then Daphne can go home with you. You're the Procter children, aren't you? I've talked often with your father when I've bought things in the hardware shop. I'm coming sometime to see his machine."

"Yes," said Suzanna, "but how did you know we were the Procter children? We didn't tell you our name. Did Graham?"

"No," said the man, "but you're the living image of your father. You look at a person just like he does, out of your big dark eyes."

Suzanna flushed. There was nothing in all the world she so loved to hear as that she looked like her father.

Little Daphne had ceased crying and her father carried her up the narrow winding stairs to their own quarters. Shortly he returned again. The little girl now wore a pretty lace-trimmed bonnet mother-made, one knew at once, and a little white cape. She was a very charming and quaint figure.

"I think, daddy," she said, "I'd like to go home right away and see the little girl's mother."

He turned his head away again for a moment, but he managed at last to meet his little daughter's eyes with a smile.

"Run along, sweet," he said.

"Can she stay to supper with us?" asked Suzanna.

"If your mother would like to have her," said the man. "And I'll come up later for her."

"All right," replied Suzanna.

Now came the hard moment for Peter, in the parting from his dog. He came reluctantly forward.

Graham, seeing Peter's distress when the animal had been delivered into David's care, said: "You can come up here often, Peter, and see the dog. I know it's awful hard giving him up."

Peter's heart was touched. Here at last was one who

understood! Here at last was one who would not condemn a dog merely because he had an unnaturally big appetite; because he got around under people's feet and had no manners.

"You're a very nice boy," said Suzanna when they were parting, "and we wish you would come to see us."

Graham's face lit. "Oh, I will come. Do you live in that little cottage with the crooked chimney?"

"Yes," said Suzanna. "Come soon, won't you?"

Graham promised he would do so.

As the Procter children went down the road, Graham watched them, but his gaze presently concentrated itself on Suzanna, who was leading the small Daphne.

"I like Suzanna," thought Graham. "I like to see her flush up like a rose when she speaks." Which was a poetical observation for a boy of twelve.

CHAPTER XV

A LENT MOTHER

Mrs. Procter was in the dining-room arranging the shelves of her small sideboard when she heard sounds betokening the children's return.

They entered the dining-room, Suzanna leading a small stranger by the hand, Maizie and Peter behind.

"Mother," began Suzanna at once, "David, the gardener, took the dog and we brought this little girl home to see you."

Mrs. Procter looked questioningly at Daphne, who stood close to Suzanna's protecting arm.

"Stay with Maizie a moment, Daphne," said Suzanna, "while I tell my mother something." Daphne smiled and did as she was told, and Suzanna went close to Mrs. Procter. In a low tone she said: "Daphne's mother went far away awhile ago, and I'm telling this to you in a low voice because Daphne cried when we asked her where her mother was. I brought her home so she could remember how beautiful a mother is."

In an instant the tears sprang to Mrs. Procter's eyes. She went quickly to Daphne, and lifted the little girl.

"Sit down in a rocking chair with her," said Suzanna, "and hold her close up to you. And then when she's cuddled down, look at her like you do at our babies."

Mrs. Procter obeyed. Daphne nestled close. "Her father knows my father, Mrs. Procter," said Suzanna.

Mrs. Procter looked up quickly at this new mode of address. Suzanna explained.

"Daphne," she said, going close and looking down at the contented little face, "I'm giving you a share in my mother while you're here today. I give over the part I own in her to you, and I shall call her Mrs. Procter whenever you visit us."

"But you can't give away even your part in your very own mother," protested Maizie.

"But I have done so, haven't I?"

"Does just saying so make a thing true?" Maizie asked.

"If you say so and live up to it," Suzanna returned.

"Well, anyway," said Maizie, "mother's not cuddling Daphne because she wants to; only because she's sorry for her."

"What do you mean?" asked Mrs. Procter. "I like little Daphne, too, and I'm glad she's come to visit us."

"But you know, mother," said Maizie, "you only find time to cuddle your own babies. And you stop just as soon as they can walk around."

"Mrs. Procter cuddles all children in her heart," said Suzanna loyally. "She'd wear her arms out if she cuddled all of us all the time."

Maizie didn't answer that. But when little Daphne finally left Mrs. Procter's sheltering clasp and went away to play with the children, Maizie still hovered about her mother.

"Mother," she said at last, "did you like to hold Daphne close up to you?"

Now mothers are very wonderful beings, and with no further word from Maizie, Mrs. Procter understood the child's unspoken wish. In a moment Maizie was held close to her mother's breast, and was looking up into her mother's tender eyes. And the mother was thinking. Was mother love selfish then in its inclusion? Weren't there little ones outside hungering for cuddling? How children went to the heart of things! She thought suddenly and perhaps irrelevantly of her husband's invention upon which he poured his heart's best treasures. And yet not once had he ever mentioned the money which might be his did success attend it. Only the good to others. His seemed a wide vision. She sighed. It was hard to find strength enough, time enough to go outside one's home doing good. "Well, at least," she thought with a sudden uplift, "I'll adopt little Daphne into our home circle."

When Mr. Procter arrived home for supper he found, playing happily about, the little addition to his family. Suzanna took her father off to one corner to explain all about Daphne.

"And so I've given my share in mother to Daphne whenever she visits us," concluded Suzanna.

Mr. Procter smiled and touched Suzanna's dark hair. Later he arranged a chair so Daphne might be comfortable at the supper table. A book and a cushion brought that state of comfort about, and the child was very happy. She was, for the time being, a member of an interesting family, everyone trying his best to entertain her. Even Peter forgot the loss of his dog and said some funny things which made Daphne laugh.

After supper David called for his little daughter. Daphne cried out joyfully as he entered.

"Oh, I've had such a good time, Daddy David," she exclaimed.

He lifted her to his shoulder, then gazed about the little family circle. His eyes lingered on Mrs. Procter.

"You've been good to Daphne, I know," he said simply. "And so good night."

"While you're here, David," said Mr. Procter, "I'll show you my invention."

"Fine!" David said; he swung the little girl from his shoulder. "I'd like to see that machine."

So they all went upstairs to the attic. The machine stood brooding in its peace.

Mr. Procter lit a lamp. Its glow fell softly upon the little group.

"Old John Massey came into the shop today," said Mr. Procter. "He promised to come in and see the machine tomorrow."

"Does he know its object?" asked David.

"No, there's been no chance to tell him."

"Why is he interested, then?" asked David. "Has his commercial instinct been aroused?"

"Oh, I think not," said the inventor, "I've not spoken to him about that part of it, only told him a great chance was his if he became interested in the machine."

"Someone's ringing the bell. Run down, Peter," said Mrs. Procter.

Peter went down and returned at once with a note.

"A man with brass buttons brought it," he said. "It's for father."

Mr. Procter tore open the letter.

"Well, that's decent of John Massey to let me know," he said. "He's ill and will be unable to come here tomorrow."

"Yes, very decent for old John Massey," said David. "Well, I must be off. And we'll come again soon, if we may."

CHAPTER XVI

SUZANNA AIDS CUPID

"Mother dear," asked Suzanna one day, "if the Eagle Man's sick, don't you think I ought to go and see him?"

Mrs. Procter hesitated. She looked into the earnest dark eyes raised to hers. "Well, dear, perhaps it would be kind," she said.

"I ought to take him some flowers," Suzanna pursued.

The time was early morning, and Mr. Procter had not yet departed for the hardware store.

"I can't think where you'll get flowers, Suzanna," he said.

"Oh, there's a little shaded spot in a field I know and there's some daisies there. I'll gather them on the way to the Eagle Man."

So that afternoon after school Suzanna admonished Maizie to be quick with her buttons because she and the baby were to pay a call on the Eagle Man.

"I have to gather the daisies for him, too," said Suzanna.

"I don't like the Eagle Man very well," said Maizie; "I'm afraid of him; and I don't see why you should take flowers to him. He has plenty in the big glass house in his yard."

Suzanna stopped short. "You don't like him after he gave you that lovely ride in the summer, Maizie Procter, and after he's interested in our father's Machine? I'm 'shamed of you. You ought to like everybody Miss Massey says, and flowers in his glass house aren't like flowers that are a present from somebody else."

Maizie did not answer this, but the look on her face indicated some defiance of Suzanna's attempted direction of her thoughts. When they were ready, they called good-bye to their mother and started away. Suzanna pushed the cart containing the baby, while Maizie walked sedately beside her.

From the field Suzanna knew, she secured a small bunch of late daisies and then the journey was continued. At length the children reached the Massey grounds. Suzanna pushed open the big iron gate and trundled the cart into the gravel path. The ground immediately began to be slightly hilly.

"You'd better help me, Maizie," said Suzanna.

"How?" asked Maizie helplessly.

"Put your hands on my back and push," said Suzanna.

So the little procession formed itself. And in this wise it reached the top of the hill. The house itself lay a few yards in front of them. The children paused to rest, and then Suzanna, looking around, beheld a small vine-covered arbor, and within, just visible through the enshrouding ivy, a man and a woman, Miss Massey and a stranger.

"How do you do, Suzanna?" Miss Massey said when she found herself discovered. "Did you want to see me?"

"I'm very glad to see you," responded Suzanna politely, "but I didn't come expressly on purpose to look at you. I came to see the Eagle Man."

"The Eagle Man?" asked Miss Massey, puzzled.

"He walks with a cane," put in Maizie, "and he coughs kind of hoarse each time he speaks."

"He's your father," said Suzanna. "He sits down on a velvet chair, and he shouts, and he gets red in the face, and he bangs his fist on the chair when a little man doesn't hurry up, though I thought he went very fast. He did all that the day the Sunday School pupils came to your party."

"Oh, yes," said Miss Massey, a smile lighting her face at the vivid description, "I did not know that you had met my father, but I'm afraid you can't see him today, dear. He's not well."

"Yes, I know; that's why I came to see him and to bring him these flowers."

Miss Massey was a little puzzled. How did Suzanna know John Massey was ill?

"Suppose you bring the baby in here," suggested the man who was sitting next to Miss Massey, and who up to this time had been silent. "And after awhile Miss Massey can find out if her father is able to see you."

"All right," said Suzanna with alacrity. She started to lift the baby from his carriage when the man sprang up and took the child from her. The baby smiled and won his way at once to the stranger's heart.

"He's sweet, isn't he?" began Suzanna, as she entered the arbor, Maizie with her. Miss Massey drew Maizie within the circle of her own arm.

"He is that," said the man earnestly, "although I don't know very much about babies. Does he cry much?"

"Well, he's very sinful when he's hungry. He's getting better now because he's growing older, but he used to shriek till his face got red. Once in awhile now he wants what he wants right away. I was trying once to learn a piece of poetry, and he suddenly shrieked and I had to stop everything and warm his milk. I'm only hoping he'll live to grow up, because if he should die now I'm afraid God wouldn't want him in Heaven."

"Are there ladies in Heaven that take care of babies?" asked Maizie interestedly, a new train of thoughts started.

"You know there are, Maizie," said Suzanna, allowing no one else a chance to answer. "There are lots of little babies that go away, and do you s'pose they'd be called if they were going to be left hungry and cold? God has it all arranged. First, he calls a baby and then pretty soon he calls a mother and she takes care of the baby."

"Any mother?" Maizie asked.

"Yes, any mother; they're all good."

"But why doesn't he leave them on earth with their own mothers?"

"Because sometimes he takes a liking to somebody down here," Suzanna said gravely. "But anyway, you needn't ask me such questions, because here's Miss Massey who knows everything," Suzanna finished magnanimously.

"She does that," said the man gravely who was holding the baby.

"Are you related to Miss Massey?" asked Suzanna. Now Miss Massey's rather faded cheeks grew pink.

"Is it a long time before the baby needs his bottle again, Suzanna?" she asked.

"Oh, not for hours," said Suzanna. "You see, now he eats crackers and bread and butter and an egg sometimes, and we gave him some before we started." She returned relentlessly to the question again, appealing to the man. "Are you related to Miss Massey?"

"No," the stranger said after a time, "we're just friends."

Miss Massey put in hastily: "Shall we go into the house, children, and I'll show you some interesting things?"

The man rose quickly, the baby still in his arms. In this manner they all entered the big house and went into the beautiful room that Suzanna remembered so well.

"Do you live here?" asked Suzanna of the man. He shook his head.

"You mean in this little town?" he asked. "I once did years ago, but I moved away to the city. I'm paying a short visit to my sister now."

"Oh," said Suzanna. "My father has a sister called Aunt Martha. She comes sometimes when we have a new baby."

"Why," said Maizie suddenly, as they were all seated, the baby contentedly sitting on the man's knee, her voice shrill with new discovery. "He *is* related to Miss Massey; he looks at her that way."

The man, after a long pause in which he gathered understanding, answered very solemnly. "Well," he said, "if loving a person makes you a relative, then I am very closely related to Miss Massey. But if lack of money keeps one from being related, then I'm only a stranger to her."

Neither Suzanna nor Maizie could understand that statement. But Miss Massey blushed till her face was like a lovely flower.

Yet when Suzanna appeared to be about to take up a new line of questioning, Miss Massey spoke quickly:

"I think you'd like some lemonade, wouldn't you, Suzanna, you and your sister? I'll go and order some for you."

She went out of the room. The man waited for a moment, then handing the baby to Suzanna, followed Miss Massey.

"Would you like to live here, Suzanna?" asked Maizie.

"No, I don't like people around with brass buttons on their coats," said Suzanna. "And then there'd be so much cleaning we'd never get through."

At the moment came an unmistakable sound.

"The Eagle Man!" cried Suzanna with absolute conviction. "I thought he was sick."

And indeed it was just exactly the Eagle Man. Straight he came to the library. He paused in the doorway at sight of the children. All the high color had faded from his face; he looked alarmingly ill.

"Oh," cried Suzanna, immediately upon sight of him. "We came to see you and to bring you these daisies."

He accepted them with a little grimace. "Thank you, little girl," he said. "Put that heavy baby down. He can crawl around."

Suzanna carefully lowered the baby to the floor. He sat with blinking eyes, so many treasures for his small hands lay within touch.

The Eagle Man spoke. "Who have you been talking with?" he asked as he looked about suspiciously.

"Oh," cried Suzanna, "there's nobody hidden away. Miss Massey and her relation went out to see about some lemonade."

"Her relation!" stormed the Eagle Man.

"Yes, the one who loves Miss Massey."

The Eagle Man recovered all his lost color. Watching his terrible expression, both children thought it a blessing that at this critical moment Miss Massey and her relation returned. But, oh, it was not the same Miss Massey, but one who had found the world. Her face was glowing like a girl's and her eyes sparkled and shone; and when she faced her father there was manifest in her aspect a certain courage that in his eyes at least sat strangely upon her.

"Father," she cried, "you should be in bed."

"What's the meaning of all this?" he shouted, ignoring her soft concern.

The new relation came forward. "My dear sir," he began, "I shall have to ask you to refrain from attempting to intimidate the lady who is to be my wife."

"Your wife?" exclaimed the Eagle Man turning upon the speaker. "She's my daughter."

"Granted," said the man calmly, "and she's also my promised wife."

"I shall never give my consent," said the Eagle Man, but his voice had fallen.

"Then, father," said delicate, timid little Miss Massey, "I shall marry Robert without your consent."

There was a long heavy silence. The baby having found a

gold-plated lizard on the hearth was contemplating it with wondering eyes.

"Very well," said the Eagle Man at last, trying to speak calmly. "You'll go your own way. Not a cent of mine do you ever get."

"I'm glad to hear that," said the man, "for not a cent of yours shall my wife need."

Into the breach Suzanna strode.

"Oh, but you will need money," she cried as she stood anchoring the baby by means of an extended arm. "When you're married and you have a big family you'll have to pay the rent, and you'll have to dress all the little children, and there'll be insurance week, and something you haven't thought of all the time, and just when you get on your feet, there'll be the doctor at your door and his bill pretty soon."

"Exactly," said the Eagle Man, as though by Suzanna's words many of his contentions had been proved.

"But we shall be together," said little Miss Massey, as though that beloved truth answered everything. The man had thrown his arms about her and had drawn her quite close, and she looked up into his face with eyes that still shone. Oh, how long she had loved him! And how long had it been since she settled to the realization that though he loved her, he was proud and would not speak. This spoken love she had craved with all her heart; and it had been withheld because he had no money and her father had too much.

"Will you tell me your real objection to me?" asked the man with frank directness appealing to the Eagle Man. "For that you have had objections to me I've sensed always."

The Eagle Man turned and looked the younger man over, carefully, critically, before answering. Indeed, he was so long about speaking that the children, at least, thought he never meant to speak again.

But at last: "My daughter," he began, "is now thirty-six. She has had thirty-six years of luxury, of merely raising her finger and receiving highly trained service. She is not a young girl who might, being more adaptable and buoyed up by romance, settle down to a new order of life; she is too used to the luxuries I have been able to give her, servants, carriages, horses, travel, fine clothes—" he enumerated them all with distinctness, giving each item a lengthy second before going on to his conclusion. "It will work real hardship on her to be compelled to give up all these things to do her own work and to make over her own dresses."

"You're mistaken, father," Miss Massey denied, "all that giving up, if giving up you can call it, will be my joy if I can be with Robert." Her voice, deep with emotion, died into a silence which reigned for moments. No one seemed to wish to break it, not even the baby. And yet, though the meaning of all the spoken words had not been clear to Suzanna, her eager, sensitive little mind seized on pictures which seemed somehow to fit in; yet pictures in their simplicity so far removed from her surroundings of luxury that they would seem but vagrant fancies.

Had she attempted to translate them, she would have failed, yet as they grew momentarily more vivid and meaningful, interpretive words, as vivid as the pictures themselves, rushed to her lips. She turned to the Eagle Man.

"Oh, on Saturday night when supper is over and the shades are pulled down and the lamp is lit in the parlor, and Robert is reading a big book with pictures in it, and the children, except the two eldest, are all asleep upstairs and it's raining outside, and you can hear the pitapat, pitapat of the drops on the window pane, then Miss Massey will be happy. Before supper Miss Massey'll have felt awful tired and she'll hurry up things and she'll make her eldest little girl hurry too, but after the dishes are cleared away, and she's sitting close to Robert, she'll be so glad she's in out of the rain with her children all in safe too, that she'll not care a bit about raising her finger for a little man to come and ask her what she wants. She'll not want to go about in a carriage, or travel in a big train!"

No one spoke. Only the scene painted so simply grew in the hearts of at least two there, so that Robert drew his promised wife a little closer to him and she glanced up in his face with eyes full of color.

Suzanna went on. She had forgotten her audience. She was just telling out the pictures that had been built into her life; supper tables with many young faces about; little babies who had stayed just awhile; hasty words and loving making up; the star-dust of the real every-day life.

"You know," she continued, "that Maizie and I crept downstairs one Saturday night because I wanted to tell daddy something, and mother was sitting right close to him, and we heard her say: 'When the children are safe in bed, and just you and I are here—then I see things clearer—' And he just looked at her and said, 'Sweetheart!' and his voice was nicer than even when he says good-night to Maizie and me."

Miss Massey turned her gaze upon Suzanna. "Little girl, little girl," she said, "come here—"

So Suzanna went and stood close to Miss Massey, whilst Maizie went after the marauding baby.

The Eagle Man cleared his throat. "That child of yours is going to sleep," he said speaking to Suzanna.

"Oh, no," said Suzanna, not meaning to contradict, but just to set him straight, "he's wide-awake. But I guess it must be time for us to go. I know you think so too, Mr. Eagle Man."

She left Miss Massey's tender clasp, went to the baby, raised him, held him under her arm skilfully, the while his legs stuck

Emily Calvin Blake

out straight behind her. She spoke to Miss Massey:

"If the Eagle Man's mad at you and he stays mad all night," she said, "you can come to our house and sleep in my bed with Maizie. Mother can fix the dining-room table for me."

Miss Massey released herself from Robert's clasp and went to Suzanna. She stooped and kissed her tenderly. "Thank you, dear little girl," she said. "I'll remember that invitation."

The Eagle Man pulled a cord hanging from the ceiling. Immediately it seemed, one of the men with brass buttons appeared.

"Carry that child to its perambulator," shouted the Eagle Man. Not a flicker disturbed the serenity of the man addressed, no matter what were his inner feelings. He put out two arms straight and stiff like rods, and Suzanna placed the baby upon them. Saying quickly their adieus, Suzanna and Maizie walked behind the uniformed man, for whom Suzanna at least felt a stirring of pity.

CHAPTER XVII

A SIMPLE WEDDING

"And so," concluded Suzanna early one afternoon as she stood on a soap box in her own yard, "the noble knight set forth on his prancing steed, having finished his deeds of blood. And all about him lay those he had slain."

The children having listened entranced to the story, now stirred; Maizie was the first to speak. "I think the knight was horrid," she said.

"I like him," said soft little Daphne who was now a constant, happy visitor at the Procter home.

"I think a brave knight is bully," said Graham Bartlett, as constant a visitor as Daphne.

"I would slay mine by the hundred," cried Peter boastfully.

Graham looked off into the distance. "I shall fare forth some day," he said, "and lead my armies to victory proudly, yet disdainfully. I shall have no love in my heart, only sternness."

"Drusilla can tell some wonderful tales of knights," said Suzanna. "Does she tell you stories when you go to visit her, Graham?"

Graham colored hotly. "I haven't been to see her lately," he

Emily Calvin Blake

answered; then, "I'll tell you, let's go today."

Suzanna bounded away to ask permission of her mother. She returned in a moment. "Mother says we may go after Peter changes his blouse. Hurry up, Peter. Don't keep us waiting."

Peter moved reluctantly houseward, and Suzanna ended: "Isn't it fine that today was teachers' meeting so we could have a holiday?"

Graham looked wistfully at her. He had a tutor, and lessons alone he felt could not be so interesting as when learned with a number of other boys and girls.

"Let's go," said Suzanna, "we can walk slowly so Peter can catch up with us. You mustn't get tired, will you, Daphne?" Daphne was very sure she would not, and Peter reappearing at the moment, they all started away. They went out into a sunny day left over from the Indian summer. Still there was crispness in the air which exhilarated them, moving Peter to sundry manifestations which Maizie coldly designated as "showing off." He stood on his head, turned somersaults, cast his voice up to the heavens, immediately spoiled the crispness of his clean blouse. He was the fine, free savage, and his sisters finally gave up trying to tame him.

"It's Thanksgiving weather, isn't it?" said Suzanna. "Come on, let's all skip."

So they all fell into Peter's spirit, and thus it was that skipping and singing they reached Drusilla's little home. It was very quiet in that spot, the garden desolate, the flowers gone. The children instinctively hushed their songs and went slowly up the front steps.

Graham rang the bell.

The kindly-faced maid answered the ring. "Oh, come in, children," she cried. "Mrs. Bartlett certainly needs cheering today."

The children, thus cordially invited, trooped in. "Is Drusilla sad today?" asked Suzanna.

"Well, she's thinking of the past," said the maid. "All day she's been talking of her early home across the ocean, talking of the familiar places of her childhood. She insisted even upon my preparing brouse for her luncheon."

"*Brouse?*" The children were interested. They wanted to know what brouse was. The maid smiled.

"Why brouse is just bread broken up into a bowl with hot water poured over it and lots of butter and salt and pepper added. One day when Mrs. Bartlett was a little girl, her mother took her to the home of an old nurse, and there she had brouse to eat, and afterwards for one joyful hour she was allowed to wear the clogs belonging to the nurse's little granddaughter."

"I know what clogs are," said Graham. "They're wooden shoes that make a lot of noise and have brass nails in them." He had looked into the sitting room and was interested in an object there. "What's that?" he asked. "Can't my grandmother walk?"

The maid's eyes followed his finger. "That's a wheel chair," she said. "Your grandmother is not so strong as she was in the summer, so I take her out in the chair when the day is bright. Well, children, go upstairs quietly. Suzanna knows the way to Mrs. Bartlett's room."

So the children on tiptoes mounted the thickly carpeted stairs. At the top Suzanna waited for the others, then went down the hall, paused and knocked softly on the panel to the right, and at the soft invitation to enter, pushed open wide the door.

Drusilla sat within, her chair drawn close to the window. Her hands were lying listlessly in her lap. She looked wilted, a flower fading to its end. She turned to the children and smiled, a very small wistful smile, but it lit her pale delicate face and made Daphne advance confidentially to the middle of the room.

"We came to see you," she said in her winsome way.

"I'm very glad," said Drusilla. "Won't you all come close to me?"

The children obeyed. Drusilla looked inquiringly at Graham, and then said, "Well, my boy, you've grown somewhat."

"Yes, two inches in six months." He wanted to say something to lift the sadness from her face, and at last he blurted out: "I think you're a bully grandmother, and I'm coming often to see you."

"Ah, then I'll tell you fine tales of your father when he was a lad of your age," she answered, well pleased. She put out her white hand and laid it on his head.

And at the touch there grew in Graham's young soul a wish to defend this dear old lady, this grandmother. He wanted to fight for her, to do something great for her. He had visions of himself, a man, wearing her colors. All his deepest chivalry was aroused. He looked longingly into her face, and with loving sagacity she read his desire.

"My dear," she said, "I wish you would do something for me."

"Oh, grandmother, what would you like me to do?" he cried.

"The day is so beautiful," she answered. "I've had my windows open and I know. Would you be my knight and wheel me out?"

"Grandmother, will you let me do that?" His voice rose. "I'll wheel you down the wide road out into the country." He straightened his shoulders, pride filled his heart. His grandmother trusted her frail body to his care!

"Well and good, my boy," she answered. And then to Suzanna: "Will you tell Letty to get my cape and bonnet. My grandson would take me riding."

Letty, answering Suzanna's call, came at once. She found a very cheerful mistress and an excited little group of children. She hesitated a moment when Graham told her he meant to take his grandmother out for a ride. But noting the earnestness of the boy's manner she made no spoken objections, but she went to the clothes press and took down Drusilla's "dolman" and small close fitting bonnet.

"Be very careful of your grandmother," said the maid, as she dressed Mrs. Bartlett and then offered her arm to steady the slight figure down the stairs.

"I shall be very careful," promised Graham. Never once in his young life had any real service been asked of him. He was experiencing for the first time a sense of responsibility and he grew beneath it.

Downstairs Letty guided the rubber-tired wheel chair out into the hall, down the front steps. She returned for Drusilla and seating her in the chair, tucked a soft velvet rug about her.

Graham took his place at the long handled bar. Gently he pushed the chair and the small cavalcade was on its way.

At first each child was quiet. Graham, ever mindful of the charge which was his, was very serious and his thoughts turned to his mother.

He wished she had taken this grandmother right into her own home to be watched over, loved and cared for tenderly. He wondered if his father, his ever busy father, would have liked that. Oh, why was it considered better for a grandmother, one who had fancies, to live alone in a small house, with every comfort it is true, but with no one of her very own close beside her!

He looked over at Suzanna. She was walking close to Drusilla, and talking earnestly as was her way. Suzanna never went out into the world but some object started a train of thought of keen interest. He could hear snatches of her talk. It was about the trees, stripped bare now, and their mood sad probably because of their denudement. Suzanna gazed with concern at their stark limbs stretching out, no longer able to shelter people or to sing softly when the wind blew through their leaves.

Drusilla contributed her share, too. She thought the trees knew that people did not need shelter from the hot sun when the snow was about to fly. And the snow could lie in such beautiful, straight lines on long, unleaved limbs.

And so they passed on from subject to subject, while Graham listened. And then little Daphne grew tired and began to lag. Graham seeing the child and about to make some suggestion for her comfort, was distracted by Peter's call. The boy had found a rabbit hole and wished he had Jerry with him to reach the rabbit, for which cruel wish both Suzanna and Maizie scolded him roundly. And he gazed at them with the same old perplexed gaze. Were these not the same sisters who looked complacently on while a homeless, helpless dog was turned out casually into an inhuman world?

Well, again he gave up the puzzle of their contrary attitudes. Perhaps understanding would come in the big-grown-up years.

But when they returned from examining the rabbit hole, they found little Daphne had curled herself up at Drusilla's feet. Drusilla had moved a little and the child hopping up on the foot-rest had put her small arms on Drusilla's knee, dropped her head and gone to sleep. Suzanna carefully covered her with part of the velvet rug.

So they started away again and came at last to a little lonely church set back from the road. It was a quaint little edifice, made of irregular purplish stone. The moss had crept up on one side softly, protectingly. You thought at once it had been built by loving hands and that loving souls had worshiped in it. And you knew that under its assumed and momentary air of expectancy it was sad in having outlived its usefulness. Its door was swung open hospitably and the children stopped to look in. Graham wheeled his grandmother close to the door so she too could gaze within.

There were pews, empty, with worn cushions. A large stained glass window with one Figure, noble despite the artist's limitations, had caught lights and sent them down in long sapphire and amethyst fingers. A man moved about the altar, changing from place to place a vase of white roses.

"Is that the minister?" whispered Maizie.

Suzanna nodded. "Yes. He's going to offer up prayer, I think."

The minister turned and smiled at the children. He seemed some way to fit into the soft atmosphere of the place, seeming to belong there. Suzanna could not fancy him moving in any merely practical environment.

And while the children lingered, and Drusilla looked in through the open church door, a man and a woman came down the road. The woman walked slowly and the man had his arm about her in a guarding kind of way.

When they neared the church they stopped. Suzanna, turning, recognized them and with a joyful cry she ran to meet them.

"Oh, Miss Massey," she cried, "and Robert. Are you out for a walk, too?"

The man looked down at her. "Yes, little girl. We are going into that old church. Did you see the minister?"

Emily Calvin Blake

"Yes, he's inside," said Suzanna. She looked at Miss Massey. "You've been crying," she said.

Miss Massey tried to speak calmly, but there was a little quiver in her voice. "Because it's all so different from what I dreamed."

"Come, dear," said Robert then, "come with me."

She seemed to take courage from his manliness and the truth of his love shining forth from his eyes, and so she put her hand into his and walked up the path with him.

At the door of the church they paused again. Suzanna who had followed quickly, said, "This is Drusilla, my very best friend."

Miss Massey looked into the sweet old face. Perhaps she thought of her own mother, for the tears came quickly again. "I'm glad to know you," she said simply. And then asked, "Won't you come in and see me married?"

And Drusilla answered: "Indeed, I should like to very much, my dear."

So Robert helped her gently from the wheel chair. He lifted small Daphne upon the vacated seat and tucked her in carefully. And then they all entered the church.

The minister came down from the altar. He had lit two candles and they sent their wavering light out upon the small audience. The Man above the altar looked down with infinite tenderness upon the pale little bride.

The minister spoke: "Robert, take your bride upon your arm!"

Thus adjured, Robert proffered his arm and Miss Massey put her small hand upon it. Then slowly they walked behind the minister to the altar. Suzanna, Maizie, and Peter followed.

Graham offered his support to his grandmother. He had pledged his fealty to her and he felt grateful that she leaned upon him as slowly she mounted the four steps which led to the altar.

There they grouped themselves about the bridal pair. Graham stood close to his grandmother, Suzanna near to Miss Massey, Peter and Maizie at Robert's right hand.

The minister began: "Dearly beloved, we are gathered here together—" and on through the beautiful old ceremony.

He came at length to this question: "Who giveth this woman to this man?" and paused simply in custom. And old John Massey was far distant, nursing his anger and yet sad, too, because he would not in his temper attend the marriage of his daughter, though most lovingly and pleadingly had that daughter begged his presence. And the girl's mother was lying out on a hillside—where she had lain for many a long year.

And the waiting bride had tears in her heart, till, suddenly, Drusilla, with a beautiful light in her eyes, stepped forward. She put her white-veined old hand softly on the bride's arm, and she said in a low clear voice:

"I do—I give this woman to this man."

And the mother spirit in her spoke so richly that the bride all at once felt happy and a little awed, too, as though her own mother had for the moment raised herself and spoken.

And the minister went on with the ceremony till came the end: "And I pronounce that they are Man and Wife."

And Robert folded his wife in his arms and kissed her while each face, young and old, pictured the deep solemnity of the moment.

Robert's wife at last turned to Drusilla. She put her arms about the bravely upstanding figure in its old-fashioned dolman. "Oh, thank you, thank you," she murmured. "I shall never forget what you've done for me today."

The color flowed like a wave up over Drusilla's face. With a quick little breath, she leaned forward and kissed the new wife. She experienced a sudden glow. It was as though Life for the moment, forgetful that she was old and laid aside, had called her forward to fill a need no other was near to fill.

They all left the church after Robert had signed his name in a big book, and his wife had written hers with a proud little flourish. Robert helped Drusilla into the wheel chair, after lifting Daphne from her place on the upholstered cushion. This time the little girl awoke. She was about to cry when Robert raised her in his arms and carried her down the road, hushing her against him, while Graham again ordered himself his grandmother's squire.

And so they went down the road together, all somewhat quiet, even Peter's exuberant spirits moderated, till they reached Drusilla's home. The maid, Letty, awaiting her mistress' return, ran down the steps, an anxious frown between her eyes.

"Come," said Drusilla. "You must all be my guests." She whispered some words in Letty's ear. The girl smiled and half shyly glanced at Robert and his bride.

Robert still carrying little Daphne, who had refused to be put down, said at once: "We should like that very much. I was so hoping you would ask us."

So they entered the little house. They went into the parlor with its portrait above the mantel and the lilies of the valley beneath it. Graham remembered with a little warm feeling that his father had once left the order at a city florist's for a daily spray of those lovely bells.

Letty, carrying the dolman and small bonnet, disappeared but in a miraculously short time returned to announce that tea was ready in the dining-room.

Drusilla flushed and happy led the way. Robert and his wife followed, and the children came last. The hostess, from her place at the head of the table, designated each one's chair, and when all were seated she bowed her head and offered up a little prayer.

And then Letty brought in hot muffins and marmalade, sweet butter and fragrant tea. And amidst much laughter and merry words the feast began:

And at the end Drusilla rose, and asking silence, said:

"Robert, today in the name of the bride's mother, I gave her into your keeping. I can see a promise in your eyes that she will never, never regret going to you. Love her always."

And Robert, standing, in a deep voice answered: "Drusilla," borrowing quite unconsciously Suzanna's way of name, "Drusilla, I have taken upon myself this day the great responsibility of a woman's happiness—" he paused and bent a look of ineffable tenderness upon his wife—"and please God I shall keep that responsibility while life lasts."

And they all pushed back their chairs, the children with a little scraping noise. And Robert looking at his watch thought it was time to leave, since the train would not wait for laggards.

Then all in a moment it seemed he was going down the path again, his wife upon his arm. And Graham, who had disappeared kitchenward, returned and flung a handful of rice after them. At which the bride turned and laughed and waved her hand.

"It was a real wedding, wasn't it, Drusilla?" said Suzanna, "even to the rice."

"A real wedding, my little girl," said Drusilla.

Graham spoke: "Grandmother, aren't you glad I wheeled you out today?"

She answered at once. "So very glad, Graham. And I feel happier tonight than for many a long day."

"And may I do so again soon?" he asked. "And next summer I'll take you out every day."

A little smile touched her lips. "Next summer—next summer—? Ah, laddie, come often this winter, if you can."

And then the children started away. And at the last moment Drusilla drew Suzanna to her. "Little girl," she said lovingly, "I'm so glad you came once to visit me—that summer day."

"Oh, so am I, Drusilla," Suzanna cried. She looked wistfully into her friend's face. "Some day I want to do something wonderful for you."

Drusilla, bending low, kissed the upturned face with its big seeking eyes. But she did not speak. For why make definite by clumsy words the miracles a little child brings to pass. No, thought Drusilla in her wisdom, Suzanna should go her way beautifully unconscious of her good works.

CHAPTER XVIII

THE EAGLE MAN VISITS THE ATTIC

A few Saturdays after the marriage in the little wayside church, Richard Procter reached home in a state of great excitement.

The family was in the dining-room. Mrs. Procter was polishing the drinking glasses. Though it was long past noon, Suzanna had just commenced to clear away the luncheon dishes. Maizie was shaking napkins, while Peter was in a corner pretending to play ball with the baby, very much to the baby's amusement.

Mr. Procter told his news triumphantly.

"At last," he cried. "Jane, John Massey is absolutely coming to see the machine this afternoon."

The color flashed up into Mrs. Procter's face.

"Oh, Richard," she cried; "perhaps—" but she did not finish her conjecture.

"He won't take The Machine away, will he, father?" Suzanna asked anxiously.

"No, not that particular one, little girl. There'll have to be others built. That is just the model."

At two o'clock Mr. Procter was in the attic working at the

Emily Calvin Blake

machine. At three, so interested had he grown, that he had really forgotten the expected visit of old John Massey. So it was a real surprise when Mrs. Procter ushered him in.

"Well, I'm here at last," said Mr. Massey. He looked over to where the cabinet stood. "Your machine is rather mysterious looking."

"Does it seem so? Here, lay your hat and coat on this table, Mr. Massey. Now I'll explain the purpose of the machine."

"Yes, that's what I'm most interested in, what it's for; what you expect to do with it."

Richard Procter turned an eager face to the capitalist.

"I'll start at the beginning," he said. "Have you ever stopped to think what would mean the greatest happiness to humanity?"

Mr. Massey coughed and moved uneasily. "Can't say I have. Food and drink sufficient for all, so I've heard your orator across the street announce."

Mr. Procter smiled. "That, yes, might bring content, but I'm speaking of spiritual happiness. Well, this is my idea of what would bring about a revolution in the sum total of world content. *Each man at the work he was born to do.*

"And having once reached that conclusion, I set about formulating plans for the building of my machine. An instrument so delicate that it could register a man's leading talent."

Mr. Massey moved away a little. He stared doubtfully at the inventor before the clearing thought came. Before him stood a madman, a wild visionary.

He looked over at his hat and coat. To stay was a mere waste of time, he realized that now. Still, there was Suzanna who had made a place for herself in his gruff old heart. The machine, he knew, could have no commercial value. Yet he remembered a few of Suzanna's values which were not based on the possession of money.

Well, for Suzanna's sake he would listen, go away and forget. So he seated himself, and waited condescendingly for the inventor to continue. He himself said nothing, for silence, he had learned, was golden.

Mr. Procter went on. "My first step in the work was to evolve what might be termed a system of color interpretation."

"I don't understand at all," said old John Massey sharply.

The inventor hesitated. Visionary, he might truly be called, but, too, he was sensitive and he had felt the capitalist's withdrawal as soon as the purpose of the machine was explained to him. But the end was a big one. He must not hesitate, so he went on.

"May I put it broadly without arousing your derision, that color sight was bestowed upon me. Just as my little girl Suzanna visualizes each day as a shape, so I've always seen people in color; that out of that sight I built my own science of color."

"*Romance* of color, you mean," returned John Massey harshly, "for so far as I can gain, there is no science about it. I deal in facts, Mr. Procter, not in air castles. Does the machine do anything, but stand there a silent monument to your dreams?"

Mr. Procter hesitated but a moment, then, "Come, Mr. Massey," he said, "take your place. Let us see what the machine says of you. Remember, please, it will register only your truest meaning, the purpose for which you were born; the part of you which never dies, which is never really submerged, regardless of a turning to false gods."

A little uneasy despite himself, Mr. Massey seated himself before the machine.

The inventor touched levers, opened and shut doors, lowered the helmet, adjusted the lens.

As the clicking sound commenced Mr. Massey stirred. "Keep very quiet," said the inventor, "and watch the glass plate."

Mr. Massey obeyed. Now a satiric smile touched his lips. He was almost enjoying this child's play.

But soon the smile faded, for in a moment there grew upon the glass plate standing between the two tubes a pillar of color, vivid yellow, tipped with primrose.

"What—what does that mean?" asked old John Massey.

The inventor lifted the helmet, and shut off his power before speaking. "According to my belief, my understanding of color significance, the reason for your being in this world, with, of course, interesting variations brought about by environment and education, is identical with that of Reynolds."

Mr. Massey started forward angrily, but he thought better of whatever he had in his heart to say. "Go on," he commanded gruffly.

"As a young man you had dreams of being a practical humanitarian," said Mr. Procter softly, "and undoubtedly with your opportunity you might have been a valuable figure in the world. You were endowed with vision. You saw the wrongs man labors under; as a youth you smarted because of those wrongs. And you saw the super-being man might become given equal chances."

"Like Reynolds—" repeated Mr. Massey after a time, on impulse—one immediately regretted.

"Like Reynolds, our great rough, fine-hearted Reynolds," said Mr. Procter, "the one whom you've had threatened with arrest because he harangued too freely on the street corner." He paused to finish impressively: "I see now that the man who throws away his spiritual birthright for a mess of pottage hates the one who keeps his in the face of all—poverty— misunderstanding—ridicule."

A silence dark as a cavern ensued. Mr. Massey at last got to his feet. He stood a long moment looking at the machine, then he glanced at the inventor, but when someone knocked softly at the door he started, revealing how far away from his immediate surroundings his thoughts had flown.

Suzanna entered. "Here's David, daddy," she said. "He wants to talk with you."

David entered. "I had some time," he said, "and I wanted to see the machine again."

"Glad to see you," said the inventor heartily. "Mr. Massey, this is my friend, David Ridgewood, Graham Woods Bartlett's gardener."

"How do you do, Mr. Massey," said David. "I've seen you before, of course. Heard of you often."

John Massey did not answer at once, since he was somewhat at a loss. He had not been in the habit of meeting socially his friends' gardeners. At last he blurted forth.

"How d' do. I've had a look at Procter's invention."

"Ah, yes, I supposed so," said David. Then: "Isn't the thought back of that machine wonderful?" Which ridiculous question quickened again all the Eagle Man's combativeness. He spoke with a fine candor.

"The thought may be wonderful, young man. I'll not pass on

Emily Calvin Blake

that. But plainly I can't see where the commercial value of the machine comes in."

David and Suzanna fell back from the cloud which gathered on the inventor's face.

"The commercial value!" he cried. "Have I spent my life working merely that the capitalist may make more money? I tell you, sir, that I have worked only for the betterment of the race. And to you, John Massey, I am giving the great opportunity."

"Well, out with it. Where's the great opportunity?" asked Mr. Massey testily. "To my mind you haven't an article with a wide enough appeal."

"Wide enough appeal!" cried the inventor. "My dear sir, it has an appeal world-wide, and you are to make it of such appeal." He paused to continue impressively: "John Massey, I offer you the opportunity of endowing an institution which shall be built to use my machine. To that institution young men of impecunious parents may come to discover their leading talent."

"If there is a leading talent, will it take your machine to discover it?" asked John Massey.

"In most cases, yes. How many young men fail to discover until too late what life work they are best fitted for, unless they possess a talent so strong that it amounts to genius. How many of necessity are sent out into the world at an unformed age to slavery in order that they and their dependents may live. What chance or time have they, grinding away at any work which brings a dollar, to know for what work they are most suited. They know only when it is too late that they are bound by chains, crucifying themselves daily at tasks they hate, and for which they have no natural adaptation."

He paused, only to continue with fire: "Or, if they have

ambitions, know what they would best like to do, how helpless they are. No money, no opportunity."

"I'll warrant, Mr. Massey," put in David, "that there are many men employed in your steel mills who by natural inclination are totally unfitted for their jobs. Now, wouldn't scientific investigation in their early manhood have helped to find for them the right place and so added to their happiness?"

"Well, I'm not interested in that part of the question; their happiness has nothing to do with me," returned John Massey. "I pay 'em their wages and that's enough. And I don't believe that every man is born with a special talent. They all look alike to me mostly."

"Every man is born with the capacity to do something in a way impossible to another," said the inventor with conviction. "There are no two persons alike in the world."

John Massey smiled. He really now felt that he was being entertained. Such another rare specimen as this inventor with his ridiculous contentions would be hard to find. So he said pleasantly: "And after the machine has recorded its findings, what then?"

"Then you, and other men like you who have accumulated fortunes—"

"Stop!" cried the capitalist. "Let me finish for you. After the machine has done its work, I'm to have the privilege of paying for the professional education or trade of these same impecunious young men."

"Exactly, sir. The institution you endow might be called the Temple of Natural Ability Appraisement. There the poor in money, but the rich in ambition may come; there the fumblers, the indecisive, may come to be put to a test. Ah, yours can be a great work."

"A great opportunity for you, Mr. Massey," emphasized David, the gardener. "I envy you."

"You'd help out, wouldn't you, Eagle Man?" Suzanna now cried with perfect faith in his good will. "You see, you'd have to when you remembered that there's a little silver chain stretching from your wrist to everybody else's in the world. It must be rubber-plated, I guess."

"What do you mean?" asked the Eagle Man, involuntarily casting his glance down to his wrist, his flow of satire dammed.

"That's what Drusilla told me; we all belong. And you can't do something mean without breaking the chain that binds you to somebody else."

"Ah, my dear," said the Eagle Man, letting his hand fall upon her bright hair, "you belong to a family of impossible visionaries." He looked over at Suzanna's father, and his face suddenly grew crimson. "Were you in earnest, Procter," he cried, "when you told me in Doane's hardware store that your machine meant a big opportunity to me—were you jesting?"

"Jesting! Why, I've pointed out your opportunity, plainly."

"Shown me how I can throw a fortune away!"

After a moment Mr. Procter replied: "We speak in different languages. By opportunity you can see only a chance to make more money."

"Any other sane person makes the same guess," Mr. Massey replied.

The inventor's face grew sad. He had dreamed of John Massey's response, a dream built on sand, as perhaps he should have known. But hope eternal sprang in his heart, and the belief that every man wished the best for his brother.

The silence continued. To break it Mr. Massey turned to David.

"Your friend seems to think he has but to put before me the need for charity and I shall thank him effusively."

David spoke slowly: "My friend should have known better. He forgot, I suppose, your slums where you house your mill hands."

"What do you mean by that?" Mr. Massey began, when an exclamation from Suzanna, who was standing at the window, turned his attention there.

"See, there's a big fire over behind the big field," she cried excitedly. "Oh, look at the flames! The poor, poor people!"

David sprang to the window. "It's over in the huddled district," he cried. A fierce light sprang to his eyes. "Where most of your men live with their families, John Massey. I wonder how many will escape."

CHAPTER XIX

SUZANNA PUTS A REQUEST

In that devastating fire which swept out of existence the entire tenement district of Anchorville two were lost, never to be heard of again, parents of a twain of children, a boy of four and a girl of three.

Mrs. Procter, finding the mites wandering away from the smoking ruins, had at once taken them home with her, fed them, found clothes for them, and rocked the tired little girl to sleep.

"Are we going to keep them forever, mother?" Maizie asked one afternoon about two weeks after the fire. No one had put in a claim for the children; they were homeless, friendless. What was to be done with them? Mrs. Procter had turned with loathing from the thought of the orphanage.

She stood at Maizie's question in deep perplexity. She could not turn the children away or put them in an institution—and yet, how could she care for them? There was the very definite problem of extra clothes and food to be found out of an income already stretched to its utmost.

"They haven't a home any more, have they, mother?" Suzanna asked, the while her earnest eyes searched her mother's face. "So we should do unto others as we'd be done by, shouldn't we?"

A vague memory returned to Mrs. Procter. What was it Suzanna had once said? "Mrs. Procter cuddles all children in her heart." And Suzanna and Maizie stood watching her, asking a literal translation of a principle laid down for man's guidance.

"We'll see what can be done," Mrs. Procter answered finally. And then she continued very carefully: "You see, it isn't only a question of giving these little ones a home, but they must be clothed and fed and educated, and we haven't a great deal of money."

"So many of those poor people haven't any homes any more, have they?" asked Suzanna. Her eyes suddenly filled with tears of pity. She looked out of the window. The sun was shining brightly. And to be in keeping with the suffering about them, Suzanna wished it would hide behind a cloud. It seemed the day itself, to be in sympathy, should be dark, depressed, altogether gloomy.

Her mother answered: "It's providential in a manner that those unsightly cottages were swept away; but they meant homes for many poor souls; and all that they possessed was contained in those homes."

Suzanna's ingenious mind settled itself to work on the problem of the bereft ones. She was no longer thinking of the two little orphans, but of the many troubled people. If only her home were large enough to accommodate them all! Her thoughts in natural sequence ran to the Eagle Man and his beautiful place, but she immediately rejected the idea. She feared he might not listen kindly to the plan of lending his home even as a temporary abode for the stricken. Had he not been a little unkind about her father's wonderful Machine?

Suddenly she remembered Bartlett Villa, and with the memory came a thousand thoughts. Impulsively she donned hat and coat, spoke a word to her mother and was off.

In a very short time, for she ran nearly all the way, she reached Bartlett Villa. She pushed open the big iron gate leading into the grounds, and stopped short, for there to the left, near a closed fountain, stood Graham. He was talking to a tall man whose back was toward Suzanna. About the two, in seeming happiness, played Jerry.

Graham cried out when he saw Suzanna. She went quickly to him. Then the man looked down at her and smiled. Suzanna decided that she liked him, but she wished his smile was more of a real one, one that should light his face. She did not know the word, but he looked, despite his smile, cynical, rather weary. Yes, she knew she should like him, for in some indefinite way he reminded her of her father. Was it the brown, rather nearsighted eyes? Surely they were keen, yet behind their keenness dwelt a softness; perhaps he, too, once had cherished a vision.

Graham greeted her demonstratively. "And this is my father, Suzanna," he said. "I've told him a lot about you."

"Yes, I know a great deal about you, Suzanna," said Mr. Bartlett; "and David has told me of your father's invention and what he expects to do some day with it."

Suzanna's face kindled. "Yes, my father's a great man," she said, simply.

Then she turned to Graham: "I came to talk to you about something very important. I was going to ask you afterwards to speak to your father about my plan."

"I may hear, then?" said Mr. Bartlett. "Shall we go on into the house? There's a little chill in the air."

So they walked toward the great house, leaving Jerry rather disconsolate. Suzanna, looking up at Mr. Bartlett, said: "I've been here twice and I've never seen you."

"My business takes me often to different cities," he replied.

They entered the house and went into a small room at the left of the wide hall. It was lovely, Suzanna decided, done all in soft gray, except the curtains at the window, which were of amber silk, hanging in heavy folds. Yes, very charming, Suzanna emphasized to herself. She liked particularly the one picture on the wall, showing a group of horses, heads high in the air, full of fire. Suzanna could see them move, she believed.

"Sit down there, Suzanna, in that high-backed chair and tell us what you have to say that's so important," suggested Mr. Bartlett.

"I'm crazy to hear all about it, Suzanna," supplemented Graham. He settled himself in anticipation, for Suzanna was always intensely interesting.

Suzanna seated herself. A quaint little figure she was, her fine head thrown in relief against the gray satin of the chair. "You know," she began, "there's been a fire."

"A bully big one," said Graham.

Suzanna turned her dark eyes upon the boy. "It was a big one, and maybe fun to watch," she said, "but it burned all the people's homes. We've got two little children, at our house. We could never find their father and mother."

Mr. Bartlett, occupying the corner of a lounge, shifted uneasily. Evidently to put forth truths so baldly was inartistic.

"My mother says it was—I can't think of the word—but she meant it was lucky those cottages were burned down; they were so dirty." Suzanna went on: "And babies played in the yards in ashes and old papers. I always hurried past when I went that way because something stopped inside of me, I felt so sorry for those babies." Suzanna paused. "I just thought as we walked up your front path how different everything is here;

your front yard is so clean, and there's so much room!"

She stopped again. She wished Mr. Bartlett would speak. He must guess now all that she meant to convey to him; all she would ask of him.

But still he didn't answer. "The Eagle Man owned those houses," she said at last.

"The Eagle Man?" Mr. Bartlett roused himself at last. "Who is the Eagle Man?"

"Mr. Massey other people call him. The Eagle Man's my own private name for him."

Graham knew his father was heavily interested in the Massey Steel Mills. But he did not speak.

"You know, it's an awful fine feeling you get when you're doing something for strangers," Suzanna pressed on. "Some way you don't feel so excited when you're doing something for your very own family."

But she was doomed to disappointment. A continued silence still greeted her words. "When people work for you isn't it as though you were their father or their big brother and had to help them when they needed it?" she asked, at length.

"Well, it's a new thought that you owe anything to the men who work for you except their wages," said Mr. Bartlett at last.

"Why, Drusilla told me that everyone in the world has a little silver chain running from his wrist to his next friend's wrist; it stretches when you run—a fellowship link my father named it when I told him. And the chain runs from my wrist to your wrist and from yours to every other wrist in the world." She leaned closer, finishing earnestly. "And Drusilla says if you break your chain you're really a slave."

"Very interesting," commented Mr. Bartlett.

"Yes, isn't it?" agreed Suzanna. She returned tenaciously to her subject. "There are many homeless families who weren't welcome where they had to go after the fire. Mary Holmes says her mother took in four people and she says as long as they stay there'll have to be stews, for in that way a pound of meat goes further, and Mary just hates stews."

"Well, what is your suggestion of a remedy, Suzanna?" asked Mr. Bartlett. At which question, though put in words beyond her, Suzanna's eyes brightened. She caught the sense unerringly and answered promptly.

"Why, I thought *you* could do something. You have so much room." And then the solution came, out of the sky as often answers came when you didn't expect them. "Why, you could put tents up in your big yards for the homeless people, till their own homes are built again."

Mr. Bartlett was greatly amused. "You ask such a little thing, Suzanna."

"Yes, isn't it, seeing it'll help out so much?" Suzanna returned innocently.

Graham rose and went close to his father. "Father," he said, "who's going to build the new homes for the poor people?"

His father answered: "I don't know, I'm sure; but I should think it old John Massey's duty to do so."

"Father," asked Graham, after a pause given over to thought and drawing on his memory for what vague facts he knew of his father's business, "if you take less money for your interests in the mill and if you speak to him, do you suppose Mr. Massey would begin at once to build those homes?" His young face was quite white with earnestness and other new emotions struggling up to the surface.

Emily Calvin Blake

Mr. Bartlett looked from one small face to the other. He smiled grimly. They could see nothing but the humanness of a situation, the need existing. Going against all precedent meant nothing to them; they simply followed ridiculous altruistic impulses. Only in their minds was the knowledge that other people were suffering; and the immediate necessity for relief.

He let his hand fall upon his son's shoulder. "How about the trip abroad, Graham?" There was an under meaning in his question which Graham got at once. His face lit.

"I'd rather help out here, father, and give up the trip. I really would."

Mr. Bartlett remained quiet for a long time again. In some mysterious manner he was now for almost the first time looking upon his son as an individual, one with opinions and the power of criticism. And there grew in his heart the very fervent desire to stand well in that son's estimation. He looked at Suzanna and envied her father. How proudly, how simply she had said, "He is a great man!"

But when he spoke, he reverted to a name used a moment before by Suzanna, a name he knew well.

"Who's your very philosophic friend, Suzanna—Drusilla, you called her."

Suzanna's eyes shone. "Drusilla? She's my special friend. She lives in a little house on the forked road. She's pretty and sweet and she has fancies, like children. She plays sometimes she's a queen. But she's lonely. She gave Miss Massey to Robert in the little church. And she has no one in all the world left to call her by her first name. So I call her Drusilla and she loves it."

Graham did not stir. Neither did he look at his father till Suzanna, suddenly remembering, cried out:

"Why, Drusilla's Graham's grandmother!"

Mr. Bartlett's face suddenly went very white. He didn't speak for a long time. Then he rose and went to the window, drew back the silken curtain and stared out.

Suzanna wondered if he would ever move again! At the moment he was far away. He was a boy again at his mother's knee, listening to that fanciful conception of the little silver chain that stretched so far. There rushed in on him, too, other memories, blinding ones that hurt. True, every day at the little house a spray of lilies of the valley were delivered; but with that impersonal gift which cost him nothing but the drawing of a check he had dismissed his mother from his busy mind, letting her stay in loneliness, live in old dreams.

A soft little swish was heard at the door and Mrs. Bartlett entered the room. She stopped in some consternation at sight of the silent trio within.

"Why, what is the matter?" she asked, impulsively.

Mr. Bartlett turned from the window. He looked at his wife, steadily regarded her beautiful face and bronze-colored hair piled high upon her small and regal head. His gaze sought the soft, white hands, the tapered fingers with pink and shining nails.

At last he spoke, very quietly, but each word seemed weighed: "'And in the morning there shall tents suddenly arise.' A quotation from somewhere, my dear, but it shall come true here."

She turned a cold gaze upon him. "Will you explain what you mean?" she asked.

"There are a few homeless people in Anchorville; their homes laid waste by a fire," he said, pleasantly. "This small messenger has suggested that we make use of our ample grounds for a time by putting up tents, for a time, I say, till more substantial abiding places may be built."

She clenched her hands. "You can't do that, Graham," she began, a note of entreaty in her voice; "you can't possibly be so absurdly quixotic."

"And why not?"

"I can't understand!" she repeated. "Such philanthropic ideas have not occurred to you before."

He went to her, standing so he could look into her eyes. "It's late in the day, but I'll try to do some little thing my mother would like me to do."

Mrs. Bartlett was about to speak again in burning protest when her glance fell upon the children, Suzanna and her own boy. And the eloquent expressions upon those small faces kept her silent. At last she turned as though to leave the room. Over her shoulder she spoke.

"At least you will not insist upon my presence here while you fulfill your preposterous plans?"

He replied gently: "As always, I ask nothing that you cannot give in perfect freedom."

She hesitated, was about to say something, stopped and took another subject: "As for your mother—"

He interrupted her, but to repeat "As for my mother—" but he left his thought unfinished.

Then he, too, went toward the door, and as he passed Suzanna he let his fine, nervous hand touch her bright hair. Once he turned. "Suzanna, as I told you," he said, "David, my fine gardener, has interested me somewhat in your father's machine; perhaps I'll make a journey to your home some day to see it."

CHAPTER XX

DRUSILLA SETS OUT ON A JOURNEY

When Suzanna, returning home on wings, opened the front door, she heard voices in the kitchen. And there, as she entered, she saw Mrs. Reynolds engaged in reading aloud the directions on a paper pattern. Suzanna, full of her story, waited almost impatiently until Mrs. Reynolds had finished.

Then she burst forth: "Oh, mother, Graham Bartlett's father's going to make tent homes in his yard for the poor people."

Mrs. Procter, leaning over the kitchen table, selected a pin from an ornate pin cushion and inserted it carefully in the pattern under her hand before turning an incredulous eye upon her daughter.

"It's for his mother's sake," continued Suzanna, who had grasped the spiritual meaning of Mr. Bartlett's offer.

Mrs. Reynolds was the first to voice her surprise. "Why, that man, to my knowledge, has never taken any real interest in anything. Reynolds says he just draws big dividends out of the mill, runs about from one interest to another, and cares really naught for anyone."

"Oh, but he's very kind, Mrs. Reynolds," Suzanna objected. "As soon as he knew his yards were too big to waste and that his mother would love to have him do good, he told his wife he meant to put up tents till new homes were built."

Mrs. Procter cast a knowing look above Suzanna's head. Mrs. Reynolds caught it and sent back a tender smile. "Out of the mouths of babes," she began, when Maizie entered. In her tow were the two shy little orphans.

Maizie spoke at once to Mrs. Reynolds. "I knew you were still here, Mrs. Reynolds," she said; "I can always tell your funny laugh."

Mrs. Reynolds laughed again. "Well, little girl," she said, "did you want something from me?"

Maizie nodded vigorously. Her face was very stern. "Yes, please," she answered. "I want you to take these bad orphans home with you. They're cross and hateful and I don't want them to stay here any more."

The two orphans stood downcast, the small boy holding tight to his sister's hand, listening in silence to their arraignment. Mrs. Procter, shocked, interposed: "Why, Maizie, Maizie girl!"

But Maizie went on. "You can't be kind to them; they won't let you. And I had to slap the girl orphan."

The one alluded to thrust her small fist in her eye. Her slight body shook with sobs. Suzanna's heart was moved. She addressed her sister vigorously. "That isn't the way to treat people who are *weary* and *homeless*, Maizie Procter," she began. "*You* ought to be kindest in the whole world to sorry ones!"

Maizie paused. She understood perfectly her sister's reference. "When the Man with the halo picked you out of everybody and smiled on you, you ought to be good to all little children that He loves," pursued Suzanna.

"Not to little children who won't play and who won't be kind," said Maizie. But her voice was low. She turned half reluctantly to the orphans and looked steadily at them, as though trying to produce in herself a warmer glow for them.

They did not stir under the look. "But naughty children have to be made good even if you have to slap them, Suzanna," said Maizie pleadingly.

"But not by you, Maizie," said Suzanna; "you never can slap or be cross. I have a bad temper and sometimes get mad. But because of what you are *You* always have to be loving and kind."

Awe crept into Maizie's eyes. It was a great moment for her, little child that she was. She was to remember all her days that she was as one set apart to be loving and kind. She gazed solemnly back at Suzanna, as she dwelt upon the miraculous truth of her heritage.

At last Maizie turned. "Mrs. Reynolds," she said, "our Suzanna once adopted herself out to you, didn't she?"

Mrs. Reynolds bestowed a soft look upon Suzanna. "She did that, the lamb, and often enough I've thought of that day."

"You liked her for your little girl because you haven't any of your own?" pursued Maizie.

Mrs. Reynolds nodded, and Maizie sighed her relief.

"Well, then, we'll adopt these orphans out to you, Mrs. Reynolds. I'm sorry for them now, and I know I ought to be kind to them, but it will be easier for me if you have them. I think you'd be awfully happy with two real children of your very own."

No one spoke. The little boy, laggard usually in movement, looked up quickly at Mrs. Reynolds. He knew that Maizie found it difficult to be patient with him, and that therefore she was offering him and his sister to the kind-looking lady.

"We like them pretty well, but we'd rather you'd have them," Maizie went on generously but with unswerving purpose. "And till you get used to children I'll come over every day and wash and dress them."

Mrs. Reynolds' face was growing pinker and pinker. She continued gazing at the boy and the girl, and from them back to Suzanna, her favorite. But whatever emotions surged through her she found for the moment no words to express them. At last she spoke in a whimsical way.

"It's not much you're asking, little girl, to take and raise and educate two growing children on Reynolds' wages." And then she blushed furiously and glanced half apologetically at Mrs. Procter. For what, indeed, was Mrs. Procter's work? With superb defiance toward mathematical rules, she was daily engaged in proving that though those rules contended that two and two make four, if you have backbone and ingenuity two and two make five, and could by stretching be compelled to make six.

"I must be going," said Mrs. Reynolds. She gathered up carefully the paper pattern, folded its long length into several pieces, opened her hand bag and thrust the small package within. "Thank you for your help, Mrs. Procter. I think I can manage nicely now," she said, as she snapped the bag together.

Mrs. Procter repeated the conversation to her husband that evening, as, the children in bed, they sat together in the little parlor. "And it might be the most wonderful happening in the world, both for the poor children and for Mrs. Reynolds," said Mrs. Procter.

Mr. Procter did not answer. His wife, watching him keenly, realized that he was troubled. She put down her sewing. "Tell me, Richard, what's gone wrong," she said.

He hesitated, caught her hand, held it tight. "I might as well tell you, dear. John Massey has bought out Job Doane's hardware shop."

"Bought him out?"

"Yes. No one seems to know why. He paid a good price and he'll probably sell again. I don't know, I'm sure."

He pressed his hand wearily to his head. "What's to be done, dear? What's to be done? There's no other opening for me in Anchorville."

She rallied to help him as always. "At least we'll not meet trouble till it's full upon us. There's always some way found."

And, as always, he brightened beneath her touch, let hope spring again within his heart. "Shall you work upstairs tonight?" she asked, knowing that companionship with his beloved machine closed his mind to other matters.

"If you will come upstairs with me," he said. "Can you leave your mending? I want you close by."

She felt strongly and joyously his need of her. "I will come," she said.

They were on the way upstairs, treading carefully that the lightest sleeper, Suzanna, might not be awakened, when the hurried peal came at the front door. They stopped. "Go on to the attic," said Mrs. Procter; "it's perhaps Mrs. Reynolds come to borrow something," so Mr. Procter went on. Mrs. Procter ran lightly down.

She opened the front door to David. Near him stood Graham and behind, his tail wagging furiously, Peter's dog, Jerry. David began at once.

"Mr. Bartlett's mother was taken ill suddenly. Mr. Bartlett is with her. She is begging to see the little Suzanna."

"Come in," said Mrs. Procter, flinging the door wide. And as they entered and stood all three in the hall, the dog feeling himself now in his new character as welcome as his human companions, she finished: "Suzanna's asleep."

"My father wished greatly you would allow Suzanna to go to my grandmother, though it is late," put in Graham.

"Could she be awakened?" asked David. And by the expression in his eyes Mrs. Procter understood that this wish of Drusilla's should not be denied.

The dog, feeling entreaty in the air, sat down and raised his voice. It was a penetrative voice, too, filling the house with its echoes, echoes that scarcely died away before a soft call came:

"Mother—mother—"

Mrs. Procter smiled at David. "There, Suzanna is awake. Jerry accomplished what he wished. I'll go upstairs and dress her quickly."

So it was that the little girl flushed, starry-eyed, appeared with her mother a little later. Her dramatic senses were alert. "Isn't it lovely and important," she began at once to David, "that Drusilla wants to see me when it's away into the night?"

"Very important," said David, but he did not smile. "Are you quite ready now?"

"Yes," said Suzanna and slipped her hand within Graham's. "Are you going too, Graham?"

"Yes. David's driving the light cart."

The night was cool, but there were big rugs in the cart. David bundled Suzanna up till only her vivid face looked out. As they went swiftly she gazed up at the stars and the soft dark sky. She loved the night fragrances, and the rustle of the dead leaves as lazy little winds stirred them.

They came very soon to Drusilla's home. David alighted, unwound Suzanna, lifted her down to the ground very carefully, Graham following slowly. David tied his horse, gave the animal a comradely pat, bade the dog remain in the cart, and then the three went on to the house. The door opened immediately for them, a light streaming out from within. The sweet-faced maid, Letty, who had been crying, ushered them in.

"I'll wait downstairs," said David.

Letty nodded, and with the children went upstairs.

They stopped when they reached the open doorway of Drusilla's bedroom. And seated in a big velvet chair, as usual drawn near the window, though the shade was pulled straight down, pillows heaped all about her, sat Drusilla. Her face seemed small, oh, pitiably small, with bright eyes quite too large for their place. But someway Suzanna, looking in, knew that Drusilla was happy.

Perhaps because, kneeling beside her, his head buried in her lap, was her son.

Her thin fingers strayed through his hair, and her tremulous voice murmured to him just as it had when as a very small, very penitent boy he had knelt in the same way, sure of her understanding, very, very sure of her love.

The picture remained for the moment, then the man kneeling, stirred and rose to his feet. He stood looking down at his mother, till impelled by a sound in the doorway he turned and saw the children.

They came forward then into the softly lighted room.

"Drusilla!" Suzanna cried, going straight to the frail figure seated in the velvet chair. "You wanted to see me, didn't you?"

"I did that, little girl," Drusilla answered. "I wanted to tell you that the land of sunshine and love is close at hand where I shall meet my king and be parted no more."

"And where you'll reign queen?" cried Suzanna, delighted.

The old head flung itself up; the faded eyes blazed; the frail figure straightened itself. "Ay, queen!" She turned to Graham, who had approached and stood regarding her, his boyish face agleam with love and a little longing, and a little sadness, for he knew better than Suzanna the great change at hand. "Who stands there?" she asked.

He answered at once: "A courtier, my Queen."

She smiled. "Approach closer then," she said with a wave of her hand. But her eyes were on Suzanna. "My favorite princess," she said softly, letting her hand fall upon the small head. "She came first one day when the flowers were all in color. She listened to me, and believed my stories of the land where I once dwelt—with my king and my young prince, who afterwards forgot me."

A sob came from the throat of the man standing near. He buried his face in his hands. A white-clad nurse came tiptoeing in, looked at her patient, nodded reassuringly and went out again.

"I knew you were a queen, Drusilla," said Suzanna, "because you were so beautiful, and so haughty." She leaned forward till her young face was very close to the old fading one. "And you told me something that day about the chain that binds everybody in the world to everyone else. I've never forgotten that. I've told lots of people about it."

"Yes, yes, I remember."

"And I told that story to the Eagle Man, and to Graham's father, and he's going to have tents put up in his yard for some poor people who have no homes, for your sake, Drusilla."

The frail figure suddenly fell back. "*Drusilla!* Who calls me that?" The pale lips trembled. "Many, many years have gone since I heard that name."

The man cried out: "Mother dear—*Mother dear!*"

She turned her eyes upon him. The light of recognition slowly returned to them. "My boy," she said gently. "Come, sit beside me. All three. The little girl who loves me, and you and your child, my grandson."

So they settled themselves, all at her knee. "Mother, dear, did you hear what Suzanna said? Your story of the chain awakened me."

"Awakened you, my boy? But that story and others I told you many years ago, and you forgot."

The tears, hard-wrung, started to his eyes. "But, mother," he said in a low voice, "is it too late? Those truths I learned many years ago from you—is it too late to use them now?" He let his head fall suddenly upon her knee: "Oh, mother, mother, how blind are men; what false gods they worship!"

She did not answer. Graham, a great pity sprung in his heart for his father, spoke: "Father's good, grandmother! He does lots of kind things for people. And he's going to take care of many families whose homes were burned."

"In your name, mother, as Suzanna says," said the man, lifting his head. "And many, many other righteous things in your name, my mother."

Her face grew luminous, with a light lent from some far place. "My boy—my little son—" she whispered.

The white-clad nurse came in again, looked sharply at her patient. "I think," she said softly, "you must all leave now."

So they rose. But Suzanna, after saying farewell, turned again. The nurse was arranging the bed. Drusilla sat, her eyes looking off into the distance. Suzanna went swiftly back.

"Is the land you're going to very beautiful, Drusilla?" she whispered.

"Fairer than you may dream, little girl," Drusilla returned. And then: "Kiss me, Suzanna, and call me Drusilla once more."

Suzanna kissed the soft, wrinkled cheek. "Good-bye, Drusilla," she breathed. "I love you with all my heart, and I'm coming to see you again very soon."

CHAPTER XXI

MR. BARTLETT SEES THE MACHINE

But Suzanna did not go to see her friend Drusilla again. For within a few days after the hurried night visit, Drusilla set off on her journey. There was but one with her when she left, all aquiver to be gone, her eyes set in the distance on visions hid from earthly eyes.

Her boy was close beside her, his arms about her, his heart filled with woe for all the years he had forgotten. And when he kissed her and begged her forgiveness, she was all love and understanding for him, even as when a small boy he had sought her forgiveness and her understanding.

The tents were up now in the big Bartlett grounds. Tents with floors and movable stoves. Children played about the grounds on the rare sunny day that Drusilla went away.

Mr. Bartlett, returning from his mother's bedside, went hurriedly through his grounds, and on upstairs to his own room. There, waiting for him, was Graham. The boy knew at once the truth.

"Father," he cried, and put his arms about the tall figure.

They stood so, the man finding comfort in the contact of his boy. And so Mrs. Bartlett, returned temporarily from a journey, found them.

Emily Calvin Blake

She started back at sight of them thus together. They seemed in their new intimacy to have shut her out, quite out of their lives. "I've been looking for you, Graham," she began, and then caught her breath sharply at the look the boy gave her; not a premeditated cold look, only one that he might bestow upon a stranger.

"Father has just come home," he said; "grandmother—"

But he did not finish. He saw that his mother understood that Drusilla had gone away. Mr. Bartlett spoke to his wife. "I heard this morning that you had returned to stay for a day. I'm afraid the tents and the children will still disfigure our grounds for some time."

His bitterness made her wince. But she answered calmly. "Yes, I returned while you were absent."

"For a day, as I was told?"

"My plans must change now of necessity—my trip to Italy—"

"Why?" he asked. "Nothing that has happened need interfere with any of your plans, your mode of living. My mother would not wish that."

She broke forth then, the color surging up into her face. "Why are you so unjust to me? Did I suggest that you neglect your mother? You could not expect me to take your place."

"No—" he spoke sadly. "No, I could not expect that. Believe me, please, when I say that I put blame on no one but myself. Money—that has been the main thing in life. Money, and more money. There was always need for all I could make." His eyes swept her lovely gown; the costly cape across her arm. Thought, much money, much time had gone into building her perfect completeness. "No. A man cannot expect another, even a wife, to fulfill his sacred obligations."

Perhaps the thought came to her that a wife need not ask so much, ask so demandingly that a man must yield his finest dreams, his every hour to fulfill her wishes. The color deepened and deepened in her cheek. Perhaps she remembered their first months together when in the grayest days he saw color, because they belonged one to the other.

They had both forgotten Graham. She looked at the boy now. He stood regarding her with that strange aloofness in his eyes, that sharp question. She felt all at once very lonely.

For Graham, she knew, was estranged from her! And now she knew that she desired most of all his love in all its purity. Her social strivings, her desire for leadership balanced against Graham's former worshipful, chivalrous love for her, dwindled to a pitiful insignificance.

And with the value of her child's love, she suddenly realized the older mother's longings—the one who had just gone on. An old mother—in her full years mourning for the child she had borne, nursed, and succored. Grieving, that in his manhood he had gone from her; that he had seemingly forgotten in his feverish striving after wealth the lessons she had sought to teach him.

Was the wife to blame for this? But some stern sense of justice derided her efforts to exculpate herself. She remembered how she had held the power to influence him in the early days of their marriage; he had believed so wonderfully in the whiteness of her ideals. He was malleable material in her fingers.

But above and beyond his love she had put wealth and fine position. He had given her both, but now before her stood her husband and son estranged from her.

She moved away at last. With new awakening power of perception, she felt she was stripped of everything of worth. When she was half-way down the wide hall she heard a step behind her. She paused, waited, and in a moment Graham was beside her.

He put his hand in hers. "Mother," he said, quietly.

Her eyes filled with the near tears. She clung to his hand as though he would protect her against her own bitter thoughts.

"Does your head ache?" he asked. There was solicitude in his voice, but still that strange, dreadful aloofness, more dreadful because he was not conscious of it.

"No," she answered. She looked down at him and out of an impulse she cried: "Do you still love me, Graham?"

"I love you, mother," he answered gravely. But she knew then that there would be work on her part before once again she stood to him his ideal.

She had dwelt in the core of his heart; perhaps in time she could once more move near to that sanctified place. The intimate human relation, husband and wife, parent and child—she knew with pain and yearning that all else— position, great wealth, worldly power—were vain beside the joy of those relations in their purest.

*   *   *   *   *

Perhaps a week later Suzanna was washing the supper dishes, and Maizie wiping them. Their mother was upstairs with Peter and the baby, Mr. Procter in the attic. As Maizie finished the last dish, the door bell rang.

Suzanna ran to the foot of the stairs.

"Oh, mother, shall I answer?" she cried.

"I wish you would," Mrs. Procter called down. "Peter has a stone bruise and I'm using liniment."

So Suzanna went to the front door. She opened it to Mr. Bartlett.

"Good evening, Suzanna," he said in a friendly voice. "Is your father at home?"

"He's upstairs in the attic. Shall I take you to him?" asked Suzanna very politely.

"Perhaps you'd better consult him first as to that, Suzanna. He may not wish to be disturbed."

"Well, I will. Won't you sit down in the parlor?"

Mr. Bartlett, half smiling, followed the small figure into the room designated. He looked about interestedly after Suzanna had gone. A kerosene lamp set upon a center table sent an apologetic light over the shabby furniture. Above the mantel with its velvet cover and statuette of a crying baby, was a picture of Suzanna, a "crayon," Mr. Bartlett amusingly surmised. The small face looked out with a distorted artificial smile quite unknown to the face it sought to represent. Yet Suzanna's aura was visible, Mr. Bartlett thought. That little girl who so simply and lovingly had called his mother Drusilla because no one in the world was left to do so! A fragrance straight from his heart made the ugly crayon suddenly a thing of beauty, showing forth a child's soul.

Suzanna returned, panting a little. She had run upstairs and down again. "Father wants you to go right up," she said. "And maybe when I've finished the dishes I'll come back, too."

So he followed her up the narrow stairs. Suzanna gravely told him that every other step creaked, except if you put your foot carefully in the middle. At the attic door she left him.

Mr. Procter looked up as his visitor entered. "I'm glad to see you, Mr. Bartlett," he said cordially. "It's not very light in here, but we can see to talk. Sit down."

Mr. Bartlett took the proffered chair. He looked about the dim room and could see in outline the machine.

"David has told you something of my invention, I remember and its object," said Mr. Procter.

"Yes, David has told me," Mr. Bartlett replied. "You're attempting a tremendously big thing, Mr. Procter. David told me about the colors and your theory of their meaning."

"Yes. Did David tell you, too, that my daughter Suzanna produced on the plate of the machine purple and gold? In my book I had written down . . . 'Purple: high talent for writing.'"

Mr. Bartlett hesitated a moment before replying.

"But it hasn't been proven that Suzanna can write. You will have to wait a few years for evidence."

"True, still she is talented. I may dare say that even though I happen to be her father. She possesses an insatiable curiosity concerning life, the divine birthright of the artist, the creator."

"Still I'm not convinced that such a machine as David drew for me is possible," said Mr. Bartlett. "I can understand that if you place a person in contact with an instrument and proceed to change his circulation by arousing his emotions that chemical change might be registered upon a sensitive plate. But how can a mere machine be so miraculous as to show forth by color or any other method one's 'meaning'? It's too big for my imagination, that's all. There are so many parts that go to make up a human being, so many points in his favor for a certain line of work, so many against it."

Still the inventor did not speak. And so Mr. Bartlett continued: "There's a man's state of health, his sympathies, his hereditary tendencies; all to be considered."

"Well, you see," Mr. Procter answered at last, "the elements you enumerate are but results of evolution, of environment, of education, and do not alter the purpose for which the man was born. And that purpose, even though given no chance to work itself out, is so vital a part of the man that it remains an undying flame going on into eternity."

Mr. Bartlett did not answer.

"Will you let me make a color test of you, Mr. Bartlett?" the inventor asked at length.

"Yes, though I am very skeptical."

He seated himself before the machine. Mr. Procter let the helmet down till it was just above the subject's head. "You see no part of the instrument touches you," he said. "There's no opportunity to say that chemical changes in the circulation are the cause of the color produced. Now please watch the glass plate." Mr. Bartlett did as directed. For some moments the plate remained clear, then rays of color played upon it.

"Green, a rare, soft green," said Mr. Procter. He went on slowly but without hesitation. "The color of poetry. That color belongs in one who lies on the grass and gazes at the sky—and dreams; dreams to waken men's souls with the beauty of his music—a poet, a maker of songs, to uplift, to keep man's eyes from the ground."

The light faded, the little clicking sound ceased, and yet Mr. Bartlett did not speak. If in his mind there dwelt the memory of an overstuffed drawer with reams of paper covered with verses, he said nothing. His face gave no evidence to the inventor of his thoughts.

At last he roused himself, shrugged his shoulders. "My dear man," he said, "did you ever hear of a poet at heart making a fortune as I have done?"

"It could be done," returned Mr. Procter sadly, "even by

Emily Calvin Blake

a poet."

Mr. Bartlett rose. "I did not aver," continued Mr. Procter, "that you could only be a poet. I said that your real meaning was to give to the world the rare visions which grew in your heart."

Mr. Bartlett gazed with some astonishment at the machine.

"The day when Suzanna was born, as I stood looking down at her, the thought came winging to me that she had come charged with a purpose which she alone could fulfill. And so was planted the first seed in my mind for the making of my machine."

Mr. Bartlett spoke again after a silence given to some pondering.

"Still, Procter, have you thought how impractical the machine must prove to be? The world is after all as it is. Suppose a man, a poor young man, has a rare gift. He must eat to live; he may have to support others. How is he going to develop that gift?"

The inventor's face was suddenly filled with a fine light. He laid his hand on Mr. Bartlett's arm. "There, sir, as I told John Massey, is where the capitalist seeking to invest his money in the highest way finds his great chance. He helps that young man to live in comfort while he is developing his talent."

"Well," said Mr. Bartlett, "it's all very interesting, and if you will let me, I'll do all I can to help you. We can talk of that at some other time." He paused, and then said: "I hear John Massey has bought out the hardware store here. I can't understand his object, but you may lose your position. Have you thought of what you could do in that event?"

"No, I haven't."

"I came primarily to see your machine, " Mr. Bartlett

continued, "but I had another object too. You know I have had tents put up in my yard for those who were made homeless by the fire. And now I find it necessary to go away in order to attend to some large interests. Can I make you my steward over these people—at a salary, while I am away?

"There will be enough for you to do," continued Mr. Bartlett. "My wife is away; my boy Graham will soon be in the city with his tutor. I shall be back here before the severe weather sets in and see that these people in some way are comfortably housed and provided for; but in the meantime I want you."

"I'll be glad to do all I can," said Mr. Procter at last; then fervently, "and thank you."

Someone knocked softly, and Suzanna entered. "This special letter came for you, daddy," she said. "Mother said I might bring it up to you."

Mr. Procter took the letter, looked curiously at it before tearing it open. He glanced through its contents, held it a second while he looked away then he went through it again. It ran:

Dear Procter:

You've known for some time that Job Doane is running the hardware shop in my interest. I bought   the place for a future purpose, never mind that purpose, it isn't of interest to you or anyone in Anchorville. I am confined to my room with an attack of rheumatism, so I can't see you to talk over a scheme which I have in mind. I will say that I have concluded all arrangements to rebuild homes for the men and their families who were burned out some time ago, and I want you to act as my agent. No sentiment in building these up-to-date houses, let me assure you. Only perhaps I've given some thought to Suzanna's little wrist chain. Come to me within a day or two and we'll talk over salary, and other things of interest to you.

Yours,
John Massey.

Suzanna plunged into the ensuing quiet. "Is there any answer, daddy?" she asked.

Mr. Procter looked at his small daughter through a mist, then at Mr. Bartlett still standing regarding him somewhat curiously. "No, no answer," he said at last, "but I want to see your mother—right away."

BOOK III

CHAPTER XXII

HAPPY DAYS

Summer once again, with the flowers abloom and all the richness of the season scattered lavishly about. The Procter house seemed more colorful too, perhaps because it had acquired within some late months a new coat of paint.

Once inside if you were familiar enough to go upstairs, you could not find the steps which had been wont to creak. And peeping into the parlor you could see that some pretty new furniture had taken the place of the shaky old lounge and chairs; one good marine picture hung between the windows and a new rug lay upon the hardwood floor.

Two years had gone since the fire, two years bringing some changes. Suzanna had shot up. She was a tall, slim girl now, though with the same dark, questioning eyes. She stood one Saturday morning in the kitchen making a cake, yes, actually stirring the mixture all by herself in the brown earthen vessel.

Her mother, hovering near, was offering comment and a few directions. Between times she attended to the "baby," a baby no longer since he was nearly four years old. Maizie, coming in from the yard with Peter behind her, stopped short at sight of Suzanna's work.

Emily Calvin Blake

"When can I make a cake, mother?" she asked. Her small face was as plump, as childlike as ever. The same sweetness of expression was hers, the same admiration in her eyes for her "big" sister.

"When you're as old as Suzanna, I guess, Maizie," Mrs. Procter answered. "What did Mrs. Reynolds say?"

Peter answered before Maizie could speak, thereby gaining a reproving look from her. "She's coming over to see you, mother. She says she wants to ask you something, anyway." Peter went to the door, gave a sharp whistle, a sharper direction and returned. "Jerry's out there. Graham Bartlett's opened up his house, and David's brought my dog back."

Still Peter's dog, you see. "Oh, I want to see Jerry, may he come in, mother?" Suzanna asked.

Mrs. Procter nodded. She was now engaged in giving the four-year-old his ten o'clock luncheon of bread and milk. "But don't let him get into anything, Peter," she admonished.

Peter promised, with a sigh in his heart for the tenacious prejudices of woman. Jerry at a word entered the kitchen door. He came in slowly, paused and regarded Mrs. Procter searchingly. He was a handsome animal now. His coat was well brushed, his hair long and glossy.

"Well," said Mrs. Procter, "you've been taught good manners, Jerry."

He wagged his tail vigorously; then further to show himself off, he sat down and held out a beguiling paw to Mrs. Procter. Maizie cried out in delight.

"Oh, can't we keep him now, mother? Isn't he cunning?"

Peter turned quickly upon his sister. "Would that be fair?" he sternly asked. His voice deepened suddenly. "You wouldn't, any one of you, even look at him when he was poor and dirty and *afraid*. And now after David has loved him and washed him and taught him how to behave, you want to keep him. Come along, Jerry."

Having thus delivered himself, Peter, with dignity, stalked from out the kitchen. He left an eloquent silence behind him. "Should we have kept the dog when he was dirty and lonely, mother?" asked Maizie, interestedly.

"Why, I don't think so, Maizie," Mrs. Procter answered slowly. "Really, you remember I'd had so much trouble that summer with stray dogs of Peter's that my patience was at an end."

Maizie was forming another question when she was interrupted by a hearty knock at the door.

"Come in," Suzanna cried. She was testing the oven as her mother had taught her and she turned a very important, if badly flushed, face to the visitor.

"I'm baking a chocolate cake, Mrs. Reynolds," she announced.

"Fine, Suzanna," cried Mrs. Reynolds heartily. She advanced to the middle of the kitchen. Two beautiful children both with large dark eyes and dark curls, exquisitely clean, followed her.

Mrs. Reynolds was a little plumper, and with a softness in her eyes which seemed of recent growth. She lifted the smaller child, the girl, upon a kitchen chair, watched the boy in his pilgrimage after the darting cat, and began:

"I'm glad to help with the christening robe for the Massey grandson, Mrs. Procter," she said; "and I think 'tis a fine idea—sort of community dress made by those who liked Miss Massey."

"I thought you'd like the idea, Mrs. Reynolds," said Mrs.

Procter. "Here, take this chair."

Mrs. Reynolds sat down. "The fine boy you have there," she said, indicating the "baby," "he's a bit like Suzanna."

"We all think he's very much like his eldest sister," said Mrs. Procter. She raised the small boy and held him close for a moment. When she put him down, he wandered off toward the popular cat.

"I wanted to ask you, Mrs. Procter," said Mrs. Reynolds, "what material you think will make up best for a Sunday dress for Margaret here." She paused, smiled, and flashing a mischievous glance at Suzanna, finished, "It'll have to have lace, says Margaret, and I suppose she'll want the goods cut away from underneath."

Suzanna, perched near the oven door watching the precious cake, turned to look at Mrs. Reynolds. A flame lit within her eyes; she had never forgotten the anguish engendered by her mother's refusal to cut away the goods from under the pink dress; then the expression softened. Was it not on that occasion, too, she had learned the dearness of that same mother?

"There, now," said Mrs. Reynolds, "I shouldn't have teased you, Suzanna." Her eyes grew tender. "I'd never have thought seriously of adopting my little children here, dear lamb, if you hadn't first adopted yourself out to me."

Suzanna's face grew luminous. "Oh, do you mean that, Mrs. Reynolds?" she cried.

"I do just that, every word, Dear Heart. Why, the night I put you to bed and you called me 'mother' I shall never forget, never. And then the truths you spoke to Reynolds!"

"He's happy now, isn't he?" asked Mrs. Procter.

Mrs. Reynolds paused impressively before answering: "Do you know," she said at length, "he forgets often to remember that the children are not his very own. The little Margaret there creeps into his lap nights, calls him daddy, and melts the heart of him. And the boy with his quaintness, follows him about the house on Saturdays, and Reynolds says often enough: 'He'll be a great man, this chap, Peggy. He says some of the things I thought when I was his age.' He's taken to calling me Peggy since the children came to make a distinction, the little girl bearing my name, you see."

Mrs. Procter nodded. Margaret stirred uneasily on her chair. "Mother," she asked, "I want to hold the Pussy, too. I'll keep my apron clean."

"And that you shall, my Sweet," said Mrs. Reynolds, her face flushing at the title as though it would never grow old to her; "come then, go to the cat, my pretty lass."

Suzanna removed her cake from the oven. It was a beautiful object, and Suzanna regarded it with pride. She took off her apron, looked around the kitchen and then turning to her mother, put her request.

"Mother," she said, "I'd like to go to the big house and see the Eagle Man and Miss Massey."

"Saturday morning?" asked Mrs. Procter, dubiously. "Well, I suppose that it won't really matter."

"I'm going to see Daphne," Maizie announced.

"Remember to be at home by noon," said Mrs. Procter. "Father may be here for luncheon."

"I'll remember, mother," said Suzanna. She kissed her mother, said good-bye to Mrs. Reynolds and started happily away. She reached the house at the top of the hill in a short time. The same uniformed man as of old gave her immediate admittance.

"Mr. Massey is in the library," he said, evincing no surprise at Suzanna's unconventional appearance.

In the doorway of the library Suzanna hesitated a moment, for the sound of voices came to her. Then she went forward, and there, standing near the white marble mantelpiece was the Eagle Man, near him Suzanna's father.

"Daddy," Suzanna cried, and ran to him.

Mr. Procter turned. His face, slightly older than when he was an employee of Job Doane of the hardware shop, was still that of the idealist, the lover of men. Yet there was a something added. Perhaps his well-fitting clothes gave him the new air of efficiency, of directness.

"I didn't know you'd be here with the Eagle Man, daddy," Suzanna cried.

Her father smiled at her. The Eagle Man spoke. "Your father is my right-hand man, remember, little girl," he answered. He brought out the sentence clearly with no strain of embarrassment.

"Right-hand man," Suzanna repeated thoughtfully. "I don't quite know what that means."

"Well, it means that your father looks after my interests in a very capable way," old John Massey returned. "Don't you remember how the new homes went up under his direction for my employees?"

"Yes, I remember," said Suzanna, "those beautiful new, brick houses, and the clean yards for the babies to play in."

"And now your father is in my mill as my superintendent, looking after the men." He paused. "How would you describe your way with them, Mr. Procter?"

"Looking after them humanly, perhaps," put in Mr. Procter simply.

"All right, we'll let it go just that way. In any event if you're making them happier by shifting them about a bit, trying to fit them by natural adaptability to their jobs and so increasing efficiency, I am satisfied with any way you put it."

Mr. Procter stood a little ill at ease. It was so very rare for old John Massey to so graciously express himself, almost unheard of.

"You see," said the Eagle Man, softly, "I'm using Suzanna as a mask; I'm telling her what I couldn't say to your face, Richard Procter." He stretched out his hand and Richard Procter let his own fall into it. The two men stood thus bound in a spirit of perfect friendship.

Suzanna went on upstairs. She found "Miss Massey" in a large room with pink curtains at the windows, pink rugs on the floor and even pink chairs and sofas. Like a sea shell, Suzanna thought. The baby lay in a beautiful rose-tinted crib drawn near the window, and above the crib the new mother bent.

She turned when Suzanna knocked softly.

"Oh, Suzanna," she cried at once, a glad note in her voice. She ran across the room and enfolded the little visitor close within her arms.

"And you've come back with a baby," Suzanna cried, after a time.

"Yes, come and see him. He's named after my father."

Suzanna went to the cradle and looked down. "He's a nice fat baby," she admitted. She really didn't think that he was pretty, but that she did not say.

"And don't you love Saturday nights when it rains and you're safe indoors with Robert and the baby?" asked Suzanna, interestedly.

"Oh, dear girl, I do, I do. What a picture you painted, and how I've tried to make it true."

"And have you a cross man with buttons to jump at your bidding?" Suzanna pursued.

"No, dear; we have a little home with a garden, where in the summer all the old-fashioned flowers bloom. I do most of my own work, and care altogether for my baby. And I'm happier than ever before in my life. And my father is no longer angry with me. He wrote asking me to pay him a visit after he knew he had a grandson named for him."

She bent above her baby for a moment, then turned her shining face to Suzanna. "And now, tell me about yourself, Suzanna, and your loved ones."

Suzanna paused to think. "Well, you know father doesn't weigh out nails any more; he's the Eagle Man's right-hand man." She remembered the phrase and brought it out roundly. "And father helped build all those nice new homes for the people who work in the Massey Steel Mills.

"My father's a great man," finished Suzanna, simply as always when stating this incontrovertible fact. "And his Machine's nearly ready now for the world to know about it."

"Oh, oh, Suzanna! And then?"

"And then many, many people are going to be happy ever after because my father thought of that machine and worked on it for years and years."

After a moment Suzanna continued: "And my dear, dear Drusilla set off on a far journey and didn't come back. And

Graham cried, and went away for a long time, and Bartlett Villa was closed. But they've come back now and it's open again. And David and Daphne are quite well, thank you. And Mrs. Reynolds has two little children of her own."

"I'm so glad," said Robert's wife. "You're a very happy little girl, then, aren't you, dear?"

"Oh, very happy," said Suzanna. "I love so many people, you see. And I have a sister, Maizie, who was once smiled upon by a very great Man." Her listener was puzzled, but she asked no questions. It didn't seem to her the right moment to ask an explanation. Some day she would. But Suzanna told the story of Maizie's rare selection, dwelling upon it with a degree of wondrous awe, for she believed the story now. It stood so clear to her, so real, that it had a fine influence upon her inner life. Often when swift anger surged through her, anger directed against the little sister, she brought to bear a strong control, as she remembered Maizie's great awakening.

She returned to her surroundings in a moment. "I must be going, Miss Massey. I wish you'd come to see us. We've got a lovely new rug in the front room and mother has two new dresses for herself. She is awfully pretty in them."

"I certainly shall come to visit you," Miss Massey promised, kissing the little girl.

Suzanna ran downstairs. She did not stop at the library, fearing she would reach home late for luncheon.

But she was just in time to set the table. Her father had not yet arrived. Mother, of course, was there and with an eager face full of news, delightful news, Suzanna guessed.

"Suzanna, dear, what do you think? Mrs. Graham Woods Bartlett was here during your absence."

"To visit us, mother? Oh, tell me all about it," Suzanna cried.

Emily Calvin Blake

"She wants to take you and Maizie and Peter to the seashore for a whole month. There, Suzanna! What do you think of that?"

Suzanna stood absolutely still. Then exclaimed: "To the seashore, mother! Why—I don't think I can stand the joy of it. Oh, mother, I'm too happy!"

CHAPTER XXIII

TO THE SEASHORE

Mrs. Graham Woods Bartlett sat in her own perfectly appointed room one morning in late June. She sat quietly, hands folded. She could hear Graham, her son, downstairs beneath her window talking to David and Daphne. She caught disconnected words. They floated to her broken like meaningless flakes of snow.

She had just returned from her call on Mrs. Procter, that impulsive call made on the wings of an impulsive, quixotic thought. There still remained sharp in her memory the picture of the little home; the busy mother, washing out small woolen garments. She had gone unconsciously prepared to patronize and had returned completely shorn of her feeling of superiority. In truth, a little envy for that sweet-faced mother was in her heart.

From the time when her husband's mother died, she had not been happy. Pursuits that hitherto had satisfied her altogether lost their power. New values were slowly born in her. Still possessing a degree of sensibility not killed by her false life, she had been by the attitude of her husband and her son, able to see herself clearly. Both had been dependent upon her in a measure for their happiness, and she had failed them. Their reaction had hurt her bitterly.

She had tried in the past two years to make amends, but some

Emily Calvin Blake

hurts heal slowly. Perhaps it was hard for her husband and son to realize that she was trying to make amends. In any event, each went his separate way, a household divided. Early in the morning had come the thought of the seashore and she had wasted no time in seeking the little home. And now its atmosphere filled her mind.

She heard Daphne's young voice, and a sudden rare pity filled her for the motherless child, her gardener's daughter. She would ask Daphne, too.

She went to seek David, and as she came upon him spading a flower bed, the two children with him, a station carriage stopped before the big iron gates and her husband alighted. He had been away on one of his long trips and was now returning home, unheralded, unexpected.

He came quickly down the path and stopped short at sight of his wife. "I did not think to find you here," he said.

She did not answer at once. He looked closer at her. "You look a bit fagged," he said, uncertainly. Perhaps he felt a softer appeal about her which took him back to their young days together.

"I am a little tired," she said.

"I thought you intended to spend the summer in the East," he went on.

"Strangely, Bartlett Villa held more fascination for me than any other place. I returned here a week ago," she hesitated before continuing. "I obeyed a whim this morning and invited the Procter children to accompany Graham and me to the seashore to spend a month."

He looked at her incredulously. "I—I don't understand," he said.

She returned his gaze, then suddenly she turned from him and hastened back to the house. Many emotions bit at her, among them anger with her husband for his difficulty in believing she had done something which would mean, some trouble to her; which in the days just behind she would have designated as impossible, or "boring."

After a moment he followed her and overtook her as she reached the small side room where Suzanna had once sat telling of the poor people who had been burned out of their homes. She knew he was near her, but she gave no heed. Instead she flung herself down in a near chair and buried her face in her hands.

He stood, looking down at her in silence. At last he let his hand fall gently on her shoulder.

"Ina," he said, softly.

She looked up at him.

"Dear," he went on, "have you and I just been playing at life?"

"Oh, it seems so," she cried. "I know I am unhappy, groping." She stood up and put out her hands to him. He took them, drew her close to him. "Ina," he said, "let me go with you and the children to the seashore. Let's try to know one another better."

A radiance came upon her, filling her eyes. She did not speak, only she held very fast to his hand, as though in the clasp she found an anchor.

There came the glorious summer day marked for the journey to the seashore. Suzanna, Maizie, and Peter waited for the Bartlett carriage which was to convey them to the depot. At last they heard it coming. At last it stood before the gate, and Daphne put her small head out of the carriage window. Then Graham opened the door and sprang to the ground. He said a word to David who was driving, and ran up the path.

Maizie began to dance, Peter to whistle. But Suzanna stood quite still, the glow of anticipation falling from her face.

"Are you quite ready, Suzanna?" asked Mrs. Procter.

At the words Suzanna's control broke. With a little cry she ran into her mother's arms. "Oh, mother, mother," she sobbed, "I can't go away, so far away and leave you—a whole month!"

Mrs. Procter held the small figure close. Her own eyes were wet, but she spoke calmly:

"Why, little girl, mother will be here waiting for your return, and longing to hear all about your good time. Come, dry your eyes and think how happy you're going to be."

"But I know you'll be lonesome, mother, and so shall I be for you."

"But when you grow lonesome," Mrs. Procter whispered, "just think how lovely it will be to return home; and remember that father's machine will be given its great test before you come back. Mr. Bartlett and Mr. Massey have made all arrangements."

Suzanna's face brightened; the clouds dispelled themselves, so she was able to greet Graham with much of her old smile.

"All ready?" he cried as he ran up the steps. "Father and mother and a maid are following in another carriage. Nancy is with us."

He was quite plainly excited by some thought deeper than the mere fact of going to the seashore. Suzanna's companionship was promised for long days to come; he knew her eye for beauty hidden from others; her quaint speech. And then, too, a new relationship had come to pass between himself and his mother. Between them an understanding that made him glow.

It seemed but a moment before they were all together in the train. Suzanna settled herself to look out of the window at the passing landscape, so exhilaratingly new to her. Maizie sat beside her, Peter across the aisle with Graham. Little Daphne was cuddled close to Mrs. Bartlett. Mr. Bartlett was in the dining-car.

Maizie whispered to her sister: "We've come to the future now, haven't we, Suzanna?"

"Why, you can't ever come to the future," returned Suzanna.

Maizie puzzled a moment. "But don't you remember, mother said we might travel on a train some time in the future? So now we're doing it, why haven't we come to the future?"

"Because you never can come to the future," Suzanna repeated. She leaned forward and spoke to Mrs. Bartlett. "When you're living a day it's the present, isn't it, Mrs. Bartlett?"

Mrs. Bartlett looked long at the two children. "Maizie thinks the future an occasion, I think," she said, and then, because lucid explanation was beyond her, she continued: "You know we have a big cottage at the seashore, and the cottage is close to the water."

Maizie it was who at last broke the thrilling silence: "Where there's an ocean? And where you can go wading and swimming?" she cried.

"And will there be sand?" asked Suzanna, hanging upon the answer breathlessly.

"Yes, there's a wide yellow beach running into the ocean where you can dig and build castles all day," said Mrs. Bartlett.

"Oh, my cup is full and runneth over," said Suzanna solemnly.

The train swept on through small towns and the children's delight and amazement increased. And when at noon the climax came, and they all went forward into the dining-car, they were one and all silent. No words great enough were in their vocabulary to express this moment.

Said Mr. Bartlett when they were all seated: "Now, children, you may order just exactly what you'd like. You first, Suzanna."

"Well," she said, without hesitation, "I should like some golden brown toast that isn't burned, with lots of butter on it, and a cup of cocoa with a marshmallow floating on top, and at the very last, a dish of striped ice cream with a cherry right in the middle."

Mr. Bartlett wrote the order rapidly on a card. Each of the children spoke out his deepest, perhaps his long-cherished desire. Some of the dishes were secretly and mercifully modified by Mrs. Bartlett, who sat in enjoyment of the scene.

"It's like a dream, Mrs. Bartlett," said Suzanna when, dinner finished, they were all back once more in the parlor car. "You don't think we'll wake up, do you?"

"No, I think not; you'll simply get wider and wider awake."

But, as the hours crept on and as she watched the flying landscape, the reaction to all her excitement came and a haze fell over everything, and she slept, to awaken some time later, full of contrition.

She spoke anxiously to Mrs. Bartlett: "Oh, I appreciated it all, Mrs. Bartlett, but my eyes just closed down of themselves," she said.

Mrs. Bartlett smiled. "It's a long journey," she said, "but we'll soon see the end of it."

At nine o'clock the train stopped for the first time since dark had fallen. "Here we are," cried Mr. Bartlett. And in a few moments they were all standing on the platform of a little railroad station waiting while carriages were being secured to take them for the night to a hotel nestling on the top of a tall hill.

Emily Calvin Blake

CHAPTER XXIV

THE SEASHORE

Morning came—a rather misty morning that promised better as the day advanced. Suzanna, sleeping with Maizie in a small room on the second floor of the hotel, woke, gazed about her unfamiliar surroundings, sprang out of bed, and in her bare feet ran to the window. There before her was a magnificent group of mountains, wooded with majestic trees whose tops seemed to touch the sky. Beneath the mountains, just at their feet, a river ran, the sun dancing on its breast. Suzanna held her breath in sheer awe; she could not move even to call Maizie. She felt as though something great out there in the mountains called to her spirit and though she wished to answer she could not do so.

The tapestry spread below the mountains of water and green slopes and velvet meadows sun-kissed too, called to her; the artist in her was keenly, deeply responsive to the call, still she could not answer, only stand and gaze and gaze, and drink in the beauty that stretched before her.

Then old Nancy came with hurrying words, waking Maizie. "We can stay in this town but two hours before our train is due," she said. "So you must dress at once, Suzanna."

So Suzanna dressed in silence, answering none of Maizie's chatter, as though she had been in a far, unexplored country and had returned steeped in the mysteries of that distant land.

Her silence still lay upon her when after breakfast they all set out for a walk around the historic old town. There were babies, happy, dirty babies, playing about doorsteps of one-storied plaster houses, or toddling about the cobble-stoned roads.

The streets were narrow and steep, the roads wide with moss edged in between the wide cracks. Suzanna kept her eyes down; she would not look up at the mountains, and finally Mr. Bartlett, noticing her silence, asked: "Do you like it here, Suzanna?"

"Yes," she said. "But I can't look at the mountains. They take my breath away and make me stand still inside. Maybe some day I'll be able to look straight at them, but not now, and some day when I'm a woman I'm going to come back here and make a poem and set it to a wonderful painting."

He smiled at the way she put it.

"And I," said Maizie, "am going to come back and take care of some of those poor little babies that play alone out on the cobble-stones."

"We'll see," said Mr. Bartlett. "Time alone can tell what you two little girls will do."

Returning to the hotel they found vehicles awaiting them. And shortly they were again on a train, speeding away.

Three hours, and they were at their destination. A short ride in an electric car, a shorter walk down a tree-lined street, and they were at the "cottage."

"A cottage," cried Suzanna, "why it's a big house!"

"Everything is called a cottage down here," said Mrs. Bartlett.

Mr. Bartlett used the brass knocker and its echo reverberated down the street. An elderly Scotch woman, Bessie, who had

Emily Calvin Blake

been long with Mrs. Bartlett's family, met them in the hall, her pleasant face alight with smiles. She said now:

"Everything is ready, and the trunks, I suppose, will be here within a short time."

"What's that sound?" Suzanna asked.

"That's the ocean booming," said Mrs. Bartlett. "Now let's go upstairs and prepare ourselves for luncheon. Nancy will show you children your different rooms."

So upstairs they went, Nancy in the lead. She threw open the door of the bedrooms. Suzanna and Maizie were given one from whose windows the ocean could be seen. Peter had a room all to himself, a small one with a cot which was much to his liking. "It's like camping out," he made himself believe. Graham occupied one next door. Little Daphne was with Mrs. Bartlett.

"There's two closets," cried Maizie, as she went on a tour of investigation. "One for your clothes and one for mine. Sometimes, Suzanna," she said, "I can hardly believe it all yet."

"That's the way I feel," said Suzanna. Nancy appeared at the door bearing snowy towels which she gave to the children. "Here, children," she said, "the bath room is at the end of the hall, and you must hurry."

So Suzanna and Maizie hurried and they were the first downstairs. The house was much more simply furnished, of course, than the big one in Anchorville, but as the children went about they found many interesting things. In one long, narrow room, the length of the first floor, was a fireplace taking up one entire end, and built of irregular stones, giving a charming effect. There were big easy chairs and sofas; tables heaped with magazines and books. On the walls were color pictures suspended by long, dim-worn chains—ocean scenes, a ship at sea, and over the piano, fifty years old as they discovered later, hung several faded miniatures of ladies of a long past age. Most interesting of all to Suzanna was an album she found in an old cabinet, an album that as you looked through it at ladies with voluminous skirts, at men with wing collars, and little girls with white pantalettes, a hidden music box tinkled forth dainty airs from a long-forgotten operetta.

In another room on the opposite side, which was entered by mounting three steps, was a large table covered with green felt and with nets stretched across it, and little balls and paddles in corner pockets, and Mr. Bartlett, entering at the moment, the children learned that many happy games were played on this big table.

Later, out of this room, the children stepped upon a wide porch, and here there burst upon them a view of the ocean.

"You see," said Mr. Bartlett, "that those of us who go into the water may dress in bathing suits here, then put on long cloaks and run down to the beach. Then when we return, we step under a shower arrangement over there near that little house. . . ."

"Please, Mr. Bartlett," begged Suzanna, "don't tell us any more now. I don't think I can stand any more joy for today."

"Well, then," Mr. Bartlett smiled, "let's start away for our luncheon. We simply live in this house and take our meals at the hotel."

And at this moment the rest of the family appearing, they all started away. A short walk brought them to the hotel where all was life and light and excitement. Children played on the wide piazzas, young girls walked about chatting merrily, and mothers and fathers sat in easy chairs reading or pleasantly regarding the children.

In the dining-room a large table had been previously ordered reserved for the Bartlett family.

Emily Calvin Blake

"We'll have," said Mr. Bartlett, when they were all seated, speaking to the interested waiter, "just exactly what you think we'd like, John."

John, who knew Mr. Bartlett well, smiled in fatherly fashion and disappeared. He returned shortly bearing a tray filled with just those things that children most love. There was cream soup, and salted crackers, big pitchers of milk, little hot biscuits, fresh honey, and broiled ham—pink and very delicious as was soon discovered. Then there was sweet fruit pudding with whipped cream and, of course, ice cream.

"Will John always know what we like?" asked Suzanna as the meal progressed.

"Well, we'll change about," said Mrs. Bartlett, who looked as though she were enjoying every moment. "Sometimes when we know particularly what we'd like, we'll give our order, other times when we want to be surprised we'll let John serve us what he thinks we'd enjoy. Don't you think that way will be nice?"

"Oh, that will be very interesting," said Suzanna; then added, "Does the water make that sound all the time?"

"Yes, it's always restless."

"Well, it seems as though it were asking for something," said Suzanna, "a kind of sad asking."

"Now," said Mr. Bartlett, leaning across and speaking softly to her, "suppose, Suzanna, you think for a moment that it's a happy sound and see how almost at once it becomes a happy sound."

Suzanna listened intently. Then her face brightened. "Why, it is a happy murmuring," she cried. "Just as though it had to sing and sing all day long."

"Exactly," said Mr. Bartlett.

"Well, then," said Suzanna, quickly drawing the deduction, "it's really just in me to make it say happy things or sad things."

"Exactly," said Mr. Bartlett again, and then they all rose and went back to the cottage.

Since the trunks which contained the beach outfits did not arrive till late that afternoon, the children did not go down to the sands till the next morning. Then with joyous hearts and eager feet, they set off, Suzanna, Maizie, Peter, Graham, and Daphne; Mr. and Mrs. Bartlett following more slowly.

A bath house reserved for their use stood, door wide open. They entered, discarded their coats and immediately appeared again clad in their pretty bathing suits for the water.

But when they reached the sands, already alive with gay children who were building houses or running gaily about, and with happy shrieks wading into the water, the Procter children stood awed, unable to speak, so many emotions beat within them.

Maizie was the first to recover her power of speech. "There's a girl down there with a shovel and pail like mine," she said.

And that broke the spell. Peter and Graham walked bravely out into the water, finally reaching their necks as they went farther and farther into the ocean. But the little girls contented themselves by simply wetting their feet and with every wave dashing up to them, leaping back with glad little cries. As the morning advanced, they returned to the older group and sat on the sand.

On the sixth day of their stay all the children were trying bravely to swim, clinging it must be confessed rather desperately to Mr. Bartlett and the beach man, secured to help them; but when he procured for them large water wings, they soon struck out for themselves. Peter really learned to swim before either of his sisters, and one morning he went out as far as the end of a quarter-mile pier.

They all grew rosy and strong, out in the fine air nearly every moment as they were. Some afternoons they went fishing, and, with a strange reversal of type, Suzanna was the patient one, Maizie the impatient. Suzanna would sit in the boat next to Mr. Bartlett, holding her line, and breathlessly wait for hours if need be, statue-like, till she felt the thrilling nibble. Maizie would grow tired immediately, and to Peter's disgust, she would wriggle her feet or move restlessly about, quite spoiling for him the day's outing. Maizie at last begged to be let off from the fishing expeditions.

"I'd rather just lie in the sand and paddle in the water, or watch the big white ships," she said.

"You're to do exactly as you please," said Mr. Bartlett, and so they did, each and every one.

Many hours they all spent on one of the large piers running out a great distance into the ocean, where always there were gaiety and music, and here one afternoon Suzanna, Peter, Graham, and Mr. Bartlett, all seated at the end of the pier saw a huge shark darting about the water. The few daring swimmers in his vicinity quickly moved away.

"A real shark," cried Suzanna. "When I go to bed tonight I'll just think I dreamed it."

Said Mr. Bartlett: "Suppose, Suzanna, I buy you a book filled with blank pages, and having a little padlock with a small key, for your very own, so that every night you may write the happenings of the day and the impressions made upon you."

"Oh, I'd like to do that," cried Suzanna, her eyes shining, "and then surely I won't forget any single little thing to tell daddy and mother."

"I'll write for the book," Mr. Bartlett promised, "when we return to the cottage."

After a time they left the pier and walked down the street, running along with the sands. The street was lined with little stores of all kinds; one where fresh fish were sold, another where French fried potatoes and vinegar were offered to a hungry multitude; a place in which handmade laces were made and sold. A florist booth kept by a dark-faced Greek was neighbor to a shop built with turrets like a castle. Here a happy-faced Italian women exhibited trays of uncut stones, semi-precious ones, explained Mr. Bartlett, and strings of beads, coral, pearl, flat turquoise, topaz, and amethysts. There were bits of old porcelain, crystal cups, and oriental embroideries, and little carved gods on ebony pedestals. The place reminded Suzanna of Drusilla's historic old pawn shop and she stood entranced.

Soon they were at the place of Graham and Peter's delight, a shooting gallery, where if one were very skillful he might, with a massive looking gun, hit a small moving black ball and hear a bell ring. Mr. Bartlett hit the ball today three times out of four, Graham once out of five, but Peter, manfully lifting the large gun and scanning its barrel, left a scar on the target four inches to the left of the little swinging ball. This occurred after eight trials.

"Well, there's another day, Peter," said Mr. Bartlett, as they moved away.

"And Mr. Bartlett practiced a long time, you must remember, Peter," said Suzanna, seeing the little fellow's downcast expression.

"Do you think before we go back to the city," asked the small boy, "that I'll be able to make the bell ring so I can tell daddy?"

Emily Calvin Blake

"Oh, yes," said Mr. Bartlett, encouragingly. "We'll come over here and practice every day."

They found the others in the cottage in the big room, resting awhile before preparing for dinner.

"Oh, Suzanna," began Maizie at once, "we're going to have a beach party on the sands tonight. And Mrs. Bartlett says we'll have a fire built so we can toast marshmallows."

Suzanna did not say anything. Then quickly she crossed the room and stood before Mr. and Mrs. Bartlett. "I wish," she said solemnly, "that all the children in the world had such dear friends as we have."

CHAPTER XXV

LAST DAYS

They held many a beach party during that wonderful month. And always they ended the evening by drawing close together and singing happy little songs. Till, when a little coolness crept into the air, they would leave the ocean and go happily homeward, to sleep deep and dreamlessly till another morning awakened them to the thought of fresh delights.

On one morning after a beach party, the children, coming downstairs to join their elders for breakfast at the hotel, found standing on the road in front of the cottage, a little brown donkey attached to a basket cart.

"Could it be, could it possibly be for them?" each child's heart asked.

And Mr. Bartlett answered the unspoken question by: "It's for you all. Peter is to drive first because he assured me the other day he knew all about horses; then Graham. And in a few days Suzanna, and Maizie, and even little Daphne, can take their turns."

He went to the small donkey and stroked its nose, and the little fellow whinnied with pleasure. The children crowded about the cart. Couldn't they have a drive now? their eager eyes asked. But Mr. Bartlett thought breakfast the logical beginning of the day, so reluctantly they left their new possession.

When breakfast was finished, Mr. Bartlett said: "I'll go for the first ride or two with you just to see how this little fellow acts, though I've been assured that he's as gentle as any lamb ever born."

And whoever it was that had given Mr. Bartlett this assurance had not exaggerated the amiable qualities of the donkey. "Little Brownie," as the children had unanimously and immediately named him, was of equable and even nature. True, as the days went by it was discovered that he was somewhat lazy, also self-willed. If he wanted to stop he would not move again until he wished to, in face of all pleading, urging, or inducements. He refused even to be led, and stood very pleasantly viewing the surrounding landscape till with a sudden jerk he would resume his usual trot. The children finally accepted Brownie's one vagary, and when they were driving home among other vehicles, and Brownie suddenly stopped and raised his right ear, a sign which meant, "I shall not move till I wish to," they only laughed, and others about them knowing the ways of little donkeys, laughed good-naturedly too, and drove around the little cart.

It is an unvarying law that the days roll on and bring to an end even periods of thrilling delight; and so there came the last evening to be spent in the cottage at the seashore. The night was early in August, but it had elected to borrow from its cooler sister September a rather chill wind which, to the children's delight, necessitated the building of a fire in the grate in the long room.

"And we'll pop corn," said Mr. Bartlett when they were all gathered together watching the roaring flames, the only light in the room.

And Nancy, who could on a moment's notice, produce anything asked of her, brought the popper and a big bag of dried corn.

After a time, when several bowls of corn were popped and buttered, salted and eaten, Nancy put on the hearth a dish of fine, rosy apples. These the children peeled and then cast the skins into the grate. A hardy fragrance came from them, but hardly pungent enough to overpower the salt-water odor that swept in from the ocean.

The flames lit all the faces, young and old. They fell on Mrs. Bartlett, touching her lovely hair to molten gold, touching her thoughtful face till it seemed a smile beyond itself rested upon it. She was thinking—"Tomorrow we start back, and in my hands lie the happiness of many. In my hands lies the keeping of the ideals of two—" She closed her eyes and asked for clear vision, for strength to keep true to life's highest values.

Graham, at her knee, looked up at her. Feeling that his eyes were upon her, she opened hers and gazed at him. She did not speak, nor did he, but she felt his heart's nearness.

And then his gaze wandered to Suzanna, Suzanna gazing into the flames, her dark eyes like glowing jewels, her soft lips parted. And into Mrs. Bartlett's heart crept a little fear and a little yearning and a little great knowledge—that composite emotion all mothers are born to know.

Emily Calvin Blake

CHAPTER XXVI

SUZANNA AND HER FATHER

At home again after the glorious month spent at the seashore! Habits, dear customs, taken up once more. The splendor of the trip had not faded for the Procter children. But home was home after all, with father and mother and sisters and brothers all sharing the common life; with short wanderings away and joyous returns; with small resentments, quick flashes, and happy reconciliations.

"It was lovely at the seashore," said Suzanna to her mother one Saturday afternoon, "but I'm awfully glad to be at home again. Were you lonely without us?"

"Very," said Mrs. Procter, "but then I knew you were all having such interesting experiences."

"Is father coming home early, mother?" Maizie asked, looking up from her work. She was sewing buttons on Peter's blouse with the strongest linen thread obtainable in Anchorville.

Mrs. Procter's face shadowed. She looked at Suzanna and Maizie as though pondering the wisdom of giving them some piece of news. Evidently she decided against doing so, for she answered:

"I can't tell, Maizie, he may be kept at the mills. Mr. Massey is growing more dependent on father every day," she ended, with a little burst of pride.

Father did not come home in the afternoon. The children lost hope after a time, and followed their separate whims.

But at six he arrived. Suzanna had noticed at once upon her return, that he was quieter, less exuberant than he had been since entering old John Massey's employ. Some light seemed to have gone from his face. Suzanna wanted always to comfort him, and he, though saying nothing, was quite conscious of his little daughter's yearning over him.

During supper his absorption continued, and immediately afterward he went into the parlor, selected a big book from a shelf, and drawing a chair near the lamp began to read. Mother put the "baby" and Peter to bed. Suzanna and Maizie, after the dishes were finished, followed father, and drawing their chairs close, looked over some pictures together.

"Saturday night"—how Suzanna loved it! It seemed the hush time of the week, the hush before waking to the next beautiful day, Sunday, when all the family were together—father in his nice dark suit, mother in her soft wisteria gown, all the children in pretty clothes; church, with its resonant organ, and the minister's deep voice reading from the old book. Then, weather propitious, the walk with father and mother in the afternoon down the country road, and at night the lamps again lit—all the homely significances of the place where love and peace and courage dwelt.

Mrs. Procter returned from putting the children to bed. "I think I'll go upstairs for a little while," said Mr. Procter looking up at her.

"Oh, do, Richard," she urged.

Suzanna went close to him, her hand sought his. "Could—could you invite us for a little while, daddy," she asked, beseechingly.

Emily Calvin Blake

"Why, yes, if you wish," he answered. "You and mother and Maizie."

It was rather a heavy consent, but they all accompanied him up to the attic. He lit the shaded lamp standing on the corner table, regulated it till it gave out a subdued glow, and then walked and stood before his machine.

He stood a long time looking at it. Once he put out his hand and touched it softly, as a mother might a sleeping child.

Suzanna and Maizie, awed and troubled, they knew not why, watched their father. Only their mother, with a little tender smile that held in it a great deal of wistfulness, went close to him.

"Richard," she said softly.

He turned from the machine. His face was strangely colorless, strangely drained of all light. She did not speak, but the loyalty and faith deepened in her eyes. Perhaps he gained some comfort from their steady gaze, his tenseness seemed to relax, his arms fell to his sides.

Suzanna unable to stand the strain longer, flew to him and put her small arms tight about him. "Oh, are you sick, daddy?" she cried, tears in her voice.

He hesitated, looked down at her, and said simply, very quietly:

"Suzanna, you might as well know the truth now as later. My machine is a failure—I am a failure!"

Her heart leaped sickeningly, her arms fell from about him. In all her life she had never lived through so intense an emotion. Her father, the Great Man, proclaimed himself a failure in tones which struck through her.

The mother's voice rang out clear. "Richard, you cannot say that." She looked about the attic made sacred by its high use, "Here while you worked we all, your children and I, have learned great lessons. You're looking at your machine, an insensate thing, and losing sight of what during its building, you put into the lives of those near to you, living stuff, Richard."

And then Maizie cried out, "Oh, daddy, it's just like being on a mountain top when we're in the attic with you. We'll never, never have to stop coming, will we?"

And Suzanna, still deeply troubled, cried: "Daddy, how could the machine be a failure when it was born because you loved all men, and wanted to make them happy? And the very thought of it up here made me happy. Why, in school on Monday I'd look down all the shapes of the week, and think of Saturday afternoon and wish it would come quick." Her voice broke and the sobs came uncontrollable, shaking the slender body. In a moment she was clasped tight in her father's arms.

After she had regained some composure she looked up at him. "It hurts me, daddy, so that I can't breathe when you forget that you're a Great Man."

A silence fell, and into it plunged a voice. "Good evening," it said.

There in the doorway stood the Eagle Man. He laughed at their bewildered expressions. "I rang and rang," he explained, "and when no one answered, I looked up at the attic window and thought you must all be upstairs."

"And was the door unlocked," cried Mrs. Procter. "I thought I attended to the doors and windows right after supper."

"The door was unlocked," said the Eagle Man, "and so I took the liberty of coming right in."

"I'm glad you did," said Mr. Procter.

"Well, I need your help, Richard," said old John Massey in an affectionate tone.

"It's ready for you, Mr. Massey," the inventor answered warmly.

Suzanna gazing at her old friend, suddenly cried out: "Oh, your eyes have changed, Eagle Man, they're all nice and shiny."

He smiled with great fondness at her. "My dear," he said, "how can a man fail to indulge in nice shining eyes after contact with a family of rare visionaries?"

Suzanna did not understand that. She knew only that the Eagle Man had greatly changed, that he seemed kinder, more understanding, and all at once she knew why. He had had of late the ineffable privilege of being close to her father. Of course, by such proximity he must grow kind and understanding.

"Richard," said the capitalist, "there's trouble threatened in the foreign section of the mills."

"Trouble?" Richard Procter's head went up.

"Yes, the men are dissatisfied, surly. It's the one department where your touch hasn't been felt. I want you to go there on Monday and begin your work."

"I'll be ready," said Richard Procter. Strength and purpose seemed to flow back to him.

The Eagle Man turned as though to go, but he paused at the door to look again at Suzanna.

"And so your father's been telling you that he has failed, that his machine refused to work in the final test we gave it at the mills."

"My father hasn't failed," Suzanna said proudly.

"No, he hasn't failed," the Eagle Man agreed. "He hasn't failed. He's the most brilliant success I know. He built into a piece of machinery his ideals, and when the machine was finished he saw in his experiments with it on those in his home ultimate triumph. But when it was taken to my mills the machine failed to register color in personalities whose chief talent by years of wrong work had been nearly strangled."

Mr. Procter spoke: "It shouldn't have failed even there. It did register, if you remember your color and Mr. Bartlett's, and both of you had pulled far away from your purpose."

"Yes, for some reason, it did register us," agreed the Eagle Man. He paused, and then his voice rang out. "Let me tell you all something that the inventor of that machine did, some miracle he brought to pass I should have thought impossible. He awakened old ideals in a hard old breast, he made hard old eyes see in men, not automatons born only to add to his wealth, but human beings to be rendered happy in their work."

"Was yours the hard old breast, Eagle Man?" Suzanna asked.

"Yes, Suzanna. A result like that is worth while, eh, Richard?"

Mr. Procter did not answer, could not, because he feared at the moment that he could not speak intelligently.

The Eagle Man turned to the wife, adoringly silent as she listened.

"Three men Richard Procter brought to me on his first day in my mills. He said: 'These men have ambitions, they are greatly talented. You must give them their chance.'"

"And what did you say?" asked Mrs. Procter softly.

"Oh, I snarled as usual, but that was really the work I wanted him to do. I wanted him to do in the circumscribed field of my mills that which he had built his machine to do. And so I snapped out: 'All right, put the burden on me! I'll give them their chance just because you say so.' And where men were dissatisfied he got at them and discovered the trouble, and down there they all trust him, and his influence will be like a river flowing on, ever widening. So there's the late history of the man who stands and calls himself a failure."

So he finished, said not another word, looked once at the inventor, and then went away.

* * * * *

Suzanna, trying in vain that night to sleep, tossed about restlessly. Maizie, a sound sleeper, did not stir despite her sister's wakefulness. Suzanna was thinking of her father, of the Eagle Man, of The Machine.

Suddenly she lay quite still. She was remembering the day when The Machine had registered her color, a soft purple, gold tipped. How stirred her father had been when the wavering color spread itself upon the glass plate. It had repeated its marvel for Maizie and Peter. Why then when The Machine was removed and conveyed to the big steel mills, did it stand brooding, sulky, refusing to make any record of any personality. She sat up straight in bed, her eyes yearning forward into the dark. And all at once the answer came to her. Only in the attic, where, piece by piece, in prayer, hope, and jubilation it had been assembled; where love and belief had formed the atmosphere could The Machine be its own highly sensitive self, reacting and responding.

With that big thought flowing through her, she slipped from the bed. The night was warm, soft little breezes coming through the open window. She went to the closet, found her slippers, put them on, and with a backward glance at the unconscious Maizie, left the room.

The hall lay quiet, the tiny night lamp flickering in its place on the small table set near her mother's room—that mother, ready at the first sound to spring to any need of her children.

Downstairs Suzanna went swiftly, and there in the dining-room, as she had thought, she found her father. He was sitting at the long table, above which hung the new lamp with its pink shade and long brass chain. His head was bent over a big book, and Suzanna knew that he was studying. She paused half-way to him. In her white night gown, her hair flowing over her shoulders, she looked like a small visitor from another higher plane. At last her father, impelled, turned and saw her. At once he opened wide his arms, and she went into them.

She lay, her cheek pressed against his, for a long time. All the thoughts that had raced through her upstairs in the sleepless hours returned to her, but she had to struggle to find language in which to tell them.

"Daddy," she began, "maybe The Machine can't work except where it was born."

"Tell me all that's in your heart, little girl," he said.

"Well, we've all thought of The Machine, and loved it and believed in it ever since I was the tiniest girl, and you've talked to us of what it was to mean."

"All true, my child, all true."

"And The Machine stood there and listened, daddy." She released herself from his clasp and stood very straight. Her dark eyes seeing pictures, were brilliantly wide. Her breath came quickly from between her parted lips: "And so it grew and grew, and soon out of its soul it sent colors. And it loved the man who made it, and it loved his little children, and made them all want to be good and do something for others.

"And then one day, they took it away from its home and into a big mill, and men crowded around it and looked at it, but they didn't love it, and they didn't believe in it. And it felt shy and hurt and the color stayed in its soul and wouldn't come forth.

"And the man who had made it felt sad and he cried, and he took his machine home. And then one day, years and years after when the man's little girl, Suzanna, was a woman and she was out in the world trying to do good, as her father had taught her, trying to make other people happy, the colors crept out from The Machine again, all gold and purple and rose and green, this time for everybody."

She finished, and with a great cry her father folded her to him. The tears came streaming to his eyes, and quite frankly now he wept. She felt the hot tears upon her face, they burned her, but she knew she had helped him and she was satisfied.

They sat on in a wonderful silence. A distant clock struck one. They heard the sound of quickly descending feet, and turning, Suzanna saw her mother standing in the doorway.

"I heard voices," said Mrs. Procter.

"Come here," her husband said. She saw his face transfigured, and she went to him and fell on her knees beside him.

"Courage—belief?" she questioned.

"Yes, they have returned," he said.

Suzanna spoke again: "Daddy," she said, in her eager voice, "I forgot to tell you of a nice happening. You know when we were at the seashore with Mr. Bartlett, John, the waiter at the hotel, said something one day about a son of his who wanted to write beautiful music, and Mr. Bartlett said right before me: 'John, let me help that boy of yours. This little girl's father has shown me the beauty of doing good for others.'"

The inventor did not speak. He sat, his arms about his wife and child, and in his eyes the radiance of new inspiration, new purpose.

At last his wife spoke. "Richard, could success as you planned it, have meant more, and wouldn't it have brushed some of the butterfly dust away?"

He took the thought, pondered it, and his wife went on. "There's the joy of striving, of waking fresh every day to hope. Can attainment, after all, give any greater joy?"

"Perhaps not," he murmured.

"So, dear," she went on, "think of what has been done, not of what you wished for. Think what you've done for our children. You took them with you into your land of dreams, letting them share with you as far as you might, that thrill which comes to the creator."

"And, daddy," finished Suzanna, "if The Machine had gone away to stay, we couldn't have any more beautiful Saturday afternoons in the attic with you."

They remained then all very still. Peter cried out a little in his sleep. His mother, alert at once, listened, then relaxed when the cry did not come again, and then Suzanna asked, "Are you still very, very sad, daddy?"

And he answered, "The sadness has gone, Suzanna. Come another Saturday, I shall take up the work again—and some day—"

"Some day all the world will say my father is a great man," ended Suzanna, an unfaltering faith written upon her face.

And so her love, like an essence, flowed out and healed his spirit.

Choose from Thousands of 1stWorldLibrary Classics By

A. M. Barnard
Ada Leverson
Adolphus William Ward
Aesop
Agatha Christie
Alexander Aaronsohn
Alexander Kielland
Alexandre Dumas
Alfred Gatty
Alfred Ollivant
Alice Duer Miller
Alice Turner Curtis
Alice Dunbar
Allen Chapman
Alleyne Ireland
Ambrose Bierce
Amelia E. Barr
Amory H. Bradford
Andrew Lang
Andrew McFarland Davis
Andy Adams
Angela Brazil
Anna Alice Chapin
Anna Sewell
Annie Besant
Annie Hamilton Donnell
Annie Payson Call
Annie Roe Carr
Annonaymous
Anton Chekhov
Archibald Lee Fletcher
Arnold Bennett
Arthur C. Benson
Arthur Conan Doyle
Arthur M. Winfield
Arthur Ransome
Arthur Schnitzler
Arthur Train
Atticus
B.H. Baden-Powell
B. M. Bower
B. C. Chatterjee
Baroness Emmuska Orczy
Baroness Orczy
Basil King
Bayard Taylor
Ben Macomber
Bertha Muzzy Bower
Bjornstjerne Bjornson

Booth Tarkington
Boyd Cable
Bram Stoker
C. Collodi
C. E. Orr
C. M. Ingleby
Carolyn Wells
Catherine Parr Traill
Charles A. Eastman
Charles Amory Beach
Charles Dickens
Charles Dudley Warner
Charles Farrar Browne
Charles Ives
Charles Kingsley
Charles Klein
Charles Hanson Towne
Charles Lathrop Pack
Charles Romyn Dake
Charles Whibley
Charles Willing Beale
Charlotte M. Braeme
Charlotte M. Yonge
Charlotte Perkins Stetson
Clair W. Hayes
Clarence Day Jr.
Clarence E. Mulford
Clemence Housman
Confucius
Coningsby Dawson
Cornelis DeWitt Wilcox
Cyril Burleigh
D. H. Lawrence
Daniel Defoe
David Garnett
Dinah Craik
Don Carlos Janes
Donald Keyhoe
Dorothy Kilner
Dougan Clark
Douglas Fairbanks
E. Nesbit
E. P. Roe
E. Phillips Oppenheim
E. S. Brooks
Earl Barnes
Edgar Rice Burroughs
Edith Van Dyne
Edith Wharton

Edward Everett Hale
Edward J. O'Biren
Edward S. Ellis
Edwin L. Arnold
Eleanor Atkins
Eleanor Hallowell Abbott
Eliot Gregory
Elizabeth Gaskell
Elizabeth McCracken
Elizabeth Von Arnim
Ellem Key
Emerson Hough
Emilie F. Carlen
Emily Bronte
Emily Dickinson
Enid Bagnold
Enilor Macartney Lane
Erasmus W. Jones
Ernie Howard Pie
Ethel May Dell
Ethel Turner
Ethel Watts Mumford
Eugene Sue
Eugenie Foa
Eugene Wood
Eustace Hale Ball
Evelyn Everett-green
Everard Cotes
F. H. Cheley
F. J. Cross
F. Marion Crawford
Fannie E. Newberry
Federick Austin Ogg
Ferdinand Ossendowski
Fergus Hume
Florence A. Kilpatrick
Fremont B. Deering
Francis Bacon
Francis Darwin
Frances Hodgson Burnett
Frances Parkinson Keyes
Frank Gee Patchin
Frank Harris
Frank Jewett Mather
Frank L. Packard
Frank V. Webster
Frederic Stewart Isham
Frederick Trevor Hill
Frederick Winslow Taylor

Friedrich Kerst
Friedrich Nietzsche
Fyodor Dostoyevsky
G.A. Henty
G.K. Chesterton
Gabrielle E. Jackson
Garrett P. Serviss
Gaston Leroux
George A. Warren
George Ade
Geroge Bernard Shaw
George Cary Eggleston
George Durston
George Ebers
George Eliot
George Gissing
George MacDonald
George Meredith
George Orwell
George Sylvester Viereck
George Tucker
George W. Cable
George Wharton James
Gertrude Atherton
Gordon Casserly
Grace E. King
Grace Gallatin
Grace Greenwood
Grant Allen
Guillermo A. Sherwell
Gulielma Zollinger
Gustav Flaubert
H. A. Cody
H. B. Irving
H.C. Bailey
H. G. Wells
H. H. Munro
H. Irving Hancock
H. R. Naylor
H. Rider Haggard
H. W. C. Davis
Haldeman Julius
Hall Caine
Hamilton Wright Mabie
Hans Christian Andersen
Harold Avery
Harold McGrath
Harriet Beecher Stowe
Harry Castlemon
Harry Coghill
Harry Houidini

Hayden Carruth
Helent Hunt Jackson
Helen Nicolay
Hendrik Conscience
Hendy David Thoreau
Henri Barbusse
Henrik Ibsen
Henry Adams
Henry Ford
Henry Frost
Henry James
Henry Jones Ford
Henry Seton Merriman
Henry W Longfellow
Herbert A. Giles
Herbert Carter
Herbert N. Casson
Herman Hesse
Hildegard G. Frey
Homer
Honore De Balzac
Horace B. Day
Horace Walpole
Horatio Alger Jr.
Howard Pyle
Howard R. Garis
Hugh Lofting
Hugh Walpole
Humphry Ward
Ian Maclaren
Inez Haynes Gillmore
Irving Bacheller
Isabel Cecilia Williams
Isabel Hornibrook
Israel Abrahams
Ivan Turgenev
J.G.Austin
J. Henri Fabre
J. M. Barrie
J. M. Walsh
J. Macdonald Oxley
J. R. Miller
J. S. Fletcher
J. S. Knowles
J. Storer Clouston
J. W. Duffield
Jack London
Jacob Abbott
James Allen
James Andrews
James Baldwin

James Branch Cabell
James DeMille
James Joyce
James Lane Allen
James Lane Allen
James Oliver Curwood
James Oppenheim
James Otis
James R. Driscoll
Jane Abbott
Jane Austen
Jane L. Stewart
Janet Aldridge
Jens Peter Jacobsen
Jerome K. Jerome
Jessie Graham Flower
John Buchan
John Burroughs
John Cournos
John F. Kennedy
John Gay
John Glasworthy
John Habberton
John Joy Bell
John Kendrick Bangs
John Milton
John Philip Sousa
John Taintor Foote
Jonas Lauritz Idemil Lie
Jonathan Swift
Joseph A. Altsheler
Joseph Carey
Joseph Conrad
Joseph E. Badger Jr
Joseph Hergesheimer
Joseph Jacobs
Jules Vernes
Julian Hawthrone
Julie A Lippmann
Justin Huntly McCarthy
Kakuzo Okakura
Karle Wilson Baker
Kate Chopin
Kenneth Grahame
Kenneth McGaffey
Kate Langley Bosher
Kate Langley Bosher
Katherine Cecil Thurston
Katherine Stokes
L. A. Abbot
L. T. Meade

L. Frank Baum
Latta Griswold
Laura Dent Crane
Laura Lee Hope
Laurence Housman
Lawrence Beasley
Leo Tolstoy
Leonid Andreyev
Lewis Carroll
Lewis Sperry Chafer
Lilian Bell
Lloyd Osbourne
Louis Hughes
Louis Joseph Vance
Louis Tracy
Louisa May Alcott
Lucy Fitch Perkins
Lucy Maud Montgomery
Luther Benson
Lydia Miller Middleton
Lyndon Orr
M. Corvus
M. H. Adams
Margaret E. Sangster
Margret Howth
Margaret Vandercook
Margaret W. Hungerford
Margret Penrose
Maria Edgeworth
Maria Thompson Daviess
Mariano Azuela
Marion Polk Angellotti
Mark Overton
Mark Twain
Mary Austin
Mary Catherine Crowley
Mary Cole
Mary Hastings Bradley
Mary Roberts Rinehart
Mary Rowlandson
M. Wollstonecraft Shelley
Maud Lindsay
Max Beerbohm
Myra Kelly
Nathaniel Hawthrone
Nicolo Machiavelli
O. F. Walton
Oscar Wilde
Owen Johnson
P.G. Wodehouse
Paul and Mabel Thorne

Paul G. Tomlinson
Paul Severing
Percy Brebner
Percy Keese Fitzhugh
Peter B. Kyne
Plato
Quincy Allen
R. Derby Holmes
R. L. Stevenson
R. S. Ball
Rabindranath Tagore
Rahul Alvares
Ralph Bonehill
Ralph Henry Barbour
Ralph Victor
Ralph Waldo Emmerson
Rene Descartes
Ray Cummings
Rex Beach
Rex E. Beach
Richard Harding Davis
Richard Jefferies
Richard Le Gallienne
Robert Barr
Robert Frost
Robert Gordon Anderson
Robert L. Drake
Robert Lansing
Robert Lynd
Robert Michael Ballantyne
Robert W. Chambers
Rosa Nouchette Carey
Rudyard Kipling
Saint Augustine
Samuel B. Allison
Samuel Hopkins Adams
Sarah Bernhardt
Sarah C. Hallowell
Selma Lagerlof
Sherwood Anderson
Sigmund Freud
Standish O'Grady
Stanley Weyman
Stella Benson
Stella M. Francis
Stephen Crane
Stewart Edward White
Stijn Streuvels
Swami Abhedananda
Swami Parmananda
T. S. Ackland

T. S. Arthur
The Princess Der Ling
Thomas A. Janvier
Thomas A Kempis
Thomas Anderton
Thomas Bailey Aldrich
Thomas Bulfinch
Thomas De Quincey
Thomas Dixon
Thomas H. Huxley
Thomas Hardy
Thomas More
Thornton W. Burgess
U. S. Grant
Upton Sinclair
Valentine Williams
Various Authors
Vaughan Kester
Victor Appleton
Victor G. Durham
Victoria Cross
Virginia Woolf
Wadsworth Camp
Walter Camp
Walter Scott
Washington Irving
Wilbur Lawton
Wilkie Collins
Willa Cather
Willard F. Baker
William Dean Howells
William le Queux
W. Makepeace Thackeray
William W. Walter
William Shakespeare
Winston Churchill
Yei Theodora Ozaki
Yogi Ramacharaka
Young E. Allison
Zane Grey